Praise for
LYN HAMILTON'S
ARCHAEOLOGICAL MYSTERIES

The Celtic Riddle

"The well-drawn characters' foray through Irish country-side and Celtic myth will delight readers."

—*Library Journal*

"A challenging puzzle . . . altogether heady stuff for the reader." —*London Free Press,* Ontario

The Moche Warrior

"With its setting shifting from Toronto to New York to Peru, this engaging story is a passport to adventure . . . richly woven descriptions . . . [a] fascinating and vividly presented subject matter and [an] artfully crafted plot."

—*Booklist*

The Maltese Goddess

"Exotically absorbing and culturally colorful . . . Lyn Hamilton is a gifted writer, who has created an intricate who-done-it wrapped inside a mystical tale . . . *The Maltese Goddess* is a terrific read that would make a tremendous movie." —*The Midwest Book Review*

The Xibalba Murders
Arthur Ellis Award Nominee for Best First Novel

"A successful mystery—and series: a smart, appealing, funny, brave and vulnerable protagonist and a complex, entertaining and rational plot."

—*London Free Press,* Ontario

"Extremely well-written . . . captivating . . . If you can't go to Yucatan, you can read this." —*Mysterious Women*

And don't miss
The African Quest,
an all-new Archaeological Mystery by Lyn Hamilton
A Berkley Prime Crime hardcover—available soon!

THE CELTIC RIDDLE

An Archaeological Mystery

LYN HAMILTON

BERKLEY PRIME CRIME, NEW YORK

THE CELTIC RIDDLE

A Berkley Prime Crime Book / published by arrangement with the author

PRINTING HISTORY
Berkley Prime Crime hardcover edition / February 2000
Berkley Prime Crime mass-market edition / December 2000

ACKNOWLEDGMENTS

Ireland is one of those special places that is not only beautiful, but where every stone, tree and place seems fraught with magic, and the sites of the great mythic events can still be found if you search for them. Those interested in exploring the mythology of Ireland might consult J. A. MacCulloch's *Celtic Mythology* or Michael Dames's book *Mythic Ireland*, which helped root Irish mythology in real places for me. Many others have helped me with the research on this book, particularly Jim Polk, Jane and Tim Marlatt, Jan Rush, Bella Pomer, Medora Sale, Catherine Clement, and Susie Wilson. I am particularly indebted to Dr. Harry Roe for his translation of "Song of Amairgen." This book is dedicated to my Irish ancestors.

Song of Amairgen

*Ic tabairt a choisse dessi i nHerind asbert Amairgen
Glúngel mac Miled in laídseo sís:*
As he placed his right foot on Ireland Amairgen of
the White Knee recited this poem:

Am gáeth i mmuir
I am the sea-swell
Am tonn trethain,
The furious wave
Am fúaimm mara
The roar of the sea
Am dam secht ndrenn
A stag of seven slaughters
Am séig i n-aill
A hawk above the cliff
Am dér gréne
A ray of the sun
Am caín lubae
The beauty of a plant
Am torc ar gàil
A boar enraged
Am hé i llind
A salmon in a pool
Am loch i mmaig
A lake in a plain
Am brí dánae
A flame of valor
Am gae i fodb   feras fechtu
A piercing spear waging war
Am dé delbas   do chin codnu
A god that fashions heroes for a lord

LYN HAMILTON

Cóich é no-d-gléith   clochur sléibe
He who clears the mountain paths
Cía ón co-ta-gair   áesa éscai
He who describes the moon's advance
Cía dú i llaig   funiud gréne
And the place where the sun sets
Cía beir búar   o thig Temrach
Who drives cattle off from Tara
Cía búar tethrach   tibis cech dáin
That fine herd touches each skill
Cía dé delbas   fáebru áine
A god that fashions weapons of glory
Commus caínte   Cáinte gáeth
An able poet. Wise am I.

(TRANSLATION: DR. HARRY ROE)

PROLOGUE

THERE'S *a story attached to that, you know. It happened a long, long time ago, before Amairgen and the Sons of Mil set foot on these shores. Before the children of the goddess Danu retreated to the sidhe. Not so far back as the plague that killed the sons and daughters of Partholan. Not so far back as that. But a long time ago, even so.*

In those days, there were giants roamed the earth, and creatures with one leg and one arm, like serpents, came out of the sea. Back then, unsheathed weapons told tales, the sky could rain fire, and the shrieks of the Hag would be heard in the night. And it was then that the fiercest of battles, the struggle of light over darkness, were fought and won by the Tuatha dé Danaan. First they routed the Fir Bolg, then banished the dreaded Fomorians in the Battles of Mag Tuired.

The tales of their heroes, their leaders in battle, we tell to this day: Lugh, luminous, shining, destroyer of the Evil Eye; Diancecht, the healer; Nuada Silver Hand; and first and foremost, the Dagda.

Now there was a god! An excellent one, by his own description. A giant, with appetite to match. It was the Dagda had a cauldron in which pigs were cooked. This was no ordinary cauldron, nor ordinary pigs. Was always a pig ready, and the cauldron never empty, no matter how many came to dine. And, to top it all, the cauldron's contents were said to inspire the poet and revive the dead.

Anyway, one day the Dagda went to the camp of the Fomorians to ask for a truce, and also, for he was a crafty one, to spy on their camp. The Fomorians, some of them giants themselves, prepared for him a porridge of eighty gallons of milk, another eighty of meal and fat. Into this they put pigs and goats and sheep, then poured it all into an enormous hole in the ground.

"Eat all of it," the Fomorians said, "or die."

"I will then," the Dagda replied, and taking his ladle, so big a man and a woman could lie down in its bowl together, he started to eat. As the Fomorians watched, he swallowed every last bit of it, scraping up the crumbs in the dirt with his massive hand where the ladle couldn't reach, then lay himself down to sleep.

"Look at his belly," the Fomorians cried, pointing at the sleeping Dagda, his gut rising like a mountain from where he lay. "He'll not be getting up from here."

And what do you think happened then? The Dagda awoke, grunted, hefted his huge bulk up and staggered away, his club dragging behind him, cutting a furrow the width of a boundary ditch. Even then he was not spent, for later that day, he lay with the Morrigan, the Crow, goddess of war. But anyway, that's another story.

I was there then, you know. Yes, I was. Who's to say that I wasn't?

Chapter One

I AM THE SEA-SWELL

ONE of the very few advantages of being dead, I've discovered, is that you can say whatever you like. Freed from the burden of exquisite politeness, you can utter whatever painful truths, cruel jibes, gut-wrenching confessions, and acid parting shots you wish, without having to endure the drama, endless protestations, embarrassment, or threats of retaliation such candor inevitably elicits.

Eamon Byrne thought as much, I suppose, but in saying what he did, he unleashed a howl of rage and bitterness so intense, perhaps not even he could have imagined its consequences. Certainly, when I heard him speak from the grave, I thought him merely churlish and insensitive, although not altogether mistaken. But that was before I had more than a passing acquaintance with the people of whom he spoke.

"I suppose you're wondering why I called you all together," Byrne began, a smirk on his face that turned into a grimace, then a gasp.

"Eamon always did like to be the center of attention," Alex Stewart whispered to me, leaning close to my ear so the others wouldn't hear.

"Eamon also had a way with a cliché, apparently," I whispered back.

"Particularly," the man went on after a few seconds of labored breathing, "particularly," he repeated, "seeing as how I'm dead."

"Bit of a comedian too," Alex added with a sigh.

The face on the videotape leaned toward the camera, blurred, then lurched back into focus, the camera adjusted by some invisible hand. It was not an easy face to look at, sunken cheeks and eyes, an oxygen tube extending from one nostril, gray hair plastered to his head, but I could see the shadow of a proud and once handsome man.

"I'm amazed he'd allow himself to be videotaped in this state," I whispered to Alex.

Alex inclined his head toward me again. "I never had the impression he much cared what people thought, Lara. Quite the contrary, as a matter of fact." As he spoke, a foot-long tortoise inched its way across the oriental carpet.

"Shhhh," the pinched-faced woman in the row in front of us hissed over her shoulder. Two other like-faced women in the same row turned at the first's admonition to glare at us, mother and daughters, like three peas in a pod, the family resemblance that pronounced. I resisted the temptation of saying something unkind, and contented myself with glaring back and thinking uncharitable thoughts.

It was an unpleasant little group, I thought: the three women, and seated between them, like spacers of some kind, two men. The men had taken their jackets off, the oppressive heat and staleness of the room vanquishing any attempt at acknowledging the solemnity of the occasion. They slouched in their chairs, two white shirts and pale necks topped by fair hair, as much as I could see of them. For a moment they made me think of the cotton batting they stick between your toes when you're having a pedicure to keep you from messing up the wet nail polish. It was a surprisingly apt metaphor I was later to learn, not just because of what it said about the two men, but because of the way they divided the women of the family in life.

To our left, the big toe, was the mother, Margaret, tall, fair and stylishly thin, neat in a suitably black nubbly-wool suit, with the short, boxy jacket and braid that one associates with Chanel. She was justifiably proud of her legs, good for her age, which she crossed and uncrossed at regular intervals. Next to her sat the first ball of white fluff, her son-in-law, Sean McHugh, then his wife, Eithne, Margaret's eldest daughter, also tall, fair and thin, with an edginess about her that suggested she was the worrier of the family; then the next ball of cotton, Conail O'Connor, seated next to his wife Fionuala, the second daughter, who looked much like the others, except not quite so tall and with a certain blousiness that marked her as the vamp of the threesome. The women were united by both a rigidity in the spine and a bitterness of outlook that had carved itself into the features in their faces, most noticeably for the mother, who looked as if she had a chronic bad taste in her mouth, but already, too soon, for her daughters. The men, on the other hand, were characterized by a softness about the chin and belly that matched what I saw to be, in the very short time I'd known them, a propensity to indolence.

The next toe, had she chosen to sit with the others, would have been Breeta, the youngest daughter. Instead, she sat slouched in an armchair, as far away as she could, in that crowded room, from her mother and siblings. She seemed a bit younger than her sisters, mid-twenties, I would have said. While the older sisters were the usual two or three years apart, there were at least six or seven years between Breeta and the next youngest, Fionuala. Breeta was, perhaps, the little surprise at the end of the childbearing years, or a last ditch effort to save her parents' marriage. If it were the latter, it was unsuccessful, I'd warrant a guess. Overweight, with a rather pouty demeanor, but pretty nonetheless, she took after her father, I thought, looking at the face on the TV screen, with her dark hair and pale eyes, and bore only passing resemblance to the other three women. Her attitude was one I'd seen in others of her generation, a kind of studied indifference to the world around her. Whether this total lack of interest in the day's proceedings was feigned or genuine, I couldn't begin to guess.

The only person in the room who showed any evidence of regret for the passing of the deceased was a young man with flaming red hair, his face, flushed by the sun and sprinkled with freckles, genuinely solemn, I thought. He looked to be a man who did physical labor outdoors, his muscles straining the seams of his plain but neat suit jacket, his worn shirt collar tight around his neck. His name was Michael Davis, I'd learned, and in addition to being one of the few in the room who mourned Eamon Byrne, he was also one of the two people in the room treated with the same coolness by the rest of them as was Alex. Appropriately enough, Michael was stuffed into the back row with Alex and me, along with the other social outcast, a man I had been told was a lawyer representing an as yet unidentified person.

The group was rounded out by two lawyers who

were looking after Eamon's estate, a maid by the name of Deirdre—I'd mentally named her Deirdre of the Sorrows because of her morose expression, whether habitual or brought out for the occasion I didn't know, and because, as a loyal retainer at the Byrne estate, she was apparently entitled to the use of only one name—and another indentured individual by the name of John, also of one name only, who smelled of stale booze and whose hands shook as he pointed everyone in the direction of their seats. John kept backing out into the hall from time to time for what I assumed to be a wee nip from a flask, something I might not have noticed, save for the fact that his shoes, black lace-ups, squeaked when he walked. Nor should I fail to include in my list of those present, the tortoise, a family pet that had the run, or should I say the slow walk, of the house. It was a new experience for me, having to keep a sharp eye out to avoid stepping on a pet tortoise, and it gave me a whole new appreciation for the way Diesel, Official Guard Cat for the antiques store I co-own, manages to stay out of everyone's way.

Aside from the tortoise, what I found interesting sitting there watching all of this reasonably dispassionately, was that, although I could not see the faces of the five family members seated in front of us, except from time to time in profile or on the rare occasion on which they chose to acknowledge our presence by hissing at us, it was still quite possible to get an impression of how they felt about everything, and everyone.

It was quite evident from the back, for example, that while they were seated together for the occasion, and despite their similarities in appearance and attitude, most notably a chilly disdain, if not outright ill will toward Alex, they didn't get along. All the marks of a warring family were there. They rarely looked at each other, all the women sitting ramrod straight, heads resolutely forward, the men slouched down but never looking at anyone except their partners next to them. They also assiduously avoided looking at Breeta, although she from time to time glanced their way, and they absolutely ignored Michael and the mystery lawyer. It must have taken a great effort of will not to look about the room or to turn one's head as the door banged, but iron will was something they apparently had in abundance.

It should be evident by now that I was not fond of these people. If any of them, with the possible exception of Michael Davis, had any redeeming qualities whatsoever, I hadn't come across them so far. As I glared back at the three women, I began to wish I hadn't come to Ireland at all, a thought I immediately regretted. If Alex Stewart felt the need of my presence here, then my presence he would have.

Alex Stewart is a very dear friend of mine, a retired gentleman who lives a couple of doors away from me and who comes in on a regular basis to help us out at Greenhalgh & McClintoch. That's an antiques and design shop in a trendy part of Toronto called Yorkville, so trendy, in fact, that we probably can't afford to be there. Some months earlier, Alex suffered a blow on the head and what the doctors described as a very tiny stroke during his convalescence. It barely slowed him down, just a little numbness on one side for a few days, but it scared the living daylights out of me. I'd been clucking and fussing over him ever since in a way that I'm sure nearly drove him mad.

So when Ryan McGlynn, solicitor with the firm of McCafferty and McGlynn of Dublin, no less, had called to tell Alex that his presence at the reading of the Will of one Eamon Byrne was required, and Alex had expressed some reservations about going, I insisted upon coming along with him. To keep from embarrassing him, I told him I needed a holiday, and indeed, much to my own surprise, the idea of me taking a vacation being an even more novel idea than a tortoise for a pet, I decided to have one. In addition, I'd managed to convince a friend of mine, a sergeant in the Royal Canadian Mounted Police by the name of Rob Luczka, and his daughter Jennifer, to come along with us. The four of us planned to tour about Ireland after the reading of the Will.

Alex said he didn't know why he'd been summoned, but I was hoping that he'd come into a minor fortune of some kind so he could spend the rest of his days in luxury. I could think that knowing he'd continue to come into the store to help out anyway, that being the kind of person he was, but at least I wouldn't have to worry about whether or not he could afford to live on his pension and the paltry sum we were able to pay him.

Alex's airfare was to be covered by the Byrne estate, apparently, and I cashed in a few thousand frequent flyer points, of which I have approximately a billion, to get tickets for myself and Jennifer Luczka. I have that many points because the merchandise Sarah Greenhalgh and I sell in the shop is purchased all over the world. I do almost all the buying, since Sarah doesn't really enjoy that part of the business, on at least four major trips a year.

I don't know why I don't use my points more often. I tell people I'm saving them for a round-the-world trip, which I know I'll probably never take. Why should I? I'm doing what I love and get all the travel anyone could want just doing my job. The truth is I'm rather superstitiously keeping the points in case Sarah and I are ever so broke that the only way we can stay in business is for me to travel free. My best friend Moira, who owns the swank beauty salon cum spa down the street, says that the accountants or actuaries who are paid to worry about such things as people hoarding enough points to bankrupt an airline will send someone to kill me one day.

We'd only been in Ireland for twenty-four hours or so, and I was already beginning to regret using those points. There we were, seated in the gloom of a room in Eamon Byrne's estate, which, according to a discreet sign out at the road, was called Second Chance. The house was quite beautiful, pale yellow stucco with black roof and white trim, an impressive long and curving drive, and acres and acres of grounds stretching toward the sea. The driveway was lined with hydrangea bushes laden with stunning pink, blue, and purple flowers so heavy they almost touched the ground. Across the back of the house was a sunroom, all done up in white wicker and green chintz, with a view of absolutely gorgeous gardens, and farther away, across a stone patio and staircase lined with white plaster urns, the blue of Dingle Bay. It was remarkably light and airy, quite in contrast with the general mood of the place.

We, however, were in the library, which suited the occasion perfectly. A rather large and impressive room also at the back of the house, off the sunroom, it was panelled in very dark wood, with oversized black leather chairs and a desk so large they must have had to build the house around it. The library had apparently also served as Eamon Byrne's study. On this occasion, the curtains, of bordello red velvet, floor to ceiling, were pulled across the very large windows to keep out the daylight, and regrettably both the air and the view, all the better to enjoy the show. The room had, to my occasionally oversensitive nose, a faint smell of anti-septic.

In contrast to the quiet elegance of the exterior of the house, this room was cluttered, almost to the point of chaos. Byrne, it appeared, was an inveterate collector and not necessarily a discriminating one. This is not to say that what he collected wasn't good—a cursory glance about me when we'd first arrived indicated he knew what he was collecting very well—but he didn't appear, at first glance anyway, to restrict himself to a specialty. If there was a unifying theme to his collecting, it was not immediately apparent to me. There were paintings, prints, books, hundreds of them, many of them leather-bound and quite old, on shelves, piled on the furniture and on the floor, which itself was covered by three oriental carpets of real quality.

The paintings that adorned the walls, oils all of them, were dark, primarily of large sailing ships battling either the elements or enemy ships at sea. Along one wall were glass cases in which were displayed some very old weapons, largely swords and spear tips, and on the bottom shelf of the case were rather extraordinary iron pots or bowls, some of them at least twelve inches in diameter, others even larger; Iron Age cauldrons, I decided. All were laid out against a red velvet backdrop, a perfect match for the curtains. I figured, as I looked about me, that it must have taken tens of thousands of dollars and about a mile of red velvet to do the room. A single sword, its blade eaten away in places by time, was mounted on the wall behind the desk, and another, obviously special, was mounted under glass on the desk. It was an impressive collection to be sure, but it did lend a rather menacing air to the proceedings. It made me think that, for Eamon Byrne, on the assumption it was he who'd amassed the paintings and the weapons, life was one long battle of some kind.

The television and VCR were placed on the credenza behind the massive desk, the TV raised on a stack of books. It was placed just slightly to one side of the desk chair, which gave the impression, from the angle at which I was sitting, squashed with Alex at the back of the room behind the more important people in Eamon's life, that the talking head was where it would have been had Eamon been alive, a sight that would normally have made me giggle, had the situation not been so lacking in humor.

With the exception of Breeta, flopped in the large armchair folding and refolding a lace handkerchief, the rest of us were perched on rather uncomfortable metal folding chairs in two semicircles around the desk. The VCR was being handled by Charles McCafferty, one half of McCafferty and McGlynn. At least I think it was McCafferty. He and his partner wore virtually identical rather expensive-looking suits, dark, nice cut, matching vests with watches and fobs, and white shirts with very starched high collars and French cuffs with silver cuff links. They also sported almost identical designer haircuts and expensive-looking reading glasses that allowed them to peer down their noses at the rest of the world. One distinguished them, apparently, by the pattern on their silver-gray ties, one diamonds, the other stripes, their idea, I suppose, of rugged individuality. I'd mentally named them Tweedledum and Tweedledee. I shouldn't do this, I know, make up monickers, often, but not always, disparaging, for people all the time. But, let's face it, I'm dreadful at remembering names. And no matter what I called them, McCafferty and McGlynn appeared to be doing quite nicely, thank you. They had that prosperous look to them, lack of sartorial originality notwithstanding. It was humbling to think that for what they had both forked out to dress themselves, I could probably pay off my mortgage.

"You'll be hearing shortly from either McCafferty or McGlynn—they're virtually interchangeable as far as I'm concerned—about the terms of my will," Eamon Byrne continued after another long pause for breath. Tweedledum looked uncomfortable with Byrne's notion that he and Tweedledee were indistinguishable, although I could not have agreed more. The three hags, as I'd already come to call them, turned their attention from us back to the television.

"Not to keep you in suspense, you will find that I have left my company, Byrne Enterprises, to my daughters Eithne and Fionuala, or Eriu and Fotla as I liked to call them when they were small, and de facto, I suppose, to their husbands Sean and Conail. Sean and Conail have, of course, been running, or should I say running down, the business during my illness, seeing as how they prefer warming the seats of their favorite bar stools to an honest day's work, in Conail's case, or swanking around like an English squire, in Sean's." The two men shuffled angrily in their seats, as the face, drawn with the effort, continued speaking. "I expect that unless my daughters see their way clear to turfing the two laggards out, their inheritance will quickly become worthless.

"To my wife Margaret I have left Second Chance, including the land, the house, and all its contents, with two exceptions, Rose Cottage, which I will speak of later, and my collection of antique weapons, maps, and manuscripts, which, by previous arrangement, I leave to Trinity College, Dublin. I have also provided her with an allowance that most would consider generous, but which she will no doubt consider miserly. Being responsible for the upkeep of the house and grounds should be instructional for Margaret, who may begin to have some appreciation for what it took to keep her in the style which she felt her due. Unless she can find herself another husband of some means in short order, I expect she'll be selling it soon." Judging by the knots at the back of Margaret's jaw, accompanied as they were by a sharp intake of breath, she was less than amused.

"To my youngest daughter, Breeta, who, until she left home in a fury two years ago, was my favorite, my little Banba—I'm sure I'm not telling my other two something they didn't know—I leave nothing. She said she despised my money, and so she gets none of it." Breeta said nothing, only bending, perhaps to hide her face, to pick up the tortoise as he began to amble under her chair. She sat stroking its little head as if this was the only thing in the world there was to do.

"I have settled upon what I hope is a generous sum for the staff of Second Chance. In addition, I have made arrangements for a monthly stipend to be paid to Michael Davis, if he agrees to go back to finish his schooling. I sincerely hope he will take me up on my offer and make something of himself. He has eased the burden of the last few weeks for me considerably." All eyes turned to Michael, none that I could see friendly. Michael looked charmingly grateful for his good fortune, but his furrowed brow indicated he wasn't sure how he'd eased Eamon's burden.

"Rose Cottage, its contents, and the land on which it sits, I leave to Alex Stewart of Toronto, who I hope is here today. It is Alex who gave me my second chance which, despite everything, I am grateful for, no matter what I said at the time, and while he has refused

my offer of compensation during my lifetime, I hope
he will accept this now. Rose Cottage has been a place
of great pleasure to me, and I hope that Alex will enjoy
it too."

Rose Cottage, I thought. Not quite the small fortune
I'd had in mind for Alex, perhaps. He certainly looked
somewhat taken aback by the notion. I had a sudden
vision of a stone cottage, its front yard ablaze with
flowers, a miniature version of the grounds at Second
Chance. Roses in profusion, that was its name after all.
White and pink, I decided, ramping up trellises, arching
over the entranceway. A thatched roof, of course. Inside, whitewashed walls and dark, exposed beams, a
huge stone fireplace, logs blazing, a carved wooden
swan on the mantelpiece. Huge comfy sofas, down-
filled, perhaps, covered in chintz in what? A soft, hazy
green? Celadon, perhaps? No, wait, rose, dusty rose. It
would have to be rose. But large and soft and squishy.
Sofas to sink way down into, a good book and a glass
of sherry at hand. Alex would have to modernize the
kitchen and plumbing, no doubt, but that would be fine.
I'd help him. And there'd be a shortage of closets, but
I'd ship over a couple of antique armoires from the
store as a present. Minor details. In short, it was perfect. The floors would probably need refinishing, wide
planks, stained dark, with area rugs, dhurries, I'd think,
that would pick up the rose, with the celadon and
cream . . .

My mental excursion through the ozone was disturbed by the crackle of psychic tension in the room.
When I came to, as it were, Margaret was so tense that
cords stood out on her neck, and even from the back I
could tell her jaw was rather firmly clenched. Breeta
sobbed just once, out loud. Her older sisters' shoulders
were hunched up to their ears. As Eamon spoke about

Alex, the anger in the room, kept in check so far, threatened to boil over. They may not have been too thrilled about Michael's good fortune, but Alex's, for some reason, really bothered them.

The face, undeterred, stopped only for a moment to sip liquid through a straw. "There is one other person who may be here, but who, fearing the wrath of my family, may send a representative instead." The hags turned and looked at the lawyer seated to our right. He nodded and smiled somewhat less than pleasantly in their direction.

"I have, with regret, acceded to my family's wishes and have left nothing for Padraig Gilhooly in my estate." The lawyer, who I surmised was representing this Gilhooly fellow, whoever he was, frowned; Margaret's back relaxed a little. The face continued. "I want Padraig to know that nothing would have made me happier than to have him accepted in our household. Perhaps he will sue for a share of the estate. It is one of the benefits of being dead that I will not have to deal with this. I leave that family squabble and all the others I have had to endure, to the living.

"It is a source of considerable pain to me that there is so much strife in this family. In an effort to address this, even in death, I have designed an exercise that will require you to work together." Shoulders stiffened all around the room.

"As unorthodox as this may be, I have some hope for it, the foolish optimism of a dying man, if you will. I have asked that after the Will is read, McCafferty and McGlynn give each of you an envelope. These two legal bookends have objected, of course, that this is not appropriate. Their protestations, mild as they were, were intended no doubt to protect their backsides should anything untoward occur, while still permitting them to collect the additional fee they require for this endeavor. They are too accustomed to the lush lifestyle of St. Stephen's Green to refuse my request, particularly when I told them I would find other executors for my estate if they did so.

"In each of the envelopes, there is a clue that, taken with the others, will lead to something of great value. One clue in itself will not get you there. Some lead to information about the object itself; others point to its location. In other words, to find it, you must work together. I am not trying to be even remotely subtle about this. If you need a reason to participate, let me remind you of what I have already said. For some of you there is nothing from me on my death, for others, not as much as they might like. Those who have received something of value from me may well find that what I have left you has become worthless. This object has, if you find it, sufficient value to help you all. I would urge you to learn to work and live in harmony. I very much doubt that you will be able to do so, but I sincerely hope you will prove me wrong. If you do not, then something truly remarkable and priceless will remain hidden, possibly forever. That is all I have to say."

With that, the face raised one hand in what could be interpreted as a gesture of dismissal, either for the cameraman or all of us. The camera drew back from the face slightly to reveal yet more tubes and hospital paraphernalia, rows of pill bottles on a bedside table. From Byrne there came no expressions of affection, not even a good-bye, just the picture of a dying man lying there, lines of pain etched into his face, slowly fading to black.

For a minute or two, we all sat looking at the blank screen as we contemplated the last words of Eamon

Byrne, no sound save a vague hiss from the television, the ticking of a clock in the hall, a muffled call of birds, the rustle of palm fronds, and somewhere far away, the faint roar of a wind-swept sea.

Breeta bestirred herself first. "Effing brill, Da," she sighed, hoisting herself out of the chair and heading for the door. "Just effing brill."

"What does effing brill mean?" Alex, looking perplexed, whispered to me, as we watched Breeta's exit.

"I think the second word is 'brilliant,' and the first begins with an f," I whispered back.

Alex looked over at Breeta's rather large departing rear and shook his head disapprovingly. I stifled a smile. Alex was, for many years, a purser in the merchant marine, no less, but I have never heard an obscenity pass his lips, nor have I ever heard him swear. I, on the other hand . . . But so much for stereotypes.

Tweedledee nervously cleared his throat as a signal that the more formal part of the proceedings was to begin. "Most unusual," he began. "I suppose it is necessary for Miss Breeta Byrne to attend?" he said, looking over at Tweedledum.

"Highly unusual. Should be here," Tweedledum replied. Tweedledee shuffled papers uncomfortably for a moment or two, as Deirdre pulled open the curtains. I could see Breeta heading down through the garden toward the sea.

"May I suggest we all take a short break," Tweedledum said. "Perhaps Deirdre," he said, turning to the maid, "you would bring us some fresh tea, and Mr. Davis," he said, thinking better than to ask John to do anything too taxing, seeing as how he'd backed out of the room several times during the proceedings, "you might go and ask Miss Byrne to oblige us by returning to the house."

The fabulous five in front of us arose as if one unit and in single file, left the room. Needless to say, no one bothered to suggest we join them or have a tour of the house or anything, leaving Alex and me and Padraig Gilhooly's lawyer to fend for ourselves, while Tweedledum and Tweedledee fussed with papers and envelopes. Gathering that we were to stay where we were, I gratefully unfolded myself from the uncomfortable chair, and being no longer obliged to watch out for the tortoise, Breeta having taken the creature with her, stretched and looked about me as Michael Davis, visible through French doors on to the patio, jogged off in the direction where we'd last seen Byrne's youngest daughter.

It perhaps goes without saying that the reason I am in the antiques business is that I love antiques, and once I'd adjusted to the chaos in Eamon Byrne's room, and freed from the acid glances of his family, the place was a real feast for the eyes and the soul for someone like me.

You can tell a lot about people from the art they collect, and while I was sticking with my snap analysis that life for Byrne was a battle of some kind, I began to see a thread of coherence in what he'd amassed. I decided after a few minutes that the paintings were the anomaly. They'd probably been in the family, his or hers I wasn't sure, for a long time, and they'd been positioned where Byrne, sitting at his desk, wouldn't see much of them.

What Byrne did like to look at were two things: the weapon collection and his maps. The weapons were, I decided, very old and reasonably consistent with a particular period, although I wasn't sure what that period would be. That is to say, Byrne did not collect weapons in general, he collected a specific period. There were

no muskets and pistols, for example, no Prussian hel-
mets or war medals, just very old swords and spear
points.

Maps were everywhere in that room, framed on the
walls, spread out on a worktable, lying about the room
in the form of large atlases. There were also several
rolls in the corner of the room, and I'd be willing to
wager that they, too, were maps. As well, there was a
cabinet with long shallow drawers that would probably
house more.

I've had old maps in the shop from time to time and
at that time was beginning to look for more of them
for a new customer who was an avid collector. Essentially, most of the maps you see on the average wall
these days are prints pulled from old atlases, and most
of them date to the middle and late nineteenth century.
Botanicals, botanical prints, have been very trendy
lately, and prices have soared, but I've found maps to
be a nice steady item. A lot of people buy them because
they look nice on their panelled den walls, decorator
art I call it, but there are serious collectors out there
who look for the rare and unusual and are prepared to
pay for it. These people are particularly thrilled by
sheet maps, that is maps that are not cut out of atlases,
but were printed or, in really rare cases, drawn, on individual sheets of paper or textile.

My customer, a normally amiable fellow by the
name of Matthew Wright who collected early maps of
the British Isles, would have killed, or at least seriously
maimed, for a couple of Byrne's. Matthew has told me
that Britain and Ireland were known to the ancients,
due to a flourishing trade with the islands, and that as
august a personage as the Alexandrian astronomer Ptol-
emy had mapped that area in the second century A.D.
All of Byrne's maps were of Ireland, and a couple of

them at least I recognized. One was a Speed map, John Speed having been a mapmaker in the early seventeenth century. It was not entirely accurate, in terms of its survey of Ireland, but it was undoubtedly the best of its time. Byrne's was dated 1610, and while it was not necessarily a first edition, because Speed's maps were usually dated then, but were copied for a long time afterward, I was reasonably sure it was an original.

Another map was attributed, according to a bronze plaque on its frame, to William Petty, who, if I remembered correctly, had produced the first atlas of Ireland sometime in the seventeenth century. There was a third map, under glass on top of the map cabinet, that was rather charming, with the lines of sunrise and sunset over Ireland for several points during the year depicted, along with drawings of monsters arising from the sea around Ireland's shores. The rest of the framed maps were also good, although not as unique as the Speed and the Petty, but an impressive collection indeed. I could see why Byrne had seen fit to leave it to Trinity College, and I expected they'd be more than pleased to have it.

What was interesting, if one were inclined to try to understand Byrne from this collection, was that in addition to the framed maps, there were hundreds of others, none of them, to my relatively untrained eyes at least, valuable, attractive, old, or particularly noteworthy in any way. There were current ordnance maps, Michelin road maps, maps of all shapes and sizes. This said to me that while Byrne collected the weapons for their antiquity, he collected maps for a different reason, one that I thought at the time I would probably never know.

After a few minutes delay, no doubt to serve the

family first, Deirdre wheeled in the tea service on a little trolley, handing cups of tea all round. I thought a sip or two of the legendary Irish whiskey would have been a considerable improvement, but understood that the occasion called for solemn sobriety.

"He died right there," Deirdre said, after handing me my teacup. "Right where you're standing." Involuntarily, I jumped, almost dumping my tea on the oriental carpet. "We had his bed set up in here," she went on, not noticing my distress. "He couldn't get up the stairs at the end. Lung cancer," she added. "Came on sudden. Very bad, it was. He liked it here, though, with his books and his maps, and the view of the garden and the sea. We put the bed where he could look out. He was alone. Sad really. The night nurse hadn't come in yet and the rest of them," she said, tossing her head in the direction we'd last seen the family, "were at dinner. And Breeta long gone." Deirdre looked even more morose, if that was possible. "In the prime of life, he was, not old at all. I thought he'd last till Christmas, you know. Lots of people do, hold on until Christmas, I mean."

"Why don't we have a look outside?" Alex said, taking my elbow.

"Fine idea," I said gratefully, and Alex and I, throwing caution to the winds, risked the ire of the Byrne family by opening the French doors and stepping outside to the flagstone patio at the back of the house. We stood there soaking up the sun while we waited, carefully sipping cups of tea so strong and hot you could feel it corroding your insides on the way down.

"What a place!" I exclaimed when we were out in the fresh air. Alex nodded.

"What did Byrne mean when he said you'd given him a second chance?" I went on. Alex had told me he'd known Byrne many years before, that's all. In fact, I'd found him a little cagey on the subject, an attitude I was soon to find out was due to a promise he'd made Byrne so long ago.

Alex gestured to me to move away from the house. "I'm not sure how much his family knows of this," he said quietly, "so let's make sure we're well out of earshot." We moved into the gardens, pausing to enjoy the scent of a profusion of rosebushes. "The first time I saw Eamon Byrne he was holding up the bar in a seedy dive in Singapore," Alex began. "My ship was in dry dock for repairs, and so I and the lads had a bit of shore leave. Eamon was drunk, of course, the proverbial drunken Irishman, and a little morose, to boot. Not a happy drunk, but a talkative one. You know how it is, people who want to talk whether you want to listen or not. Went on and on about Ireland, how beautiful it was, but none so fair as the woman he loved and lost, that kind of thing. Real drivel, I thought. In fact, I'd have to say he was a crashing bore. But I went back the next night, same place. The booze was cheap, and they didn't water it down too much. Eamon was there again, just as drunk.

"This time he wasn't nearly as talkative. Just stood there holding up the bar, downing glass after glass of cheap Irish whiskey, crying into his glass. Hard to say, isn't it, which is worse: a talkative drunk or a morose one. The only thing he told me was how he'd let his family, his mother, I think, down. He was a disgrace, really. Smelled bad, and it was not just the booze. Hadn't bathed in days. I just wanted to get rid of him.

"One minute he's got his head on the bar, then, in a flash, he's straightened his back, as if he's reached some resolution, some conclusion, and he staggers off the bar stool and out into the street. I have no idea why

I did it, he was so unpleasant, a sixth sense maybe, but I followed him. He walked down to the water and stood for the longest time on the pier, brooding, staring into the water. I was about to pack it in, when suddenly, quick as a wink, he threw himself in. Even in the dim beam from the light at the end of the pier, I could see he couldn't swim. He didn't even try. Just sank like a stone. Well, what was I to do? Just stand there and watch him drown? I went after him."

"Are you saying he couldn't swim, or that he wouldn't?" I interrupted.

"Probably couldn't. A lot of sailors refuse to learn to swim. Figure if they go overboard in the North Atlantic, or somewhere like that, they might as well go straight to the bottom as struggle hopelessly on."

"But you're saying he was trying to kill himself. That it wasn't an accident."

"It was no accident, of that I am certain. It was really hard to find him in the dark, and I can't tell you how heavy he was, but I managed to haul him out. The poor sod was trying to fight me off, but he was too drunk. I dragged him back to a filthy little hotel, him cursing at me—his daughter comes by her choice of language honestly, I must say—put him to bed, and watched over him while he slept. The next day I made him wash, and we had a little chat about life, the one I had from time to time with the young lads on the ship who went somewhat astray, shall we say. We had a terrible row, actually. Somewhat comic, I'd think, in the overall scheme of things, if it wasn't so desperate. Here I was trying to think of reasons why he shouldn't kill himself, and him arguing with me.

"I told him a life was a terrible thing to waste, and he told me his wasn't worth saving. Then I told him he was a coward, doing what he did, no matter what had happened to him. He said it was his life, and up to him what he did with it. I wasn't making too much headway until I noticed he was wearing a small cross around his neck. I told him he'd roast in hell if he died by his own hand. I remember he just looked at me, then said he'd roast in hell for much worse things than that. But it seemed to do the trick. He pulled himself together. In the end, he forgave me for saving him, I guess. He said something to the effect that it wasn't my fault because a man could only go when he was called, and that he hadn't been called that day in Singapore. Nice fatalistic touch, really, the idea that your day of death is preordained. Superstitious people, the Irish, in many ways."

"No hint of what he'd done that was so terrible, then?" I asked.

"He said he'd broken something actually, although I can't recall what it was."

"Just a minute," I said. "Are you telling me he tried to kill himself because he'd knocked over the family's favorite Royal Doulton figurine, or something?"

"It would be more likely to be the Waterford crystal here in Ireland, don't you think?" Alex smiled. "No, I think it was something more like a taboo. He used a word I didn't recognize, it wasn't English. I wish I could remember it, because someone around here might be able to tell me what it was. Maybe it will come back to me. The memory isn't what it used to be, unfortunately. Old age, I'm afraid."

"It's still better than mine," I replied. "So then what? Obviously you were successful in talking him out of suicide."

"I got him a job as a deckhand, and for the next few months we sailed together. It's backbreaking work, you know, on those ships, but it was what he needed,

I guess, and he was a good worker. When we got back to Europe, he took his wages, which he'd managed not to drink, and left the ship. He made me promise I'd never tell anyone about what he called his moment of weakness, and I never have until this very moment. And I don't think I'll tell his family now, quite frankly, even though it doesn't much matter, I suppose, now that he's dead.

"I can't say I really got to know him, we'd never be close friends, and we lost touch soon after. I'd never seen him again until today. If you count that video as seeing him, that is. That and his picture in one of those business magazines about five years ago: he was being touted as a big success in one of those international roundups or whatever they call them. I recognized him, although he looked a whole lot different. To be honest with you, I have no idea why he should remember me in his Will, really. I did very little for him, and I certainly wasn't expecting to be given anything when he died."

"He said you'd refused compensation before," I said.

"He sent me a letter about ten years after we'd parted company with a check for ten thousand Irish punt in it—his fortunes had clearly improved over the intervening years—but no return address. I never cashed it. There was no reason for him to do that, really."

"It makes perfect sense to me," I said. "As he said, you gave him a second chance. He even named his house and property Second Chance, didn't he? It was an important moment, a watershed of some sort in his life." Alex shrugged. "I wonder where this Rose Cottage of yours is," I added. "I hope it's nice."

At this moment Michael Davis hove into view. "I didn't find Breeta," he said. "I looked everywhere. What'll we do?"

Michael's news required a major consultation on the part of Tweedledum and Tweedledee, but in the end they opted to proceed with the reading of the Last Will and Testament of Eamon O'Neill Byrne of County Kerry, Ireland. There were no surprises, except perhaps to learn that both Deirdre and John had two names, like the rest of us: Flood in Deirdre's case, Deirdre Flood, and Herlihy in the case of John. Michael Davis looked suitably grateful for the gift Eamon had bestowed upon him, John Herlihy surreptitiously poured himself a congratulatory drink from a crystal decanter on a side table, and even Deirdre of the Sorrows showed something akin to a small smile when she heard what she would get. They were reasonably generous sums, Deirdre's not being as large as John's, which I took to mean she had joined the staff at Second Chance rather later than he had. The lawyer for Padraig Gilhooly sat stone-faced through the whole affair, and shoulders stiffened once again when Tweedledee came to the part about Alex and Rose Cottage. The sons-in-law squirmed with pleasure when their wives' inheritance of Byrne Enterprises was confirmed and Margaret looked suitably shocked, as her husband had predicted, by the mere pittance, though plenty by most standards, that he'd left her. There were the usual puts and takes: an unbelievably complicated formula on how, if any of them died, where the remaining funds were to go, and so on. I confess I didn't pay much attention.

Then came the moment, considered unorthodox even by Byrne himself, when the two lawyers went about the room handing all those named in the Will, an envelope with their names on it scrawled in a shaky hand: Eamon Byrne's, no doubt, written with one last dying effort. Margaret got one, as did both Eithne and Fionuala, and also, surprisingly, since this was to have been

a family exercise, Alex, Michael, and Padraig Gilhooly's lawyer. Only one envelope remained un-
claimed: Breeta's, since she wasn't there to receive it.
Tweedledum took that one and, with fanfare, locked it
in the safe in the wall of Byrne's office.

Everyone sat looking at their envelopes, nice creamy
linen ones with the initials EONB embossed on the
flap, as if opening them might set off a letter bomb.
All except Alex that is. He opened his immediately and
stood up. "I'm not sure I approve of this," he said, "but,
in the interests of getting it over with, mine says 'I am
the sea-swell.' "

The rest of them all sat there for a moment staring
at their hands, not looking at Alex, nor anyone else for
that matter. Then they got up, every last one of them,
and clutching their envelopes, unopened, hastened from
the room.

"NICE," I sighed. "Very nice," I added. "Lovely people. I think I've had about enough of this place for now. How about you?" I said, turning to Alex, who like me was watching the family beat their hasty, and nasty, retreat. "Why don't I buy you a drink back at the Inn?" I went on. "Rob and Jennifer are probably back from sight-seeing by now, and we can hear about their adventures. There isn't anything you need to do here right now, is there?"

"I don't think so, although I suppose I should ask," he replied, tucking the envelope and its obscure contents into his jacket pocket. We looked about us, but Tweedledum and Tweedledee were nowhere to be found. "I can always telephone later," he said. "A drink sounds like a very good idea."

We were well along the driveway and almost to where I'd parked our little rented car, when we heard footsteps hurrying across the gravel, and turned to see Michael Davis approaching us. "Mr. Stewart, Ms. McClintoch." He waved. "Wait for a minute."

He smiled as he caught up to us. "Don't you want to see Rose Cottage, Mr. Stewart?" he said. "I could show you where it is."

I looked at Alex and shrugged. "Why not? Is it far?"

"Not far," he replied, "but," he said looking rather dubiously at my feet, "it's a bit of a climb, Ms. McClintoch."

"Call me Lara, and I'm sure I'll be fine," I said tartly. I had eschewed my normal comfortable flat shoes and squashed my feet into something a little more fitting for such a formal occasion as the reading of a Will at Second Chance, a decision I'd been regretting long before this.

"Okay, Ms. McClintoch," he said, ignoring my attempt at familiarity, and making me feel rather old. "This way."

We went around to the back of the house, and down toward the water, then followed a path that led beside a hill on the right. The path started to climb, affording us a magnificent view of both the sea and the grounds of the Byrne estate. To one side of the house was a very large kitchen garden, four square beds of vegetables and herbs surrounded by a low hedge of what looked to be rosemary, and bisected by a stone path. An arch, almost obscured by white climbing roses, led to a cutting garden, I supposed, filled with a profusion of flowers. An almost perfect lawn divided that from the rose garden on one side, and a tropical setting of palms and flowers. I thought of the rather patchy swath of grass I called a lawn at home and felt more than a tinge of envy.

"Do you like them?" Michael asked. "The grounds, I mean?"

The gardens were exceptionally beautiful, and I said so.

"I'm really quite proud of them myself." He grinned.

"Are you . . . ?" I paused. Should I say gardener? I wondered.

"The groundskeeper," he said. Of course, I thought. People like me might have a gardener. Should have a gardener, I corrected myself, thinking of my pathetic attempts at making something of the backyard. The Eamon Byrnes of this world, however, have groundskeepers.

"You've done a wonderful job," I said, and Alex agreed.

"Mr. Byrne says I have the touch," he went on. "Said," he added. "He always said I had the touch." He looked out to sea for a moment. "He could be a mean old bugger, I know, but I'll miss him."

"Are those orchids?" I asked, pointing toward the palm grove, and trying to change the subject.

"They are," he replied, turning back to me. "This is a tiny ecosystem," he said. "A little tropical paradise where you might not expect it. This part of Ireland is warmed by the Atlantic currents, and some rather unusual plants and animals are the result." He went on to talk knowledgeably about various aspects of horticulture as we continued our climb up and around the side of the hill. I could see why Eamon Byrne thought Michael Davis worth supporting and sending back to school.

The path continued to curve around to the right and away from the house, until we reached a headland, high above the water. Here, the wind was in our faces, waves dashed the rocks below us, and a mass of yellow gorse and purple heather stretched as far as we could see, a feast for the eyes of a different kind from the carefully tended gardens around the house. This was the wild side of the hill. I looked back, but the house was now obscured from our view. Ahead of us was a small cluster of houses, derelict, roofs gone, and abandoned.

"It's not far now," Michael said. We continued along the path, which followed the edge of the cliff, occasionally veering too close to the edge for someone as uncomfortable with heights as I. The water lay rather far below us. It was spectacularly beautiful. Though it was still clear, as it had been all day, dark clouds were forming close to the horizon, and the sky on this side was a very dark gray, almost black. From time to time, the sun would pierce through the cloud, almost like a spotlight, and a bright circle of light would appear on the water below. As I watched a heron swooped low, skimming the water below us, "Next stop is America," Michael said, pointing out to sea. It was true, when I thought about it. There really was nothing but water between this point and North America. "I'd like to go there some day," he said wistfully, then more practically, "Rain coming. Weather comes up very fast here. We won't stay long."

Stay where, I wondered, but then I saw it. It was not quite as I'd imagined it: Rose Cottage. In every way, in fact, it was quite inappropriately named. Heather House, perhaps, or even Gorse Cottage, but not a rose to be seen. Instead, there was a wind-weathered house a hundred yards inland, its face to the sea, and its back to a mountain. It was not large, not compared to Second Chance, that is, and in many ways rather plain. Instead of the thatched roof of my reverie, the roof was slate. The walls were whitewashed and two rather tired-looking wooden chairs sat out front.

I turned to Alex. He stood almost transfixed by the sight of it, as if he could not believe his good fortune. He loved the place, I could tell, and even though I knew this might mean I'd lose his company back home, I felt a rush of happiness on his behalf.

"Take a pew, why don't you?" Michael said, gesturing to the chairs, "while I get the key." Alex sat on the sturdier-looking chair of the two and gazed about him. I looked around as well, out to sea, and then beyond the cottage to a patch of trees. When I looked back, Alex had a small smile on his face and was nodding his head.

"It's great, isn't it?" I said, feeling just so pleased for him.

"Quite wonderful," he replied, having found his voice at last.

Michael continued his search, lifting a couple of old pails on the porch and feeling up into the rafters. "What's the problem?" I asked him.

"The key," he replied. "It's usually around here somewhere. I thought Mr. Stewart would like to see inside."

I tried the door, and it opened. Michael shrugged. "Last one here forgot to lock up, I guess. No harm really. There's never anyone about, and there's nothing in here worth much."

We stepped inside into the main room. It may not have been the little jewel I'd imagined, but I immediately fell in love with it. On our left was a stone fireplace, cold stubs of candles stuck in wine bottles on the mantel, melted wax making little sculptured beehives at their base. Facing it was an old couch, not the perfect chintz I'd pictured, but satisfyingly comfy, and at right angles to it, two large chairs, the kind you yearn to flop down in. Another chair had been placed beside one of the two windows facing the sea, turned slightly so as to best capture the view. And what a view it was, across the heather to the cliffs and then as far as you could see over the water. I turned my gaze out to sea. It was one of those times when the light is extraordinary, when the sun is shining, but the sky and the water are almost black, the circling gulls slashes of white against the approaching dark. The wind dropped suddenly, the shriek of gulls as well, and the world fell silent, a kind of morbid stillness, as if breathless, waiting for something terrible to happen.

Thinking that even an hour or so locked with the Byrne family in that dark room with the red velvet and the war paintings and the swords and spears had put me in a dreary frame of mind, I wrenched my attention from these gloomy thoughts and turned back to the room.

In contrast to my unease about the world outside, the room had a very ordinary and comforting feel to it. To the right of the door was a rough-hewn table pushed against the wall, with two wooden chairs on either side. There was a pile of books on the table, and a well-worn sweater had been placed over the back of one chair. At the back, there was a tiny open kitchen, rather primitive in terms of appliances, just an icebox and a gas cooktop with two burners, which I took to mean there was no electricity. There was water, though, an enamel sink with a pump, and mismatched dishes stacked on open shelves. A doorway led off to the right, to what I assumed was the bedroom.

I looked about me. "Breeta," I called out. "Come and say hello."

The two men looked perplexed. After a few seconds, Breeta sidled through a door to the right of the fireplace. She was the kind of young woman, I thought, that people always made a point of saying had a pretty face, by way of ignoring her excess weight. She did have many good features, beautiful dark hair set against flawless pale skin and blue eyes, but at this very moment, she looked dreadful. I wanted to take her home to my friend Moira's beauty salon and get her straightened out. Her dark hair was unkempt, and she kept twisting a lank tendril round and round her finger. Dressed in black jeans and a baggy and rather unflatteringly-colored brown sweatshirt, she looked lumpen. Her pale skin was blotchy. She was suffering, it suddenly occurred to me, despite her uninterested demeanor, but whether it was from sorrow at the death of her father, or disappointment at being cut out of his Will, I couldn't say. "How did you know?" she asked accusingly.

I pointed toward the floor. "The tortoise. I saw its little brown head poking out from under the sofa," I added.

"He," she said getting down on her knees and reaching under the sofa. "It's a he, not an it. His name is Vigs." That appeared to be all she was prepared to say.

"Vigs," I agreed, as I walked to the kitchen counter. A half-empty bottle of whiskey sat on the counter. I opened it and sniffed. It smelled just fine to me. I grabbed four tumblers, and turned to the others. "How about a get-acquainted drink?" I asked. "We might as well, it's starting to rain," I added, as the room grew suddenly darker.

"Should these young people be drinking this?" Alex asked severely, eyeing the bottle of Bushmills.

"This is Ireland, Mr. Stewart," Michael laughed. "We'll be getting this in our mother's milk. Whiskey was invented here, you know. Irish monks. For medicinal purposes, of course. Took the recipe to Scotland, where they've made a bit of a botch of it."

Wisely I think, Alex and I chose not to get into a

discussion of the relative merits of Scotch and Irish whiskey.

Seconds later, the wind was blowing sheets of rain almost horizontally against the window. Breeta slumped once again in one of the chairs in front of the fireplace, a large wing chair covered in a cabbage rose print, and stroked the tortoise's head. I poured. Breeta sulked.

I felt myself getting irritated. Words cannot express how much I dislike people who sulk all the time. Mercifully, Jennifer Luczka has grown out of such a phase. Actually it was not so much growing out of it as a miraculous transformation when her father's then live-in girlfriend Barbara vacated the premises. Barbara is a perky blonde I call Ms. Perfect on account of how she designs her own clothes, irons everything, even socks, runs marathons, and never serves a salad that doesn't have a flower of some kind in it, all the while holding down a job as a vice president of a bank. Come to think of it, I like perky even less than I like sulky. Perhaps Jennifer does too.

"How about a fire?" Michael exclaimed. He peered into the wood box, shrugged, and headed for the door. "I'll be right back," he said.

I stood by the window peering out into the mist. It was impossible to see more than a few feet from the window, and Michael had disappeared from view almost immediately. The rain drummed on the roof, and made splintering sounds against the windowpanes. In the distance I heard a squawk, a gull perhaps, or an animal scurrying from the wet, a sound that for a moment brought back the edginess I'd been feeling earlier.

In what seemed rather longer than I would have thought necessary, Michael returned, soaking wet and very dirty, a pile of dark lumps about the size and shape of bricks in his arms. "Turf," he said, noticing my expression. "You'll need to get more, Mr. Stewart. I had to crawl on my hands and knees to reach the last of it under the house. We'll have a fire." In a few minutes he had the fire smouldering away, and stood, his back to it, drying out. Turf, I decided, was the famous Irish peat.

"Oh, I forgot," Michael said suddenly, taking a rather sodden piece of paper out of his shirt pocket. "My clue. I didn't tell the others because they wouldn't tell after you told them yours. They may get over it," he added. "He gave them hard of his tongue, Mr. Byrne did, on that video. Maybe put them a bit out of sorts. Anyway, here it is: The furious wave."

"I am the sea-swell. The furious wave," I said, very much doubting that the family would get over it, as Michael hoped. They seemed way too set in their miserable ways for that. "How very obscure. And speaking of obscure, who, by the way, is Padraig Gilhooly?"

Dead silence in the room: Breeta's hand paused in midstroke over the head of the tortoise.

"Nobody," said Michael. "Now, my clue has a two beside it. Do you think that means something?" Deft change of topic, that was.

"I don't know," said Alex, taking his envelope out too. "Mine has a one."

"Of course it means something," I said, abandoning my attempt to ferret out Gilhooly. "The clues are in some order. Eamon Byrne was, I surmise from his comments on the video, occasionally nasty as they may have been, a reasonably astute judge of character." I hesitated for a moment before going on, realizing that he had judged Breeta too. She gave no indication that she was paying attention at all, though, just went on stroking the head of the tortoise in a monotonous way.

"Knowing you both, he assumed you'd give your clue first, Alex, and that you, Michael, would be next."

"But what's it mean?" Michael said.

We, and by we I refer to the three of us, Breeta continuing to pretend we weren't there, went on for a few minutes, speculating about what it might mean. It was pleasant enough with the flames licking around the turf, the rain pattering against the windows, the Bush-mills sliding down quite nicely, and entertaining, in a kind of mindless way, to try to guess what this was all about: a game of twenty questions with the person who knew the answer gone from this world.

Michael was particularly enthusiastic. "Maybe it's about a shipwreck, some old ship off the coast here loaded with gold bullion," he said.

"Could be," Alex agreed.

"But it's the sea-swell and furious wave, both on top, and not under the ocean. I wonder if we have to take it literally. Perhaps its an anagram, a cryptic clue of some sort."

Breeta sighed loudly. "It's a poem," she said, look-ing at the three of us as if we were members of a subhuman species, several notches below that of the pet she still held in her arms.

We all looked at her. "Ah, come now, Bree," Mi-chael said in an exasperated tone. "Don't just say 'it's a poem' and leave it at that. What poem? What's the rest of it?"

Still Breeta said nothing. I felt like shaking her until her eyes bugged out, but resolved not to get emotion-ally involved in all this. Alex had his lovely little cot-tage, I told him, he'd done his part in giving the rest of them his clue, and now we should get back to having a holiday and ignore this horrid family.

" 'Song of Amairgen,' " she said finally.

"What?" we all said.

"'Song of Amairgen.' Pronounced Av-ar-hin, spelled A-m-a-i-r-g-e-n, or sometimes A-m-h-a-i-r-g-h-i-n. It's very old. Amairgen was supposed to be a file, that is a poet, of the Milesians, the first Celt to set foot on Irish soil. He's claimed to have chanted this poem when he first stepped off the boat in Ireland. It's all bullshit, of course."

"Who are, or were, the Milesians?"

"Don't you know anything?" Breeta replied. My, she was an annoying young woman. I told myself to be sure to tell Rob how lucky he is to have a daughter like Jennifer, who was not all that much younger than Breeta, as difficult as he may occasionally find her. "It's in the *Leabhar Gabala*," she said, "if you want to find out."

The *Leabhar Gabala*. Now that was helpful, almost as useful as the reply to the question about Padraig Gilhooly. This might be a good moment to remind myself how glad I was I'd never had children. Being, like many of my women friends, most of them in business like me, a little ambivalent in that regard, it was good I had such opportunities to clarify my thoughts on the subject from time to time.

"Well, if you're so smart," Michael said, sounding as irritated as I felt, "what's the next line?"

"The roar of the sea," she said smugly.

"Sure must have something to do with water," Michael said.

"The next line is about a stag," Breeta said acidly. At least she was talking.

"But we don't know that Eamon was using the whole poem, now do we?" Alex said. "We'd need to see more clues for that."

"Breeta has a clue. Mr. McCafferty—or was it Mr.

McGlynn?—put it in the safe in your father's study, Bree," Michael said. Breeta continued to look bored.

"Come on, Bree," Michael said, shyly leaning over and touching her hand. She pulled her arm away. Undeterred, he carried on. "Let's go and get your envelope. It might be kind of fun to look for this thing, whatever it is. And if it really is worth something, like your Da says, and you find it, then everything will be all right. You'll be set, you know, maybe for life." But Breeta ignored us.

Just as suddenly as it had begun, the rain stopped and the sun came out. Alex and I went outside to look about. Behind the house, inland, clouds still hovered over black mountains, but where we were was a world of bright, lush colors, greens predominantly, but also yellow and purple, and the intensely dark blue of the sea.

"I could get used to this place," Alex said, looking about him. "It wasn't what I expected, with a name like Rose Cottage. I was thinking of something more like an English country garden, or something. But this suits me better, I think."

"I'm pleased for you Alex," I said. "We can make it really nice."

He smiled. "I think I like it just as it is."

Michael came out to join us. "Don't mind her," he said, gesturing back toward the house. "She's missing him terrible no matter how it looks." Breeta appeared at the door, and he quickly changed the subject. "Right, we'd best be off. We're in for some weather again," he said, pointing to a new set of black clouds out to sea, and waving us back to the house.

"Is there another way in here?" I asked looking about me. "Another road?"

"No," Michael replied. "Although you could put a

lane in from the main road up there," he said pointing toward something I couldn't see. "You'd have to do a bit of clearing though," he added gesturing toward brush and rocks. "Set you back a few punt, that's for certain.

"The easiest thing to do is to come in the way we did. Park your car out at the road near the gate to Second Chance and walk in. They can't stop you from crossing the property," he added. "There's a right of way."

But they could make it pretty miserable for us, I thought to myself. Michael watched my face. "I'd want to put a road in, too," he said, smiling slightly.

Inside, I collected up the glasses and went over to the sink to rinse them out, Alex right behind me with a towel, ready to dry. Michael turned his attention to dousing the fire. As we worked, I sensed rather than saw Breeta get out of her chair and go over to the table on the other side of the room. The three of us, coming to the same realization, all quietly turned to watch as she picked up a book, leafed through its pages, then with one arm, held it to her chest. With the other hand, oblivious to our glances, she reached slowly for the sweater on the back of the chair. After studying it for a few seconds she brought it up to her nose and breathed deeply, then held it against the side of her face, a large tear rolling down her cheek. It's her father's, I thought, her father's sweater. His smell would still be on it, would remind her of him. Missing him terrible, indeed.

She noticed us watching her at last. She looked directly at Alex. "I know the Will says the house and its contents," she said, her voice breaking, "but would it be all right, would you mind, if I kept the sweater?"

"Of course you may, my dear," Alex said softly.

"Keep the book too. Please take anything you like."

"Just the book, and the sweater," she said, holding both tight.

We were a subdued group as Michael locked up, handing Alex the key, and we began our trek back to the big house, each lost in our own thoughts. Breeta would not let go of the book and sweater, so Michael took Vigs and went on ahead. I rather pensively watched as the rays of the late afternoon sun caught drops of rain on the leaves and blossoms of the gorse and heather, transforming them to glittering amethysts and citrines. It was late afternoon by now, and gulls circled offshore looking for dinner, or bobbed on the surface of the waves, slashes of white against the dark water. "Take care," Michael, ahead of us, yelled. "It's really slippery here." It was indeed. The rain had made the path very slick and more than once I caught myself sliding down the incline. I made my way carefully along the edge of the cliffs, turning back from time to time to see how Alex and Breeta were faring.

Although I was trying not to look down, something below caught my eye and I stopped. "Alex," I called back to him, several yards away. "What was that clue of yours again?"

"I am the sea-swell," he called to me. "Why?"

"Hang on a sec," I said. I was standing over a small cove at the foot of the cliffs. While on either side of me there was a sheer drop, in front of me there was a steep pathway, part grass, part mud, that lead down to the water. Gingerly, considering my choice of foot-wear, I began to pick my way down, slipping and sliding on the wet earth and grass. I was two-thirds of the way down when I lost first a shoe, then my footing, and rolled down the grassy slope, gathering momentum as I went. I heard the others shouting above me. For

some reason, I wasn't afraid. I knew, somehow, I
would stop in time, and was rather more worried by
how undignified I must look, rolling ass-end over tea-
kettle, than by the possibility I'd be dashed to smith-
ereens on the rocks. And indeed, the ground soon
levelled out a little on a sandy dune, and I rolled to a
stop.

I was lying on sand, or rather pebbles, on a rocky
beach at the foot of the cliffs, a few feet away from
the water where a little rowboat, a skiff, was anchored,
bobbing in the surf. The boat was white, where the
paint hadn't peeled away, and the gunwales were blue.
It had, as I had suspected from the top of the cliff, the
name *Ocean Crest* painted on its prow.

Michael started down the path after me, slipping and
sliding as I had, but so far still on his feet. "Stay there,"
he shouted. "I'll come down and help you back up."

"It's called *Ocean Crest*," I yelled up to him and the
others. "Do you think it has anything to do with the
clue?"

I looked about me. The boat's owner was nowhere
to be seen. I found my shoe and carefully picked my
way across the rocky shore toward the skiff, which was
just offshore under a large underhang of rock. The boat,
as far as I could see from land, was absolutely empty.
I thought I should take a better look. After all, if this
was the answer to the first clue, there might be something in it that would lead us on, a note stuck in a
fishing basket or something. A little voice was telling
me that I was forgetting my resolve to stay out of this
game, but I ignored it, the tumble down the hill having
robbed me of good sense.

The water was too deep and the boat a little too far
out for me to wade out to it, so I thought I'd try something else. I carefully scrambled up a large rock on the
shore, hoping from its height to have a better view of

the inside of the boat. It was, as I'd thought, completely empty, without so much as an oar to be seen.

As I looked about me from the vantage point of the big rock, I saw at the foot of a steep rocky cliff toward the end of the cove, what looked to be a shoe, partially hidden by a large rock. Perhaps it's floated ashore, I thought, lost overboard on a yacht, or something. But as I climbed down the rock and moved toward it, I had a flash of recognition, followed by a sense of being in the grip of a terrible dream that I couldn't stop, a dream that impelled me, slowly, unwillingly, toward the shoe. When I got there, I saw the shoe was attached to a leg. And the leg belonged to the broken body of John Herlihy.

Chapter Three
THE ROAR OF THE SEA

"I've been thinking," I said. This was cause for deep relief for me, thinking again I mean, after a couple of days of walking around in a kind of shocked and vacuous haze in which even the slightest mental effort seemed beyond me. I was still feeling a little shaky, as if I'd seriously overdosed on caffeine or adrenaline, and jumped at every loud noise. But I felt at last as if I was starting to come around, all things considered, the shock of finding John Herlihy gradually fading. Apparently, however, Rob was not as keen as I was on my return to relative mental acuity.

"Why do I think this is going to be trouble?" he groaned, setting two foaming pints of Kilkenny cream ale in front of us on the small glass-topped table in the bar in the inn where we were all staying. "We're on vacation, remember."

"I know," I replied, thinking that this was not exactly the vacation I'd been hoping for, thanks to John Herlihy's unfortunate demise. "But we came over here to keep Alex company, and this is about Alex. What I've been thinking," I continued before Rob could stop me, "is that it might be kind of fun to look for this treasure, this item of great value that Eamon Byrne talked about."

Rob made a face. "Bad idea," he said.

"Why?" I said.

"You have a rather short memory," he said. "Shock, I suppose, although imminent middle age can do that to you too. John Herlihy. Dead. Cause of death still under investigation."

"But he fell," I said. "Drunk as a skunk, if you ask me."

"Something of a tippler, you think?"

"It went way beyond tippling," I replied. "I overheard Deirdre of the Sorrows refer to Herlihy as the old souse."

"Am I safe in assuming that you are referring to someone other than the Deirdre of J. M. Synge's unfinished play by that name?"

"Deirdre, the morose-looking maid," I said, "and don't try to distract me with your erudition." Although I have known Rob for a few years now, comments such as these never fail to amaze me. I know I'm guilty of a gross and unfair generalization when I assume policemen don't read playwrights like John Millington Synge, particularly when the only policeman I know, at all well, does.

"So you're assuming he just fell over the edge in a drunken stupor, are you?" Rob asked. There was a tone in his voice that meant I was in for a bit of a lecture. "You can't just assume that, you know," he went on, launching himself fully into the topic. "You have to investigate it thoroughly. Did he just fall, or is there any evidence to support a suspicion that he was pushed, or even that he threw himself over the edge? Footprints, signs of a struggle, marks on the body, that kind of thing."

"I thought you said we were on vacation," I interjected.

He laughed. "Hard to get out of the work mode, isn't it?"

"Not for me," I replied blithely.

"So you weren't eyeing any of the furniture in that fellow Byrne's manor house, thinking you just might pick up a piece or two if they were auctioning any of it off now that he's gone?"

"Nope," I replied.

"Didn't you say he was something of a collector? You didn't think a few items in his collection might find a home in your shop?"

"Not at all," I replied. "Objects of destruction on red velvet are not quite the look we strive for at Greenhalgh & McClintoch." Well, maybe one or two of those maps, I thought to myself.

He looked suspiciously at me. "And you have not even once worried just a little about the shop while we've been here? I did notice you eyeing the pay phones in Shannon Airport the moment we got off the plane, did I not?"

"I'm not worried at all," I replied. That was patently untrue, and both of us knew it. I had indeed been eyeing the telephones at the airport. I did realize, however, that it was the middle of the night back home, and had managed to restrain myself.

Normally there are always two people in the shop, one to be at the cash, one to help the customers. When I'm off on buying trips, Alex stays in the shop with Sarah; when she's on holiday, it's Alex and I, and so on. But with two of us away, that left Sarah on her own, and Sarah, who's a whiz on the business and financial side of things, but not comfortable on the sales side, was a bit nervous about it all. For a while, I found myself with competing loyalties: looking after Alex or minding the store.

In the end I asked my ex-husband Clive Swain, who had the supremely bad taste to open an antiques store right across the road from Greenhalgh & McClintoch, to keep an eye on the place for me, and give Sarah a hand if she needed it. This is much akin to Custer asking Crazy Horse to hold the fort while he goes off for a little R&R, of course, but Clive, the rotter, had also dumped his second wife and, when I wasn't looking, taken up with my best friend, Moira, a very successful businesswoman who, I reasoned, was not so far gone in her affection for Clive that she would allow him to ruin my store. I just tried not to think too much about it.

Rob and I were quiet for a minute or two, sipping our beer. I sat admiring our surroundings, the somewhat prosaically named Hunt Room, with glowing fireplace, nicely worn green, gold and red-striped sofas and chairs, the dark green walls lined with prints of English hunting scenes, and a rather valuable, if not to my taste, oil painting of a stag cornered by a pack of hounds, over the mantelpiece. I knew what would happen next, and right on cue, Rob sighed theatrically. "Okay, so after almost twenty-five years in law enforcement, I can't help myself. What makes you so sure that fellow Herlihy just fell?"

"Well it was slippery enough. I should know. I took this something less than graceful tumble down the hill myself, did Alex tell you?"

"He did. He was obviously being very tactful, though. He didn't mention anything about lack of grace."

"It was quite undignified, I assure you. I was lucky to fall on mud and wet grass. It made a mess of my clothes, but I wasn't hurt. The slope was not all that steep, and there were no rocks at the bottom. A few yards either way, though, and I'd have ended up like Herlihy. On top of that, I'd only sipped a small whiskey. And Herlihy, as I mentioned, not only had a reputation for drinking regularly, if Deirdre's comments are anything to go by, but I noticed he kept nipping out of the room for a few seconds at a time. At the time it was quite clear to me that he was sneaking out for a swig or two of something or other."

"Maybe he was going to check the door, or he had a bladder problem, or didn't want the others to see he was overcome with grief or something," Rob interjected.

"I don't think so. His shoes squeaked, and he stopped after a few steps, just about as far as a sideboard in the hall on which there were several bottles of booze, I'd noticed. He had another drink, a rather large one, when Tweedledum or Tweedledee, whichever it was, said how much he'd get. It was about fifteen thousand Irish punt, by the way, which these days is worth more than twenty-five thousand dollars. That should rule out suicide. Why kill yourself the day you come into some money? When Alex and I left to go to the car, he was helping himself again, quite liberally, to the drinks on the sideboard in the hall. It's a wonder he could even stagger to the edge of the cliff!" I concluded.

"There!" Rob exclaimed. "What did I tell you? You've just added an element of doubt to your own theory."

I glared at him. "My point, if only you would allow me to get back to it, is that we're here for a while, pending the results of the autopsy, so why not look for the treasure?"

"But why would you want to?"

"Well, for one thing it wouldn't bother me a bit to beat those po-faced women to it," I replied.

Rob winced. "Aren't you being a little hasty in your judgment of them? What did they do to deserve that?"

"Since you ask, they were horrible to Alex," I said. "When we first arrived, we were left hanging about the front hall for ages, and I overheard Byrne's wife Margaret telling Tweedledum or Tweedledee—those are the lawyers—that she wouldn't have that man in her house. I assumed she was talking about Alex, although come to think about it, it could have been the other lawyer, or Padraig Gilhooly, whoever he is. In any event, Alex went over and introduced himself when we were finally allowed in, and they wouldn't even shake his hand when he offered it."

"It was a bad time for them, don't forget," Rob interjected. Sometimes the man is way too nice.

"I know. But Margaret and the two daughters all have the same expression on their faces, like they've just encountered a bad smell, or something." I paused. "And there's another reason."

"I thought there must be. The real one, this time, I hope," Rob said.

"Alex just loved the cottage. I could tell, without him having to say a word. It's a dream come true for him."

"I'm very glad of that. But he has the cottage. What's your point?"

"My point is, now what? How is he going to look after it? Pay the taxes or water bills? Put in some electricity? Make repairs? Those old places need a lot of upkeep. And unless he wants to keep crossing the property in front of the house, which heaven knows, I wouldn't, he's going to have to put a road in that will cost more than a penny or two, I can assure you. He's on a pension, Rob! If we could find the treasure for him, and it really is worth something as Byrne said it is, Alex could really retire, not just sort of retire and work part time in the store the way he is now.

"We're here now, aren't we?" I wheedled. "And we're not going too far until the police conclude their investigation into John Herlihy's death, although what could take them so long, I can't imagine. Anyway, we'd get to see a little of the countryside around here, while we looked, and we might just have some fun."

"I do understand how you feel about Alex, and maybe he does need the money, but what makes you think we could find it? We don't know the place at all, or the people."

"Piece of cake," I replied. "After all, you are a policeman. You're accustomed to tracking down clues. Already we have two of them, and we know they come from a poem called the 'Song of Amairgen.'"

Rob looked baffled and I felt mildly triumphant, having produced the name of a poem he didn't know. As rare as the occasion might be, I tried not to gloat. "Michael Davis is going to try to persuade Breeta to get her clue out of the safe at the house, and tell us what it is. We'll then have three of the clues. I think there were seven—the mother and three daughters, three more counting Michael, Alex, and someone by the name of Padraig Gilhooly, who incidentally would be about as welcome in that house as a rattlesnake at a garden party, should he choose to show his face there—so we're almost halfway there."

"Halfway where?" Jennifer said, sliding into a chair beside her father. She tossed her windbreaker, a pinky-purple number with the words "Take no Prisoners" emblazoned across the back.

"Half the clues handed out to Eamon Byrne's family yesterday. I'm trying to persuade your father that we should look for the treasure in the Will."

"Brilliant!" Jennifer exclaimed, having managed to pick up the local slang within minutes of our touchdown at Shannon Airport. Or rather, she said something that sounded like ten-ale-erb. Jennifer had taken a class in what was called creative thinking in her last term, in which the teacher had encouraged them to free their minds to think outside the box, to use that odious expression beloved of management consultants, by speaking backward. Jennifer had readily taken to this suggestion, a development her father found intensely irritating. I, however, had a dim memory of school chums doing the same thing, secret societies and the like, and I assumed this was a stage that would pass. I did not wish to stunt her creative thinking, of course, but I hoped it would be soon. "Tiod stel, Dad," she added.

"Not both of you," Rob grumped.

"Have you seen Alex?" I asked.

"Yes," she replied. "He's down at the docks renting a boat. I've come to ask you both if you'd like to go sailing with us."

"Wonderful idea!" I replied.

"Sailing!" Rob exclaimed, feigning horror at the thought. "You forget I'm a Ukrainian from Saskatchewan. My idea of relaxation is to sit on a porch and watch fields of wheat stretching as far as the eye can see. Now there's a vacation for you. Why risk seasickness, when you could have the taste of dust in your mouth, and not so much as the tiniest breeze to mess up your hair?"

"What hair?" Jennifer grinned as she reached over and patted a small bald spot on the top of her father's head. I noticed she switched to regular speech when she wanted to tease her dad, so he wouldn't miss the jibe.

"Given the absence of dust here, and wheat for that matter," I said, "what are you going to do this afternoon while the rest of us are sailing?"

"I don't know," he replied. "I'll think of something."

There was something in his tone. "Rob!" I said.

"I was thinking maybe I'd just pop down to the local police station—what do they call themselves? Gardai is it?—introduce myself."

"Would you know a vacation if you tripped over it?" I asked. "You wouldn't be planning to prove your theory that John Herlihy met with foul play, would you?" I can't believe this man, I thought. He's absolutely obsessed by his job. How can people be like that, thinking about crime and criminals every waking moment, and maybe even dreaming about it, too? It's a sickness.

"Will you look who's talking like she's an expert on vacations all of a sudden?" he said mildly. "When she hasn't had one in all the years I've know her. No, I'm just trying to improve international relations, inspire a little goodwill between police forces, that sort of thing. Now get going, will you, so I can get on with this noble activity? And try and stay out of trouble, both of you." He gave his daughter an affectionate hug.

Jennifer and I turned left as we exited The Three Sisters Inn, as the guest house where we were all staying was called, and with Jennifer chattering away about all the things she'd have to tell her chums about when she got home, we ambled along a cobblestoned street that wound its way down to the sea past charming little houses, shops, and pubs painted sunny colors, yellow, red, blue, and green.

To save money on the trip, I was sharing a room with Jennifer, and Rob and Alex were doing the same. It was not my idea of the perfect holiday, bunking in with an eighteen-year-old, but I found I was enjoying her company, and, as we made our way down to the harbor, I got caught up in the enthusiasm she brought to everything about her. Although she'd been reluctant to come with us at first, she was clearly having a good time now that we were in Ireland. She was on the cusp of adulthood, a little young for her age in some things, in my opinion, but very worldly in others, a whole new life ahead of her at university when she got home.

Jennifer's mother had died when she was very young, and Rob had raised her on his own. He'd not remarried. The way he told it, he and Jennifer had never found a woman they agreed on. So Jennifer had the combination of self-reliance and yet the essential loneliness of the only child. The big problem with her life right now, I'd quickly ascertained, was that she hadn't yet had a serious boyfriend. As painful as this was for Jennifer—she claimed she was the only girl in the western hemisphere who hadn't had a date for the prom—this state of affairs suited her father just fine, considering as he did all his daughter's potential suitors to be lascivious louts, to use his own words. After a couple of days sharing a room with Jennifer, I began to realize it was time I had a serious talk with her father, something along the lines of his reserving his interrogation and intimidation skills for the people he came across in his chosen line of work, rather than the young men who came calling on his daughter. It was not a conversation I was looking forward to, but what are friends for? And certainly Rob has never held back from telling me things about myself he feels I need to know.

The town lined the mouth of a river at the head of a large bay that provided snug harbor for the dozens of boats, large and small, moored there. We found Alex waiting for us at the end of the pier, aboard the *Maire Malloy*, a rather old and lumpy little wooden craft painted a dreadful pea green. The sea was perfect for sailing: a good stiff breeze, but not too much of one. The sky was clear in all directions, so it looked as if the weather would hold. Gulls squawked and wheeled after us as Alex started the engine and we putt-putted out of the harbor, past fishing boats, large and small. When we cleared the edge of the harbor, Alex cut the engine and gave orders to hoist the sail. The wind caught us immediately, and appearances to the contrary, the boat surged forward very nicely.

"Oohay!" Jennifer yelled. Sailing was a new experience for her, and her excitement was contagious. I found myself starting to enjoy myself, pushing the picture of John Herlihy's black boot back to the furthermost corners of my mind.

"Oohay!" I agreed. From the sea, the land was even more spectacularly beautiful: blue mountains in the distance, cut by the enormous gashes of valleys, rolling hills that swooped down to sheer cliffs at the sea, farther out, the wild columns of spray where the sea met the shore. And everywhere, tiny isolated houses stark against the most extraordinary shades of green.

"Where to?" Alex called to us, the wind whipping his words away.

Jennifer shrugged. "Dnaleci," she shouted.

"I have a more practical idea," I called back.

It was relatively easy sailing, hugging the coast, past little bays and coves, some with houses visible, others deserted, others with the same derelict and abandoned houses we'd seen near Rose Cottage.

Few of the homes were as beautiful as Second Chance. From the water it was spectacular, the pale yellow of its walls in sharp contrast to the dark, dark green of the hills way behind it, and the well-manicured lawn and gardens sloping down to the sea. It looked like a little paradise, and even Jennifer, burdened very slightly by a late adolescent angst that had a tendency to show itself as chronic cynicism, looked impressed.

As we followed the coast past Second Chance, the wind whipped up, as it had when we'd hiked to Rose Cottage, and we had to tack several times to make headway. It was exhilarating, though, as the little boat crested the waves, then fell into the trough, the rugged shoreline, high cliffs at whose base the waves pounded and above which seabirds flew, receding off into the mist miles away. And high on the cliff, Alex's newly acquired cottage sat snugly facing out to sea. "Is that it, Uncle Alex?" Jennifer called out pointing toward the shore. "Oooo," she exclaimed, as Alex nodded proudly. "It's brilliant. Can I come and visit summers?"

"Of course you may," he replied.

The little wooden boat was still bobbing in the cove when we got there. Alex skillfully maneuvered our craft past some rocks and pulled alongside.

"I don't see anything," Jennifer said, peering into the *Ocean Crest.*

"We'll need to board her," I said.

"Be quick about it, Lara," Alex said as he pulled alongside. "It's time we were getting back," he added, pointing to the sun now dipping toward the horizon.

"Just give me a few minutes," I said, easing my way

into the other boat. Once I was aboard, Alex shoved off and anchored several yards away.

I started at the stern and moved forward. I checked for wire or ropes over the side, thinking there might be a watertight package hidden in the water. I pulled the boat up to the buoy where it was moored, but found nothing there. I ran my fingers under the gunwales in case a tiny piece of paper had been stuck there. I checked the oar sockets and I felt under each seat, before moving toward the bow. I checked under that seat, too. Still nothing. Then I reached up into the prow of the boat, and came up empty again.

I was about to give up when I noticed that one of the boards in the bow looked freshly painted, in contrast to the rather worn quality of the rest of the boat. I gave the board a little tug and it came away to reveal a piece of white plastic sheet, part of a plastic bag, I'd have said, rolled up tightly and wedged into a groove between the boards, then taped to hold it in place.

"Got it," I yelled to Alex and Jennifer, slowly peeling away the tape, being careful not to tear the plastic or its contents.

"Ynapmoc!" Jennifer called out, waving her arms toward the shore. I looked up in the direction Jennifer was pointing. At the top of the cliff, round about where John Herlihy must have gone over, Conail O'Connor, son-in-law number two, stood, arms crossed, one leg propped up on a rock at the edge, looking down at us, like a bird of prey readying to strike. At that moment, I knew two things: One was that if looks could kill, I'd have keeled over right then and there. The other was that some people were taking this treasure hunt way too seriously.

"Let's get out of here," I called to Alex, who weighed anchor and navigated over to me. I stuffed the plastic roll in the back pocket of my jeans and scrambled on board the *Maire Malloy*. Alex started the little engine, and we slowly made our way out of the cove and into the wind.

The trip back to the harbor should have been a fast one. The wind was with us, and as soon as the sail was up our little boat leapt forward. The setting sun was to our right and behind us as we sped along.

We were about halfway back when a trawler, engines at a deep throaty roar, blasted out of the late afternoon shadow of the bay, heading directly for us. It was not a sleek boat, but it was a powerful one, its course bringing it inexorably closer and closer. "Come about," Alex yelled, as Jennifer and I ducked to avoid the boom, and scrambled to the opposite side. The other boat changed direction and continued to bear down on us. We were yelling and waving, trying to catch the attention of the driver, whom we couldn't see, before it was too late. At the last moment, Alex, an excellent sailor and remarkably calm in a crisis, did a quick maneuver, and the trawler, which was about to hit us broadside, instead just grazed the stern. It was enough, however, and, swamped, the *Maire Malloy* rolled over, hurling all of us overboard.

As we went over the side, I grabbed hold of Jennifer, but I hit the water so hard, I was dazed for a moment, and she was wrenched from my grasp. There was a roaring in my ears, either the shock of the water or the underwater sound of the powerboat, and my nose and mouth were filled with water as I was swept up in the wake. I struggled my way to the surface and looked about for the others. I saw Alex immediately, but Jennifer was nowhere to be found. A panic so intense it was almost a physical pain gripped me, and I started screaming her name and flailing around in the dark, cold water, desperate to find her, a glimpse of her purple jacket, or her blonde hair.

And suddenly there she was, first her head, then her shoulders, she rose coughing and sputtering, a few yards away. "Gip!" she gasped, shaking her fist at the departing trawler, already far away, a small black shadow retreating in the shimmering path of the sun on the water. "Mucs!" she yelled again, this time much stronger. I figured she was okay.

Together, we tried to right the boat, but it was difficult, exhausted as we were by our narrow escape, and in the end we just clung to the side of it, waiting until help arrived. It came mercifully soon in the person of Michael Davis who pulled alongside not long after in a small motorboat.

"I saw you from the cliff," he said after he'd hauled us all on board and attached a line to the sailboat to tow it to shore. "Bloody ijit driving that boat!" he exclaimed. "You could all have been killed!"

"Did you happen to see who the bloody ijit was?" I asked him, after I'd caught my breath.

"No," he replied, but he looked away as he said it. I had a feeling that even if he couldn't actually see, at that distance, who was driving the boat, he had a very good idea who was responsible. And recalling vividly the malignant look on Conail O'Connor's face, so, for that matter, did I.

Chapter Four

A STAG OF SEVEN SLAUGHTERS

"APPARENTLY you were right," Rob said, nodding in my general direction as he passed his daughter the marmalade. Breakfast was served each morning in a little glassed-in porch overlooking the little garden at the Inn, and we started our days together there.

"I'm always right," I said, as Jennifer giggled. Alex raised his eyebrows skeptically.

Rob chuckled. "That may be, but I don't often admit it, now do I?"

"That's an understatement," Jennifer teased. Rob made a motion as if to box her ears, and she ducked, laughing.

"What particular instance of my being right are you referring to this time?" I asked. I was happy to see Rob and Jennifer getting along so well, and that she was beginning to speak English in its normal order once again.

"John Herlihy," he said. "Blood/alcohol readings over the top. Guy had been drinking for several days solid. It's a wonder he could stand up at all, but people who drink pretty consistently can be like that."

Now I'm always glad when Rob agrees with me about something. I like to think that on the important things in life we pretty much agree right down the line. On the smaller details, however, we hardly ever see eye to eye. It's the source of bouts of bickering from time to time. Sometimes, I think we carry on like an old married couple, even though we've never been anything more than friends. Having him admit I'd been right in this instance was, indeed, a victory. Trouble was, in the meantime, I'd changed my mind.

"What about the other things you talked about: marks on the body, that sort of thing?"

"According to the garda I spoke to, pleasant chap by the name of Minogue, Herlihy's injuries are pretty consistent with having fallen forty feet onto a pile of rocks," Rob said. "All rather neat and tidy, actually. After all, they can pinpoint the time of death with great accuracy. You walked by the spot minutes after the proceedings at Second Chance ended, that is about three-thirty, and about forty-five minutes or so later, by all accounts, you walked back, and there he was. His clothes were wet, from the rain presumably, under the body too, although that doesn't mean much on the seashore. He might have been lying down there when you first went by, I suppose—you wouldn't necessarily have seen him—but it's more likely he fell during the rain. Either way, it doesn't change the time much, and during that time, everyone is more or less accounted for, not every second perhaps, but no one was alone for very long."

It wouldn't take very long, I thought to myself, just a short jog to the edge of the property and around the corner where no one could see. And from our end,

Michael had been gone rather longer than I had thought necessary to get a little fuel for the fire. "What about the other stuff? Footprints? Signs of a struggle?"

"Downpour pretty well took care of that. Also, all of you tramping around and looking over the side of the cliff when you found him." He looked mildly annoyed as if we should have known better. "Not much sign of anything, I'm told." He paused for a moment. "Do you take the opposite side of every discussion with me for sport, or have you changed your mind?"

I shrugged. How could I tell him that for a moment or two the world had stood still, soundless, and that I'd had a premonition of something awful about to happen? How could I say that just as it was beginning to rain I'd heard an unnatural animal sound that at the time I'd thought was a bird, or an animal fleeing the wet, but now thought, despite every effort to persuade myself otherwise, might have been the scream of a dying man going over a cliff? "Just wondering," I said.

"Well, wonder no more," he said reaching for the *Irish Times*. "Do you think my arteries will survive two weeks in this country?" he asked, eyeing the empty plate in front of him that just a few minutes ago had contained the innocuously named heart attack on a plate, the Irish cooked breakfast: two eggs, a few rashers of bacon, two breakfast sausages, two kinds of blood sausage, and toast with Irish butter. I gathered he was changing the subject.

I couldn't let it go like that. The sound I'd heard, the edginess I'd felt, wouldn't go away. If indeed that awful sound had been Herlihy, then he hadn't slipped on the mud. It had barely begun to rain when I'd heard it. And why, exactly, had it gone so quiet? The wind had dropped, yes, just before the rain, the lull before the storm. But what about the birds that only seconds before had been wheeling and shrieking above us. Why did they suddenly stop too? Was it the approaching storm, or had something else, a struggle on the cliff, perhaps, made them go silent?

Before the boating incident of the day before, I might have been prepared, indeed have welcomed the chance, to accept the official explanation. But I couldn't believe that what had happened to us had been an accident, not after seeing Conail O'Connor's face. That in itself made me look at other so-called accidents with suspicion. But I couldn't tell Rob that, either. Jennifer had related the story with great dramatic flair when we got back, and Rob had looked perturbed, but she was at the age where she exaggerated everything, and Alex and I had downplayed it. I would have liked to talk to him about it, about my panic when I lost hold of her, those horrible seconds before she surfaced, but I knew I'd be doing it to make myself feel better, not him. Parenthood is frightening enough, I decided, without having to be terrified by what might have been.

When breakfast was finished, Rob and Jennifer announced that they were off sightseeing to Killarney, if anyone wanted to come. Alex said he'd met someone who'd offered to take him fishing. I said I was just going exploring around town.

"Promise me you're not going anywhere near Second Chance," Rob said severely.

"I promise," I said. It was an easy promise to make because I had something else in mind. Not something he'd be any happier about, mind you. There was a specific bit of exploring I proposed to do, and when the others had left, I headed down, once again, to the pier. It took me about an hour, wending my way up and down the docks, but eventually I found what I wanted. It was down by a sandwich sign advertising something called St. Brandon Charters offering fishing expeditions, scenic tours of Dingle Bay, trips to the Blasketts, the islands off the Dingle coast, and both fly-fishing and sailing lessons. The proprietor of St. Brandon Charters, whoever he or she might be, was obviously a versatile sort. Multi-skilling, I think they call it in the corporate world, another of those vile made-up terms like downsizing and rightsizing that are euphemisms for unpleasant results, in this case, presumably, fewer employed people doing a lot more work.

"Nice boat," I said.

The man barely looked up from his work. "Yeh. Thanks," he replied.

"Who owns it, do you know?"

The man ignored me, continuing to painstakingly clean the gunwales, inch by inch.

"Anybody know who owns this boat?" I said, turning to three old men sitting on a bench on the pier.

"Paddy Gilhooly," said one of them. This was not the name I was expecting, but an interesting one nonetheless.

"Do you know where I might find him?"

"He's not far," the old man said. The second man cupped his hand around his ear to hear better and laughed.

"Yer lookin' at him," the second man shouted, pointing to the man working on the boat.

I suppose I should have known from all the guy-and-his-boat behaviour, which is remarkably similar to the guy-and-his-car ritual, that this man was the owner, even if he didn't look as if he could afford it. In vain, I searched his face for a glimpse of Eamon Byrne, having decided that the reason the family despised him was because he was an illegitimate son of Byrne. If the resemblance was there, I couldn't see it.

"Is that true?" I asked him. "Are you Padraig Gilhooly?" The man ignored me still. I took that to be a yes. "I've been looking for you."

Still the man said nothing.

"Too bad about that pea green paint scratch on the bow," I went on. "Unusual color. You should be more careful."

"Have we met?" the man said suddenly, and not just a little belligerently, tossing his rag into his pail and standing up. He was tall and wiry, a little too thin perhaps, dark hair and very dark and intense eyes, and dressed in overalls and a white shirt, sleeves rolled up, and heavy work boots. For a moment I almost lost my nerve.

"Yes," I said, taking a deep breath. "As a matter of fact we have. To be more accurate, it was our boats that met, this one and the one I and a couple of friends of mine were sailing, the *Maire Malloy*."

"So you've come to apologize for hitting my boat, have you?" he glowered. "And to offer to pay for repairs, no doubt?" There was a sarcastic edge to his voice.

This conversation wasn't going exactly the way I had intended. "This is your way of pretending that you didn't notice you hit and swamped us, I suppose," I said. I was getting so annoyed, I was no longer afraid of him. "Not only swamped us, but left us to drown, I might add."

Gilhooly stared at me. "What are you goin' on about?" he said at last. "I never hit nobody. And if I did, I most certainly wouldn't leave them to drown."

"Then where'd you get that pea green scratch on your boat?"

"Did those fecking bastards up at Second Chance put you up to this?" he asked. "Because if they did . . ."

He raised his fist and I backed away quickly.

"No," I replied from a safe distance, "the fecking bastards, as you so delicately put it, did not. The truth of the matter is they wouldn't put me up to anything at all, and frankly I expect they'd just as soon I went back home. Now, could we start again, do you think?"

He glowered at me for a second or two and then slowly lowered his arm. "How do you do," he said finally. "I'm Paddy Gilhooly, owner of this here boat, the one called *Lost Causes*. And you are?"

"Lara McClintoch. How do you do."

"A Yank, are you?"

"I'm here visiting from Toronto."

"Canadian. Not a friend of that fellow, Alex something or other who got Rose Cottage by any chance?"

I nodded. "His name is Alex Stewart. He's a friend of mine."

"Aye," he said. "I heard there was a woman with him. My solicitor told me," he added. "He was there, but you know that, seeing as you were too. Now what's all this about my boat. Beautiful, isn't she?"

"She is," I said, "unless you happen to see her first coming right at you, and then later disappearing into the distance as you swallow gallons of seawater from her wake."

"And this supposed event would have been when?" His tone turned aggressive again.

"Yesterday afternoon. Ask your pals here," I said gesturing toward the three men on the bench. "They'll tell you the *Maire Malloy* got towed in late yesterday afternoon, with the gash in her stern, and her crew rather damp."

"That so, Malachy?"

One of the old men on the bench nodded. " 'Tis so, Paddy."

Gilhooly frowned. "So was *Lost Causes* docked then?"

Malachy thought slowly and carefully about that. "Difficult to say, Paddy," he said finally. "Difficult to say. Close on sunset. We'd been over at the pub for a spot of refreshment. Lots of the boats coming in, and this one," he said, pointing at me, "being towed. Plenty of excitement all round." The second old geezer cupped his hand to his ear and looked at Malachy. "Do you recall if Paddy's boat was in when they towed this one in?" Malachy yelled at him.

"Can't say as I recall," the second man said after a moment or two of contemplation.

"No use asking this one," Malachy said, pointing to the third man, who had turned away from us and was looking out to sea. "He's elsewhere most of the time."

"Well, Malachy, since you'll be on telling me about her story," Gilhooly said, "perhaps you'll also be verifying mine."

"Which is?" I asked.

"Cork," Malachy said. It sounded more like Cark to my ears, but I figured it was Cork. "In Cork, he was, our Paddy. Took the train first thing. Not a sight of him here all day. Not that I can see so good, mind you. But Kev can, can't you Kev?" he shouted. Kev nodded.

"So now that we've got that out of the way," Gilhooly said, "I'm sorry to hear about your boating accident, but it's got nothing to do with me."

"Any chance Conail O'Connor could have taken your boat?"

"Conail O'Connor!" Gilhooly exclaimed. "Conail O'Connor can kiss my royal Irish arse!"

" 'Tis James Joyce he's quoting," Malachy said solemnly. *"Ulysses."*

"Was that a no?" I said acidly, James Joyce or not.
"How about Sean McHugh?"

Gilhooly remained silent, but I could see his jaw
working, and he looked as if he was about to burst a
blood vessel.

"I assume your lawyer told you about Eamon
Byrne's little game," I said.

"He did. Bloody nonsense. I'd have credited him
with more sense. Though I suppose you can't blame a
dying man."

"I'll tell you our clue if you'll tell me yours," I said.

"You mean the one about the sea-swell? My solicitor
was there, remember."

"I know another one, Michael Davis's," I replied.
Actually I had two, if you counted the one that was
currently being painstakingly dried out in my room at
the inn in hopes that something remotely legible could
be found, but it didn't seem to be a good idea to give
everything away at once with this bunch. "A couple of
us thought it might be entertaining to try and find this
thing, whatever it is."

"Entertaining, you call it? There is nothing entertaining about those people up at Second Chance, I can
tell you. Nothing whatsoever." Gilhooly tossed his rags
into the bucket and started to walk away.

"Are you going to sue the family for a share? Byrne
suggested you might, and your solicitor was there.
What's his name?"

"Dermot Shanahan. And I would be paying his legal
fees how?" he asked bitterly.

I was tempted to suggest he could sell his beloved
boat, but decided to be nice. "Can I buy you a beer or
something?" I asked him. Maybe, I thought, his tongue
would loosen and I'd learn what the bad blood between
him and the Byrne family was all about.

"Where I come from, girls wait to be asked!" he called over his shoulders as he left.

"I'm not asking you for a date, Padraig," I retorted to his retreating back. "Just for a drink. Sullen men with chips on their shoulders are not my cup of tea. I mean do you fight with everybody on principle, or are you just having a bad day? And by the way, I don't care what girls of your acquaintance do." And don't call me a girl, I added to myself. He ignored me and kept going.

I looked back to see the old guys on the bench laughing so hard the tears were running down their cheeks. Two of them, that is. The third, who'd not yet spoken to me, appeared to be having a long discussion with either himself or a post on the pier.

"If yer not interested in sullen young men," Malachy said finally, wiping the tears from his eyes, "how do you feel about happy old ones? Dere's tree of us," he added, dropping the "h" in "th" the way many of the people in these parts appeared to. "I don't see so good, and Kev don't hear so good, and Denny, well, as you can see, Denny's a bit special, if you know what I mean. But put us together, we're someting."

I had to laugh, too. "Come on," Malachy said. "Take a pew." He gestured toward a broken-down old chair a few feet away. "Drink?" he said, pulling a bottle of whisky and a couple of tin cups out of a little bag beside the bench.

"A little too early in the day for me," I replied. "But thank you. I'm Lara," I said, shaking their hands in turn, before risking the chair. Even Denny broke off talking to himself long enough to shyly shake my hand. Malachy, Kev, and Denny, all dressed in gray wool pants, white shirts, and black fishermen's hats: "Brothers?" I asked. Malachy and Kev nodded in unison.

"Kev and me's brothers. Denny's our mate. We're all named for saints, you know: me for St. Malachy, Kev for St. Kevin, and Denny for St. Denis. Paddy too, of course, for the greatest Irish saint of them all, St. Padraig. He's not so bad, our Paddy," Malachy added when he'd stopped laughing long enough to catch his breath. "Bit of a chip on his shoulder, maybe. You might be right about that." The other two agreed.

"He'd do no such ting as run you down in the water," Kev said.

"And leavin' you dere to drown," Malachy added. He set the cups on the ground in front of the bench and carefully filled them, handing one each to his brother and friend, keeping the bottle for himself. "May you find yourself in heaven before the divil knows yer dead," he said, raising the bottle in a toast, and then taking a long swig. The others did the same.

"Paddy doesn't get along too well with the people at Second Chance, does he?" I asked. If Padraig wouldn't tell me himself, maybe these three would.

"Not so well at all," Malachy agreed, "but those boyos up dere at the big house don't much get on with anybody these days. Now Eamon, he liked the young lad. Gave him the boat, didn't he?" I waited, but he added nothing more. I was wondering how far I could push this line of inquiry before they got mad at me and clammed up. I had a feeling that, as a foreigner, I would be tolerated only as long as I behaved myself.

"It's nice here, and a lovely day," I said looking about me. And it was: the sea, the boats, the rocky coast stretching out in both directions, part of it shrouded in mist.

" 'Tis, tank God," Malachy agreed.

"Do you tink she'd like to hear a story?" Kev asked Malachy. "Denny tells a good story," he said to me.

"No, she wouldn't," Denny said, suddenly, as if he'd come out of a trance.

"Sure, I would," I replied.

"Come on, Denny," Kev said. "Tell this nice young girl a story." I considered how irritating I found it when Gilhooly called me a girl, but how sweet I thought it was when Kev did. The path of feminism is not always simple.

"The young ones don't listen to Denny's stories anymore," Malachy whispered. "That's why he tells them to the post and the pier. So he won't forget them."

"What did you say?" Kev said, elbowing his brother. "Speak up!"

Malachy glared at him.

"Why doesn't he just write them down?" I asked.

Malachy looked horrified. "Dey can't be written down," he said. " 'Twould spoil them. They're too special for that."

"Tell her the one about the golden ring," Kev said, reaching over to poke his mate.

"No, that's no good," Malachy said. "Everybody knows that one. Tell her the one about the mirror. That's the best!"

Denny didn't say a word. "Okay, Denny," Malachy said in an exasperated tone. "Tell her whichever one you want."

"One of the old ones," Kev added. "I don't suppose you'd have someting to help Denny wet his whistle, now would you?" he said, looking dolefully at the now empty bottle. "A little liquid libation to get him going?"

"No, I'm afraid not," I replied, "not knowing that I was about to make your acquaintance. But I'll be sure to bring something next time I'm here," I added. "What does Denny like?"

"Whiskey, of course," Malachy said.

"Me too," Kev said. "It doesn't have to be really fine. Just about any whiskey will do."

"No, don't bring us the good stuff," Malachy agreed. " 'Tis no use acquiring the taste for that, our circumstances being what they are. A shame they keep perfectly good whiskey around so long without drinking it, anyway."

We all looked over at Denny.

"You'll just have to wait," Malachy whispered. "Denny talks when he wants to."

As we waited to see whether the spirit would move Denny, we all sat in companionable silence. I, of course, thought about the treasure hunt, as it had come to be called in my mind. I thought again about John Herlihy and the plunge to his death. It had to be linked to the treasure in some way, although how was not immediately apparent. Neither Deirdre nor Herlihy had been given an envelope to participate in the treasure hunt. It was a team-building exercise, to use that nauseatingly overused business term, a ploy to get the family to work together. But Alex, Michael, and Gilhooly were included, for reasons I simply didn't know and couldn't guess.

On the surface at least, the ploy seemed to be working, with the family sticking together. We were seriously outnumbered, Alex and Michael against the rest: Breeta, Margaret, Eithne, Fionuala, Sean, Conail, and Padraig Gilhooly. I'd had unpleasant run-ins with two of the seven, if you counted Conail's nasty glance and the run-in with the boat as one, and counted Paddy as the second. If events unfolded the way they'd started, I had five more unpleasant encounters to go.

On the other hand, it was pretty hard to imagine that if Herlihy had been helped over the side—and I had to admit the jury was still out on that one—it could have to do with anything else but the treasure hunt. Alex had read his clue aloud, and everyone had heard him, Herlihy included. Perhaps Herlihy immediately linked it to the little boat, the *Ocean Crest*, in the cove and had made his way there as fast as his drunken legs would carry him, hoping to be cut in on the deal. If that had been the case, maybe one of the family had raced him to it, with deadly consequences. Once Herlihy's body had been found, the police were all over the site, and it would be difficult for any of them to get to the boat.

Maybe that's what Conail was up to. He'd been biding his time until the police left and was about to make his way down to the cove, when we breezed in from the sea. Or perhaps he'd been there already, but hadn't been able to find it. Seeing me pulling the little plastic packet out of the bow would certainly explain the ugly look on his face.

The other problem was the sodden scrap of paper I'd pulled out of the boat. I'd assumed that with only seven clues handed out at the reading of the Will, finding the treasure wouldn't be all that complicated: Put seven clues together, and presto, the treasure would be found. But if each clue led to another, did that mean there were fourteen clues, or even more? Or did it mean that there were seven separate trails that led to the treasure? I decided that the latter wouldn't be the case, because for all of them to pursue their separate ways would not accomplish the family salvation Byrne was hoping for. Maybe, I thought, the clue in the *Ocean Crest* wasn't a clue at all. I'd had a look at it, of course, as soon as we'd got to shore safely. It didn't look like much at all, although the writer had had the foresight to use ballpoint pen, so there was still ink to be seen. More like doodling than a clue. But if it was just doodling, why wrap it in plastic and hide it in the boat?

It occurred to me that there were more questions than answers in this little mental exercise I had taken upon myself and that proof of any of this speculation was in rather short supply.

I looked over at Denny. He'd put his hands flat on his thighs and was starting to rock slowly back and forth on the bench. The rest of us waited.

"I'll tell you a story about someting very strange that happened to someone around here," he said finally. "Now I'm not saying who. No, I'm not saying who 'tis I'm talking about. If you know, then you know. If you don't, then you won't hear it from me. No, you won't be hearing it from me.

"Once there was a Kerry man who'd a wife and beautiful daughters."

"Now this is a good one," Kev said. "Very mysterious, I'll tell you."

"Don't interrupt." Malachy scowled. "Let him tell it."

"But he wasn't happy, for he wanted a son. Soon it was too late, if you take my meaning, his wife getting on to middle age. He was nigh on desperate for a son, and some say he made a pact with the divil so's to have one. Whatever 'twas he did, to everyone's surprise, his wife presented him with a fine lad. A beauty, the boy was. All pink and gold, and eyes so blue. How he doted on that boy. Wouldn't hardly leave him alone for a minute."

"Hardly a minute," Malachy agreed.

"But one day he had to go to Cork to see to his affairs, and while he was away, and his little son, only a few weeks old, was rocking in his cradle out in the garden, a very strange boy, old-looking, came to the place. The maid, she seen him, and this strange creature hopped into the little boy's bed. When the man came home, he found his son gone, and this strange-looking creature in his boy's cradle. 'Twas a terrible ting happened, really 'twas. And he says to his wife, 'what's happened here?' And she says, 'what do you mean?' 'It's the fairies,' the man exclaims, 'they've taken my boy away.' 'Yer crazy,' the woman says. But I tell you 'twere true. The fairies had switched the boy for one of their own. And the man raced to find the boy before he ate the fairy food, because as everybody knows, once you eat their food, you're with them forever, the fairies."

" 'Tis true," Kev asserted. "If they take you, don't eat what they offer, not even a little bite, no matter it looks so good."

"Shh," said Malachy. "Let him finish."

"But the man had a pact with the divil, as I've just told you," Denny continued as if the others hadn't spoken. "So he went back to the divil and says to him, 'you promised me a son,' he says to the divil, bold as brass, for what'd he have to lose what with his son being taken and all? 'I gave you one,' the divil said. 'I didn't say you'd have him forever.'

"Now this Kerryman was no slouch in the head, if you know what I mean, no slouch at all in that department. 'So what do you tink people will be saying about you, if you don't keep your promises,' the Kerryman says. 'I'll be telling everybody what you done to me. There'll be no more pacts with the divil around here when I'm done.' 'Hush your tongue,' the divil says. 'You're worse than a woman for all your complaining. But I'll tell you what I'll do. You go back and get rid of the ugly child in your boy's bed, and I'll save your boy. But you'll have to find him yerself, because I've already promised him to another.'

"The Kerryman accepts the divil's offer. What else could he do? He goes home, and takes a sword and goes to whack the ugly boy over the head with it, and what do you know, the ugly child, seeing what he's up to, jumps out of the cradle and runs away so fast no one can catch him no matter how fast they run.

"And the man looks all over the countryside for his wee boy, the real one, but he can't find him for many, many years. But then he does, when the boy's almost growed. But then the man's wife, who's brooded all these years over her lost boy, she won't recognize her son, says he's not him. But the man, he knows it's his son, who's been lost, and just before he dies, is reconciled with him. So 'tis a strange story, but a true one, and a happy ending of sorts."

Denny stopped talking, and then rocking. The tale, such as it was, was over. What a peculiar story, I thought, and would have made a point of forgetting if it had not been for what was said next.

"Denny has lots of stories like that one," Malachy said. "But that one, 'twas one of Eamon Byrne's favorites. Brought a tear to his eye every time, didn't it, Kev?"

"Aye, a tear to his eye every time. Very close to his heart, 'twas."

I was about to probe this further when I heard my name yahooed from the top of the hill leading down to the pier. Michael Davis came running toward me. "They told me at the Inn they thought you'd come down here," he puffed. "It's gone!"

"What's gone?"

"Breeta's clue!" he exclaimed. "Someone's got into the safe and stolen Breeta's clue."

Chapter Five

A HAWK ABOVE THE CLIFF

As *wondrous as the Dagda's cauldron might be, 'twas only one of four great gifts from the gods, one for each of the cities from which the children of the goddess Danu sprang, and each with a tale to be told.*

The cauldron, the one that was never empty, was from Murias. From Falias came Lia Fail, the stone that roared and sang when the true king of Ireland stood on it. Brought, some have said, from the East by the goddess Tea to Tara, the stone, for that is what it is, the stone of destiny, is to rest wherever the high king of Scotic reigns. Many the man thought he would be king at Tara, but only a few heard the roar of Lia Fail.

It should never have left Ireland. Never have left. But Fergus, son of Erc, begged his brother, Murtagh mac Erc, to send it to him in Iona so that Fergus might be crowned king there. Filled with a care for his brother, Murtagh sent it across the sea. Then Kenneth took it to Scone.

And what happened then to it, this gift from the

gods? The bloody English took it! The things the English done to us! The evil Edward carried off the stone of destiny and put it beneath the English throne. Edward thought he took the power with it, but have the English ever heard it roar, I ask you? Have they ever heard it roar?

There's some would say the stone that rests at Tara now, right close to its center, is Lia Fail. But that one too is silent, and should it be Lia Fail, then the magic's left us.

And then there's them that say the English have set their royal arses over a plain old chunk of stone. And Lia Fail is hidden, waiting for a better time, waiting to be found.

"I'm afraid you may think us ungracious," Margaret Byrne said, as she poured tea into delicate ivory cups with a practiced hand, having peremptorily dismissed a rather nervous Deirdre, who'd clattered around with the teacups in an irritating way. "The circumstances . . ." she said, dropping her eyes delicately. "I hope you understand."

Despite the refined setting, and the hoity-toity manner in which we were being served, the room was awash in tension. I had a feeling that Alex and I, who had hied ourselves off to Second Chance at the request of Michael and Breeta to ferret out the details of the disappearance of Breeta's clue, had interrupted a scene of some drama when we'd arrived. If true, there was no mention made of it.

Margaret looked toward me, awaiting my response. She was neatly dressed, Chanel again, and black again, in a silk blouse and skirt, with expensive-looking pumps: snake, appropriately enough. The expression on her carefully made-up face was one of perpetual faint surprise, the result, I thought maliciously, of one too many face-lifts. But she was an attractive woman, nonetheless. She looked to be in her late forties, but I assumed she was probably ten years older than that. She sat framed against two oil portraits on the wall behind her, one of Eamon Byrne in happier and healthier times, another a man who was, if the thin lip line and resolute jaw was anything to go by, her father.

Seated next to her was her eldest daughter, Eithne. Eithne, who looked almost the same age as her mother, also dressed very much like her, but in a subdued shade of blue. Where Margaret looked rather smart, however, Eithne instead looked a bit old-fashioned, even frumpy, for her age. She restricted her interaction with the group to nodding favorably whenever her mother spoke and frowning when her mother did, which was often.

On the other side was Fionuala. Daughter number two had not inherited her mother's elegance and good taste, it was plain to see. Her dress, while expensive, I'd imagine, was way too tight for someone with her tendency to softness about the middle. Her jewelry looked just a little gaudy, a rhinestone pin that might be best for evening. Her attention was focused almost entirely on her hands.

Ungracious! I thought, pondering Margaret's opening words and the general unpleasantness of having to face the three hags across a tea tray. On the way to the house, we'd been virtually forced off the road, finding ourselves and the car in a close encounter with a fuchsia hedge, as Conail O'Connor, the predator on the cliff of the previous day, had come rocketing down the lane, his face contorted in what I took to be rage. He didn't even slow down when he saw us. "I'd say he drives very much the way he sails," Alex said mildly, voicing the same thoughts as mine, as I pulled the car back on the road again, the scratching of branches along the car door accompanying the maneuver. Alex and I shared the same conclusion as to the identity of the skipper of the boat that had run us down.

As well, Margaret was clearly in a very bad mood when we arrived. One of the family's two solicitors, which one I wasn't sure, was just leaving as we approached the front door. "I am truly very sorry about this," I heard him say as he shook her hand, holding it rather longer than necessary, I would have thought. "Truly sorry. I will see what I can do." He nodded curtly at Alex and me as he brushed by us.

Whatever it was he had to be sorry about, it had blackened Margaret's already dark outlook on life. She barely spoke to us as we were ushered into the house. No, the word *ungracious* didn't quite cut it when it came to describing the Byrne family.

"Of course," I replied to her request for understanding, however. "Alex and I feel very badly that our presence may have added to the stress you and the family are feeling at such a sad time." Really, butter wouldn't melt in my mouth sometimes.

"Indeed," Alex agreed. We all nodded at each other, giving a completely erroneous impression of consensus.

The conversation continued in much the same vein for a few minutes, insincere pleasantry heaped upon cloying sentiment, Eithne nodding in support of her mother's every word, until exhausted by the effort of being nice to each other, we edged our way toward the business at hand. As we sipped our tea, I tried to take in my surroundings. I watched through the back windows as Sean McHugh, Eithne's husband, crossed the grounds to the rear. He was looking rather tweedy, leather patches at the elbows kind of thing, with big boots and a cap. I remembered Eamon's description of McHugh as an English squire, and could see it was apt. Michael Davis, who was also in view, was working in the gardens casting surreptitious glances back toward the house, perhaps in a vain attempt to see how we were doing. He bent and straightened, pulled weeds, straightened plants in a nice rhythm, and I found it comforting to see him out there. He was quite the nicest thing about Second Chance.

"I understand from Breeta that there's been a robbery at Second Chance," I said at last, sipping tea awkwardly from the cup and saucer she'd handed me. I really dislike those delicate little teacups that don't give you enough room to put even one finger through the handle, forcing you to hold on for dear life lest you dump the contents on the wool rug at your feet. But everything about Margaret Byrne was like that. The room was filled with delicate little ornaments of crystal and china, some balanced breathlessly on the edges of glass shelves and side tables with delicately carved legs. I found myself wondering what she and Eamon Byrne, who favored dark wood and ancient swords, had ever found in common.

"Yes," she replied, eyes downcast once more. "At such a time . . ." her voice trailed off again. It was a favorite conversational gambit of hers, I noticed, to allow others to finish off sentences for her, without having to voice the hypocrisies personally.

"Breeta says her clue was stolen from the safe in your husband's study," I said, ignoring her attempts at delicacy. "Who would do that, do you think?"

"But she, you, couldn't think this robbery was about a clue," Margaret said, her chronic expression of surprise heightened at the thought. Eithne raised her eyebrows the same way her mother did. "They were looking for money, surely."

"Was money taken?" I asked,

"There was very little money in the safe," she said. "Just a little housekeeping money. But yes, it was taken."

"Was anything else stolen?" I asked.

"Nothing of value, just some of Eamon's things," she said. Then, thinking perhaps that might sound callous, she added, "Though, of great sentimental value, of course."

"Of course," I agreed. "How dreadful for you. I hope you called the police." At least on this score I was sincere. I could hardly wait to send Rob back down to the garda station to inquire about signs of forcible entry and so on. Not that I thought there'd be any. I was prepared to bet the store this had been an inside job.

Margaret shook her head. "There was really no need to bother them about something so minor."

"What things of your husband's did they take?" I asked, trying to sound sympathetic, which in many ways I was. Not about the robbery, perhaps. I just didn't believe her on that score. But the situation, her deceased husband's rather callous remarks, and the little treasure hunt he'd concocted for his heirs must have been truly upsetting for them all. I told myself to be more understanding about their general demeanor.

"His diary, and two of his maps."

"Surely the maps are worth something?" I went on doggedly.

"But they weren't any of the old ones," she said. "Perhaps the thief was unaware of the value of what he missed. My husband's collection of weapons and manuscripts is quite valuable. Regrettably, he has left these things to Trinity College." Her tone hardened.

"Now," she said setting down her teacup and looking straight at me, so that I saw for the first time her eyes, hard as polished diamonds, and the firm lines around her mouth that even surgery couldn't erase. "If I have satisfied your curiosity, I have a request to make of you. Please leave us to our grief. This treasure hunt of my husband's is cruel and inappropriate, and the family has decided we will have nothing whatsoever to do with it."

Really, I thought. And maybe pigs can fly, babies are brought by storks, and the Little People do live at the end of the garden. She was right, though, about her husband. His cutting words on that video must have been truly awful for them. I decided I should be more tolerant.

"I would ask you to do the same," Margaret went on. "Please leave us to deal with our grief as best we can. Which brings me to one more matter we wish to discuss with you." She said we, but so far, she'd done all the talking.

"Rose Cottage is a place of considerable sentimental value for the family," she continued. Eithne nodded vigorously, and even Fionuala looked up from her study of her hands. "It was a place where Eamon . . ." she paused for effect. "Where Eamon spent a great deal of time. We were somewhat surprised that someone whom Eamon had known so slightly, and so long ago, should come to possess it. We would ask that you consider returning it to the family."

Alex looked startled, and after a second, he opened his mouth to speak.

"I don't think we'll be doing that," I said quickly, before he could say anything, and as any glimmer of sympathy I'd felt for the widow Byrne vanished in an instant.

"Then you will understand the family will feel compelled to pursue whatever legal options we have to bring Rose Cottage back where it belongs. My husband was very ill and didn't know what he was doing. Otherwise, I am sure he would never have left the cottage to Mr. Stewart." She spoke as if Alex wasn't even in the room.

I was about to say "see you in court" or something, when Margaret set her teacup rather firmly on the silver tray in front of her and rose from her chair. The other two stood up immediately as well. Fionuala, who had not uttered a single word, not even a hello, got out of her chair and left the room without so much as a backward glance. The audience, apparently, was at an end.

There was one more defining moment, however, in the revelation of Margaret Byrne's character. As she stepped forward, the slow and steady Vigs lumbered out from under the sofa, causing her to start and lose her balance for a moment. She clutched at the tea trolley, and one of the delicate teacups fell over and broke. "Deirdre!" she hissed. "Deirdre! Get this dreadful creature out of here—permanently." There was no reply from the maid.

"Thank you for coming," Margaret said in an imperial tone, gesturing toward the hall. I gathered we were supposed to let ourselves out. I was very close to losing my temper, and had to stifle an impulse to say something truly nasty. I kept seeing in my mind the expression on Alex's face when he first laid eyes on the little cottage. It was not enough, I thought, that the Byrne family should have this palatial home, more villa than house, their servants, and acres and acres of land, with their roses and orchids and palm trees, and a stunning view of the water. No, they had to have Rose Cottage, too.

Over my dead body, I thought, glaring at Margaret. I was suddenly absolutely determined that Alex would not only get to keep his cottage, but he would have the money he needed to live there comfortably. If that meant going to court, I thought, so be it. And if living comfortably meant snatching the treasure right out from under their noses, then we were going to do that too.

The trouble was, to do that we needed all the clues, and I was going to have to think of another way of getting them. I had thought for a few golden moments that we wouldn't need them. When I found the clue in the little boat off shore, I had thought we were home free. We knew the first two clues, and they pointed us to a poem by an ancient poet named Amairgen. If each line of the poem led to a real clue, then we didn't need their clues. We had only to try to guess the location that would correspond to the lines of the poem and go get them.

The clue in the boat was, however, a disappointment. It was from Eamon Byrne, all right. At least it was his personal memo paper, with his initials and Second Chance printed across the top. But the clue, if that was what it was, was far from what I was hoping for. I didn't expect something as definitive as, say, a note that told us that the key to the safety-deposit box in Killarney train station was under the third flowerpot on the left side of the driveway, or anything. I had, however, expected more than the doodling that I'd found when the paper had finally dried out, just a series of lines that looked vaguely like a railway track, or the bones of a fish, perhaps. I'd kept the piece of paper, if only because I couldn't believe that Eamon Byrne, or anyone else for that matter, would bother to wrap up doodlings in plastic, either wade, or wait till the tide was out, to the boat, and carefully conceal it between the boards. But my illusions about a quick end to this treasure hunt had been dashed.

I think at that point I'd have been inclined to drop the whole matter, but the convergence of a number of events made me change my mind. One, of course, was this interview with the Byrne women, along with their stated intention of trying to take the cottage away from Alex.

Added to that were a couple of developments that meant I had a little time on my hands, and we know what they say about idle hands. First was Jennifer's decision, with her father's reluctant acquiescence, to take sailing lessons every morning, from Padraig Gilhooly, no less. Apparently, her damp and frightening introduction to the sport had merely whetted her appetite for it. As far as her father's opinion on the subject was concerned, he wasn't exactly keen on his daughter being anywhere near someone involved, even peripherally, with a murder suspect, but Padraig, it seemed, had an ironclad alibi, vouched for by his lawyer in Cork, no less.

The other was a realization that I wouldn't be seeing much of Rob for the next little while, a turn of events that had been immediately obvious the previous evening when I'd entered a bar on the main street of town with Alex, to find Rob chatting up an attractive woman, slim and rather fit-looking, with a halo of reddish hair around her face, and attractive green eyes.

"Lara," Rob exclaimed as I'd walked up to the bar. I wasn't sure what the tone meant. I suspected it wasn't Lara as in Lara-I'm-so-delighted-to-see-you. He'd picked this bar a couple of blocks from the Inn, in hopes I wouldn't find him, I'd warrant. "Lara, I'd like you to meet Maeve Minogue. Maeve, this is my associate Lara McClintoch."

Associate? I see. "How do you do," I said, shaking her hand. She had a very firm handshake.

"It's grand to meet a friend of Robert's," she said. "We're all enjoying having him here."

Who is we, I wondered. The name Minogue was familiar, but it took a minute or two for me to twig to it. This woman was the "chap" Minogue Rob had talked to at the police station. It gave a whole new meaning to the term "improving international relations," to use Rob's own words, and the fact that he'd used the term chap to describe her spoke volumes of his intention to keep her a secret from me.

"Well, Robert," I said, sweetly. "Perhaps you'll excuse me while I go and sit with another of your associates. Lovely to meet you, Maeve."

I went and sat with Alex, trying not to huff. This was a development I found intensely irritating, although I don't know why it incensed me so much. Rob is, after all, free to do as he pleases. I have no claim to his affections. Occasionally, I wonder if he might make a suitable partner for me, but really our lives don't seem to work out in that direction.

When I first met him, he was living with Ms. Perfect, and I was in a long-distance relationship with a Mexican archaeologist. Then I was free, which is to say I got dumped, but Rob was still with Barbara. Then Clive, my ex-husband, persuaded his second wife, Celeste, to buy him the store across the street from Greenhalgh & McClintoch, setting me off into a fury and putting me off relationships with the opposite sex for some time. After a while Clive ditched Celeste and took up with my best friend Moira, about the time Rob and Barbara parted company. Rob expressed mild interest in me at that time, at least I think he did, but I was so traumatized by Clive and Moira, that I ignored him, or at least chose not to notice.

As I think about this, I am beginning to wonder if I might have a career as a scriptwriter for afternoon television, drawing from my own life experience for the plots, should the antiques business, perilous at the best of times, not work out. I do know that as someone who has seen the dark side of forty, I should probably just reconcile myself to the single life, and take up needlepoint, or something, to fill the long evenings, but I don't. Like many of my generation, I feel younger than my years—or at least I delude myself that I do. I no longer feel as if I could live forever, but I don't feel old, either. I am, however, at the stage in life where men my age appear to prefer younger—much younger—women. That made Ireland, that through some demographic anomaly having to do with emigration rates and such, has a population 50 percent of which is under the age of twenty-five, pretty much a paradise for forty-somethingish guys like Rob.

But I digress. The final and deciding factor in my renewed resolution to find the treasure was a series of events that took place as Alex and I left Second Chance after our unpleasant session with the inhabitants, to head back to the village. It was late afternoon as I negotiated the rental car down the long driveway toward the main road. It had begun to rain quite hard, and Michael was nowhere to be seen, having presumably gone indoors for shelter. The windshield wipers were waving hypnotically in front of me, and the defroster was working overtime to clear the fog from the windshield. As I rounded a turn a hooded figure stepped out from dense brush at the side of the road and into the path of the car. I slammed on the brakes but, forgetting I was driving a standard shift, didn't depress the clutch in my hurry. The car jerked along then stalled a few feet from the figure.

I rolled down the window and peered out at the face under the hood. It was Deirdre, and she looked genuinely frightened, a trembling little bird on scrawny legs, her hair matted from the rain, despite the hood. "Stay away from Second Chance," she said breathlessly. "You have no idea what's going on here. This family is cursed!" Then she looked over her shoulder and quickly stepped back into the brush and disappeared.

Then I saw what might have startled her. Sean McHugh, son-in-law number one, was walking down the drive toward the house. He was, like his brother-in-law, fair, but a little softer looking, a little jowly perhaps, and less threatening in demeanor, though not, in this case, in stance. He was still in his tweeds and high boots, but he'd added a rain cape swirling behind him—the aforementioned country gentleman look—except that he wasn't looking particularly gentlemanly. He was carrying a gun, a rifle, slung over one shoulder. Even though it wasn't pointed at us, it was an unpleasant moment.

"What are you doing here?" he demanded.

"We've had tea at the house," I replied.

"What are you doing snooping around on the road?"

"I'm not snooping," I replied haughtily. "The car stalled. A rabbit ran in front of us, and I had to stop suddenly." I was speaking, I suppose, metaphorically. There had been more than a little of the frightened rabbit in Deirdre.

"Get moving," McHugh said, looking as if he didn't believe me for a moment. Maybe there weren't any rabbits around here. Regardless, we did what we were told. I consider it a good rule not to argue with a man who holds a gun.

I looked over at Alex. "All rather Gothic, wouldn't you say?"

"Gothic, yes, but part of it is true," he said. "To Deirdre's point, I have no idea what is going on here."

"I feel sorry for Vigs," I said. "I figure he's doomed. What do you think she'll do to him? He's too big to flush down the toilet."

"I don't even want to think," Alex murmured. "We should have brought him with us."

"Maybe we should have brought Deirdre, too," I replied. Alex smiled.

"We're going to have to do something about a road into Rose Cottage," I said, seriously. "We can't have Sean McHugh waving a rifle at you every time you try to get there."

"I'll think about it," Alex said. "I haven't decided what to do about the cottage just yet."

"But you know you love it," I said. "And we can't let those awful people intimidate you out of your inheritance!"

Alex just shrugged and took to looking at the scenery. I gathered this was a topic he didn't wish to pursue at the moment.

"Pull over," he said suddenly. "Can you back up? About a hundred yards?"

Surprised, I complied. "What is it?" I exclaimed.

Alex pointed down a little road off to the right. I looked but couldn't figure out what he was talking about. It was just another lane, as far as I could see.

"What?" I said to him, mystified.

"Look at the signs," he said. There were a number of signs hammered into a tree, one of them for a B&B, another for a vegetable stand, others individual names. At the very bottom, however, was a crude hand-lettered wooden sign. The Breakers, it said.

"Worth a try," I said.

We slowly made our way along the road, checking all the houses as we went. After about five minutes, the pavement ended, and we bounced our way around muddy potholes, then made a sharp left turn down an even worse road.

At the very end was a little house, a shack really, with smoke swirling from the chimney. Beyond it was the sea, huge breakers crashing against black cliffs, the spume rising high up before dissipating into a mist that blew across the little bay. The sign on the gatepost was almost illegible, but apparently we were at The Breakers.

I looked at Alex. We got out of the car and made our way to the door, a little black and white dog yipping at our heels.

I knocked, then knocked again. I heard steps inside and the latch being opened, then a familiar face peered out at us.

"Malachy!" I exclaimed.

"Lara!" he replied. "Kev," he shouted. "Put on some tea. It's that nice young girl we talked to at the pier. Lara. And her friend," he added, looking myopically in Alex's direction. I introduced the two of them. "Did you bring some whiskey, by any chance," he whispered.

"Sorry again," I replied. "I didn't know I was coming here." I hoped I didn't wear out my welcome with these two before I got them whiskey.

"Where's Denny?" I asked to change the subject.

"Denny lives with his sister and her family in town," Malachy said. " 'Tis just Kev and me lives here."

Malachy cleared a space on the sofa, sweeping aside papers, and taking unwashed plates to the sink. "We weren't expecting company," he said. "Please excuse the mess."

"It's fine," I replied, taking a seat and accepting a mug of hot tea.

"To what do we owe the pleasure of your company?" Kev asked loudly.

"Shush, don't be rude," Malachy said, wagging his finger at his brother.

"I just want to know," Kev replied peevishly.

"That's a fair question, Kevin. Actually, we didn't know you lived here. We were just touring around. You have a fabulous view," I said, trying to figure out how to broach the subject I wanted.

"The best," Kevin agreed.

"Grand, isn't it?" Malachy added.

"But now that we're here," I went on, "I have a question for you. Did Eamon Byrne leave anything with you to give to his family or a friend?"

"What did she say?" Kevin said, cupping his hand around his ear.

"She's asking if Eamon Byrne left anything here," Malachy shouted.

"How would she know that?" Kevin asked. Both men turned to look at me.

"Byrne gave everyone who got something from his Will, well, almost everyone, anyway, a riddle to solve. Alex here was one of the people who was included in this riddle, and when we saw your sign for The Breakers, we thought maybe it was a clue." I decided honesty was the best policy, as unlikely as the story might have sounded.

"What did she say?" Kevin said again.

"She said Alex here is one of the people looking for Eamon Byrne's clues," Malachy repeated.

"Good," Kevin said. "I like her better than some of

the rest of them. But she has to say the magic words, doesn't she? Does she know the magic words?"

Both men turned to look at me again. "The furious wave," I replied.

"She got it!" Malachy exclaimed. "Get the clue, Kevin. It's hers."

"Where'd we put it?" Kevin said, looking perplexed. My heart sank. For a few minutes the two men shuffled about, pulling open drawers, looking under cushions. I was in despair.

"I got it!" Malachy exclaimed at last, pulling a slim white envelope out of a book. "Here 'tis," he said handing it to me. I resisted the temptation to rip it open on the spot.

At that moment, the little dog started yapping again outside, and we could hear footsteps coming up to the door, then a loud banging.

"Goodness me, another one," Malachy said. "Tree years since somebody came to visit, and now dere's two in one day!"

He opened the door slowly, then tried to close it again. A foot stopped it from closing. "Have you got something from Eamon Byrne?" Conail O'Connor asked harshly.

"No, I don't," Malachy said, rather craftily I thought. I had it, he didn't. But he must have looked suspicious, because O'Connor thrust the door open roughly and grabbed Malachy by the collar. The older man staggered and started to fall, but O'Connor held him up. Kevin grabbed a frying pan. I grabbed the teapot.

"Now see here," Alex said stepping forward, arms up, his hands balled into fists, in a kind of a boxer stance. "You have no right to treat these people this way!"

"Get out of my way, gobshite," O'Connor said, let-ting go of Malachy and stepping toward Alex menacingly. I swung my arm back with the teapot and started to move toward them.

Alex stepped to one side, dodged O'Connor's arm, feinted with his left, then his right hand snapped forward. There was a loud crack, and Conail O'Connor went down for the count.

Chapter Six

A RAY OF THE SUN

"Now Mr. Stewart," Ban Garda Maeve Minogue said. Her tone was severe, but there was a hint of a smile playing about the corners of her mouth. Minogue was in her early thirties, I'd say, with reddish hair, now pulled back and tucked neatly into her cap, and that flawless complexion so many women in Ireland are blessed with. "That is quite a punch you throw."

"I wish I'd hit him too," Kevin grumped.

"You should be glad you didn't, Kevin," Minogue said sharply. "If you'd hit him with that frying pan, O'Connor might be dead, and you'd be in a fine mess. As it is, he won't be eating solid food for days. Last I saw of him, he was down at Tom Fitzgerald's pub, taking in his daily requirement for calories in liquid form.

"Now, Mr. Stewart," she began again, "seeing as there are three witnesses here who claim you were provoked and the fact that you have a member of a sister law enforcement agency here," she said gesturing to Rob, "who can attest to your good character, as well

as several people around town who can speak to
O'Connor's less than exemplary behavior of late, we
will not be laying charges. Conail O'Connor is threatening to bring assault charges on his own, which he is
quite entitled to do, but I do believe he will change his
mind, seeing as how he's already been the butt of several jokes regarding the difference in his and your ages,
to mention nothing of size. We will not be laying
charges against him either, unless you wish to make a
case for it. Extenuating circumstances."

I wondered what these extenuating circumstances
might be, but decided it was better not to ask.

"I won't be laying charges," Alex said.

"Me neither, I guess," Malachy said. "Though that
boyo better not come 'round to our place again."

"Right, then. Now if you gentlemen will agree to
behave yourselves for the balance of the evening," the
garda said, "I'll be away." She glanced at her watch.
"Off duty at last," she sighed.

"Can I buy you a drink in that case?" Rob asked.

"That would be grand," she said. "I'll call in and
then be off home to get changed and come back, if
that's all right?" Rob smiled his assent. I got the distinct impression he was smitten.

"Well, can I buy you two the whiskey I've been
promising?" I asked, turning to Kevin and Malachy.
Rob may have found himself a new woman, but I had
my two new men.

"You can," Malachy said. "She's buying us a drink,"
he said in Kevin's ear.

"And how about you, Alex?" I said. He was favoring
his bruised knuckles.

"I believe I will," he said. I ordered three whiskeys
for the men, a cola for Jennifer, and a glass of wine
for myself. Rob declined my offer and headed off to

his room, to beautify himself, no doubt, for Garda Minogue's return.

"Who's that woman at the bar?" Jennifer asked me. I looked across the crowd.

"Fionuala Byrne O'Connor," I replied. "Why?"

"One of the hags, you mean?" Jennifer said. "That makes it even worse."

"Makes what worse?"

"She's been chatting up Dad," Jennifer said. "Fortunately, he didn't seem to notice."

She sounded annoyed, and I had to smile. Fathers and daughters, I thought. The jealousy seemed to go both ways. She had a point, though. Fionuala was definitely out for a good time. She was holding down a stool at the bar, her tight, short skirt riding provocatively high on her thighs, and a cigarette, held delicately between brightly painted fingernails, sending swirls of smoke around her head. I wondered if she'd heard about her husband's jaw's intersection with Alex's hand.

I was also speculating whether Jennifer would like Maeve Minogue any better, when Michael and Breeta joined us.

"What happened to your hand?" Michael said, eyeing Alex's knuckles, now an unbecoming shade of blue.

"It came in contact with Conail O'Connor's jaw," Malachy proffered.

"He was trying to kill Malachy at the time," Kevin piped in. "O'Connor, I mean. He had his hands around Malachy's neck and was throttling him. Malachy was almost unconscious." My, I thought, how these stories grow! Denny would be telling this one to the post on the pier before long. "Alex and I went after O'Connor, Lara too."

"Knocked him out cold." Malachy grinned. " 'Twas a fine sight to see. I think we should drink another toast to Alex's right hand." I ordered them another round, but passed myself. It was beginning to look as if this was going to turn into a long night, and I thought I might be called upon to do a little chauffeuring later.

Michael looked at me. "Can you enlighten us a little? We saw O'Connor leaving Tom Fitzgerald's place. Face all swollen, and in a right bad mood. Staggering drunk, of course. Headed off down one of the laneways," he added.

"Not in this direction, I hope," I said, thinking that a drunk Conail O'Connor might be a real problem.

"He might be," Michael said. "But if he is, it's going to take him a while to get this far, the shape that he's in. So tell us what happened this afternoon."

I told them the story, with a lot of help from Malachy and Kevin.

Throughout this conversation, Breeta said nothing, although she looked shocked enough when she heard the story. She seemed sort of out of it, somehow, her mind somewhere else entirely. I'd offered her a drink, but she didn't take me up on it, and sat, instead, holding a glass of soda water, which she barely touched, as she stared into the flames of the fireplace across from us.

"I've lost my job," she said, suddenly rousing herself from her torpor.

"Oh dear," I said. "That's too bad. What happened?"

She was silent for a moment or two. "I've been working in a dress shop," she said finally. "A very fancy dress shop, in Killarney. I think," she said slowly, "I think—they didn't say so, but they didn't think I looked good enough to work there. They wanted someone who looked better in the clothes." Her lip trembled, but she didn't cry.

"What do you mean, Bree?" Michael exclaimed. "What do you mean you didn't look good enough to work there?"

"I've put on so much weight," she said. A tear slipped out of one corner of her eye. She brushed it away angrily. "And they're right. I don't look good in the clothes. I don't care about the job. It wasn't very interesting," she went on. "But I'll have to give up my flat in a couple of weeks, and I don't know where I'll go."

"I think you're just beautiful, Bree," Michael said, his voice hoarse. "And you can stay with me. I know I'm not good enough for you, working on your family's estate and everything. But I have that little flat in the staff cottage. Now that John Herlihy's gone, maybe I can get his. It's bigger, with a little kitchen and everything. There's room for . . ." He stopped and looked down at his rough hands. "There's room for all of us."

I wasn't sure who all of us were, but I thought his offer was very nice, and Breeta could do a lot worse. Michael wasn't exceptionally bright, maybe, but he was smart enough, and he was also kind and generous, and obviously sweet on Breeta.

"Thank you, Michael," Breeta said softly. "I appreciate your offer. Very, very much. It's the nicest thing that's happened to me in a long time. I will have to think about it, but . . ." Her voice trailed off, and they both sat looking at each other.

Ain't love grand? I thought. Certainly it was thawing Breeta, which was nice.

"That settles it. We'll have to look for that treasure," Michael said suddenly. "Really look for it. I mean it. Everything will be all right, Bree. There'll be lots of money. We can all look together. I'm sure there will be enough to go around when we find it. You can have my share." He paused. "I forgot," he said, turning to me. "What happened when you went to ask about Breeta's clue?"

"We were stunningly unsuccessful," I said, as Alex nodded. "Your mother," I said looking at Breeta, "insists it was an ordinary robbery. Some money was taken from the safe along with the clue, if we believe the clue is really missing, and a map or two. She also said the family has decided to have nothing whatsoever to do with the hunt for your father's treasure."

"I don't believe that," Malachy said indignantly. "What was that shite Conail O'Connor doing at our place if he wasn't looking for the treasure?"

"But we don't need them, do we?" Michael persisted. "Breeta knows the poem. Come on, Bree. Tell us about the poem. Please!"

"Oh, Michael, you're such an optimist. Touched in the head. Maybe Da was just making a joke, teasing us all."

"And maybe he wasn't! It's worth a try, anyway. What do we have to lose?"

Breeta looked over at him affectionately. "All right," she said at last. "It's called 'The Song of Amairgen,' and it is supposed to be the words spoken by Amairgen of the White Knee as he set his right foot on Ireland's shore. My father made me translate it from the Old Irish, and to memorize it. It goes something like this. I am the sea-swell, the furious wave, the roar of the sea." The sound of her voice was lovely, the Irish lilt and cadence carrying the words along.

"Her Da taught her well!" Kevin exclaimed, his hand cupped over his ear. "Young people today, hardly any of them are interested in the old tales, want to pretend the past doesn't matter, but Breeta always was. She's like her Da in more ways than one."

"Hush," Malachy said.

"I am a ray of the sun." As she spoke, Michael reached out and took her hand. This time she did not pull it away.

"I am the beauty of a plant." These were lovely images, and I found myself falling under the spell of the words. And so it went until she came near the end. "Who drives cattle off from Tara," she said. "That fine herd that touches each skill." She paused for a moment. "That's the translation, but there are some who have interpreted these phrases about the cattle as being about the stars, rather than the herd. It's a question, almost, like 'Who calls the stars? On whom do the stars shine?'"

"I hope they shine for us," Michael said fervently.

One thing was certain, the stars were not shining for Conail O'Connor. The door of the bar burst open, and a very drunk Conail lurched in. His hair was matted down by rain, and his jaw looked swollen and sore, his face flushed with alcohol. I felt a surge of panic as I saw him look our way. But it wasn't us he was looking for.

"Nuala," he roared. "Get your coat. We're going home! As for you, gobshite," he said, grabbing the man next to Fionuala, one who'd been the object of her charms since Rob had left, "keep yer fecking hands off my wife."

The man stumbled as Conail pulled him off the bar stool.

"Now, Conail," Aidan, the proprietor and bartender, said. "Calm down now, will you?"

"I wasn't doing nothin'," the other man said. "Just talking, that's all."

"Talk to somebody else," Conail shouted. "Come, Nuala. Now!"

"I'm not going anywhere with you, Conail," she replied. "And it isn't your home, anymore. You and I are finished. Don't you dare darken my door or come anywhere near Second Chance ever again!"

Conail grabbed her arm, his face contorted with rage. Several people stepped back. I sensed rather than saw a few people slip out the door preferring to brave the rain than to be involved in this nasty little scene.

"Mr. O'Connor," Garda Minogue's calm voice said. She was out of uniform, looking softer and rather pretty, in fact, but there was no ignoring her tone. "Might I suggest you get a room at the hotel down the street before you find yourself spending the night in jail. Let go of Mrs. O'Connor's arm, please."

Conail, still holding Fionuala's arm, ignored her and started yanking his wife toward the door.

"I believe Garda Minogue has asked you to let go of Mrs. O'Connor and leave the premises," Rob said. I hadn't seen him come back, but I made a mental note to tell him his timing was impeccable. "I suggest you do exactly as she says," he said, with an emphasis on exactly. He was standing very still, arms down at his side, but there was a degree of readiness there, I could tell, to move very fast if he had to. There was also something in his voice I'd never heard before, something that said Conail had better comply. Conail apparently heard it too, because after a second or two, he let go and left the bar, shoving a table by the door very hard as he did so, sending several glasses crashing to the floor.

Absolute silence greeted his abrupt departure. A few more guests followed Conail out into the street. The Conail O'Connors of this world could not be said to be good for business.

"How about a jig or two, Malachy," Aidan said finally, grabbing a broom and dustbin. "Free drinks all evening for you if you'll help me entertain my guests here."

"Done," Malachy said. One of the waiters took the broom and started working away at the trail of broken glass Conail had left behind. Aidan disappeared into a back room for a moment and came back with a fiddle and a Celtic drum. "Where's Sheila?" someone called from the crowd.

"In the back, where else?" Aidan said. "But I'll get her out for this."

Sheila, Aidan's wife and co-proprietor came out of the back room, her face pink and steamy from the kitchen. "Where's your flute?" the man in the back called. Sheila grinned. "We're having a bit of a ceilidh, are we?" she said, pulling a tin flute out of her back pocket. "I had a feeling we might when I saw Malachy and Kevin come in. It's grand to have you back, Breeta," she said.

"What's a ceilidh?" Jennifer asked.

"A musical event," the man at the next table said. "Brought your dancing shoes, have you?"

Aidan watched as Malachy pulled the bow across the strings a couple of times, tuning his instrument. "Pick the tune, Malachy," he said, "and we'll follow you."

"Best call your uncle," Kevin shouted to one of the young men at the bar, who nodded and headed for the phone. "One of Denny's sister's boys. Denny should be here."

Malachy launched into a rousing number, followed by Sheila on the flute. Aidan marked the beat on the bodhran. It was a real toe-tapper, and pretty soon the crowd was swaying in time to the music, and one of the older women in the crowd started to dance. Within a minute to two, the furniture was moved back against the wall, and Malachy was fiddling as fast as he could. Jennifer grabbed Alex's arm and pulled him up. Breeta shyly reached over and took Michael's hand. Maeve even convinced Rob to get up and dance, an event I considered extraordinary. Kevin stood up, a little shakily, and bowed very formally. "May I have the pleasure of a whirl around the floor?" he asked me. I didn't know the steps, but it didn't really seem to matter. In truth, it seemed impossible to sit still. Everyone who was able to was laughing and drinking and dancing enthusiastically. Those too old to dance were smiling and clapping in time to the music and singing along. Everyone that is, except Fionuala, who stood for a few moments at the edge of the crowd, clapping half-heartedly in time to the music, her face a study in conflicting emotions. After a few twirls with Kevin, I turned to look for her again, but she was gone, and soon both she and Conail were quite forgotten, as the music and the conviviality restored everyone's spirits.

When most of us were breathless, Aidan yelled above the din. "We'll have to take a break for a moment!" he shouted. "I have to make a living, don't I? So who's for another drink, and for some of Sheila's food? Best bar fare in town!"

Breeta and Michael collapsed, laughing, onto the stools at our table. Jennifer and Alex joined us shortly thereafter. "That was brilliant!" Jennifer gasped. "Absolutely brilliant." And it was. The whole evening had an exuberance and spontaneity to it that was sadly lacking in much of the music and dance that is promoted as Celtic these days. This was the real thing. Jennifer reached over and hugged me. "I'm having the best time," she said. "Ever!" I hugged her back.

"There'll be a music festival on here in two, three weeks," Michael said. "There'll be music and dancing

everywhere in town. Too bad you won't be here. Or
maybe you will. Maybe you'll be enchanted by the
place—plenty are—and want to stay forever. It happens, you know."

"Let's stay!" Jennifer said. So much for the girl who
hadn't wanted to leave her friends in Toronto even for
• a week or two.

Malachy and Kevin were up at the bar, now, and
Aidan was pouring them both a drink, and one for
Denny if he'd promise a story. "All right then," Aidan
shouted over the din a few minutes. "If you'll fortify
yourselves with a little liquid libation, we'll be hearing
a tale from Denny." There was a roar and some foot
stomping approval.

"Tell about the time you heard the banshee, Denny,"
a young woman at the back called out.

"Someone get Denny's chair," Aidan said, and a
rocker was quickly pulled up in front of the fire.

"In honor of Breeta's return to The Three Sisters,
she can pick the story," Denny said.

"Pick a good one, Breeta," a man called out.

Breeta thought for a moment. "In honor of my Da,"
she said at last, "I'd like one of the old ones, Denny.
Tell us the story of how the Good People came to rule
Ireland."

"Good choice, Breeta," Malachy said.

Denny rocked back and forth in his chair for a moment or two.

"The tale I'm telling you now happened a long, long
time ago," he began. "Before Amairgen and the Sons
of Mil set foot on these shores. Not so far back as the
plague that killed the sons and daughters of Partholan.
Not so far back as that. But a long time ago, even so.

"In those days, there were giants roamed the earth,
and creatures with one leg and one arm, like serpents

came out of the sea. Back then, unsheathed weapons told tales, the sky could rain fire, and the shrieks of the Hag would be heard in the night.

"And it was then that the fiercest of battles, the struggle of light over darkness, were fought and won by the Tuatha dé Danaan."

The bar was absolutely silent. Three small children, sons and daughter of the innkeepers, crept into the room and sat on the floor, transfixed. Driving rain splattered against the window, and the fire cracked and hissed.

"Now there's many a story about how the dé Danaan came to be here in Ireland. Many a tale. Some say they came from Scythia, driven out by the Philistines; others say they came from northern realms, from four glorious cities where they learned magic and druidic skills.

"There's more than one tale about how they arrived. Some say they arrived in a mist, others that they came in ships which they burned so they would not fall into Fomorian hands or so they themselves would not be able to flee.

"However they got here, when the smoke or mist cleared, the Fir Bolg, for it was them who lived in the western reaches of our island, found the Tuatha dé had already fortified their place.

"The two groups met. They inspected each other's weapons, those of the Fir Bolg heavy and fierce-looking, the Tuatha dé's light and agile. 'We should divide up the island equally,' the Tuatha dé told the Fir Bolg.

"But the Fir Bolg were not impressed by the weapons of these newcomers, and they decided not to accept the offer, but instead to fight. And thus it was that the first mighty Battle of Mag Tuired was fought on a plain near Cong. At the head of the Fir Bolg was Eochaid, son of Erc; leading the Tuatha dé was the prince Nuada."

"Nuada Silver Hand," one of the children called out.

"Nuada Argat-lam, Nuada Silver Arm," Denny agreed. "But he wasn't called that just yet, not till after the battle, and I'll tell you why. The battle was fierce, and there were heavy losses on both sides. But the Tuatha dé won victory and pressed the Fir Bolg northward, where eleven hundred were slain, among them Eochaid, son of Erc.

"But there was a price to pay. In that wondrous battle, Nuada lost his hand. Diancecht the healer and Credne the brazier made for him a silver hand, which worked just like the one you have," Denny said, grabbing one of the children's arms. "For the Tuatha dé had the magic, didn't they?

"But this was a great loss for the Tuatha dé, for Nuada could no longer be their king, Tuatha dé kings having to be perfect, and even though the silver hand worked so well, Nuada was no longer considered perfect. So the kingship fell to Bres, the beautiful, who was not only half Fomorian, but a very bad king. And the Fomorians exacted so much tribute from the Tuatha dé that they suffered greatly, even their gods, like the Dagda and the rest. Just when it seemed darkest, a new champion arose, the greatest of them all, Lugh Lamfada, Lugh of the Long Arm, and he, along with the other gods, and Nuada, with a real arm now, through magic made, fought the second great battle of Mag Tuired, more vicious than the first, the battle for supremacy over the dreaded Fomorians."

What followed was a wonderful tale, of magic harps, swords and spears, of gods and goddesses, of prophecies and promises broken, of bravery and treachery, of fathers killed by sons, and sons by fathers, and in the end, the death of Nuada on the field of battle, and a prophecy, from the Morrigan, goddess of war, of the end of the world.

"And this is only one of the tales of the Tuatha dé," Denny concluded. "There are many more, until, as you all know, they were defeated at last by the Sons of Mil and banished to the sidhe, the islands and the underworld, where they live to this day." He paused for a moment. "And how about a little something to wet the whistle, barman?" he said.

The crowd applauded, then turned back to their friends and their drinks, and soon the room was a din of conviviality.

As the others chatted away, I couldn't help my mind wandering a little, back to the unpleasant episodes with Conail earlier in the day. Extenuating circumstances, Garda Minogue had said, in explaining why they wouldn't be laying charges against O'Connor. If the recent ugly scene was anything to go by, those extenuating circumstances included a bad fight with his wife, one which could have signalled the end of the marriage, a fact that could have resulted in O'Connor's reckless exit from Second Chance that afternoon as we were arriving, and his ill humor later on. Just as his wife inherited half of Byrne Enterprises, by all accounts a very successful business, and one he'd had a hand in running, or running down, to use Byrne's own words, Fionuala turfed him out. No wonder his excessive fervor in searching out the clue: He'd want to beat that family to the treasure, whatever it was, even more than I did.

"Have you thought about what your father's treasure might be, Bree?" Michael was asking as I returned to the present from my reverie.

"Of course I have," she replied. "I've thought about it and him a lot."

"So?"

"I think he was telling us that whatever it is is very, very old. He chose Amairgen's chant after all. That makes it Celtic, that I'm sure of, or maybe something from the time of Amairgen."

"So when exactly is that?" Jennifer asked.

"Any time after about 200 B.C.," Breeta replied. "It could be as late as the twelfth or even the fifteenth century, when the 'Song of Amairgen' was written down."

Jennifer's eyes widened. "But that could be almost anything. Illuminated manuscripts, gold, iron, bronze, anything."

"It could," Breeta replied.

"Surely you could narrow it down for us a little more than that," Michael sighed. "What about all those old maps and weapons of your Da's? I know he said he was giving them to Trinity College, but could it be another of those, an especially old or important one? Are those things worth anything?"

"Oh yes," I said, "they are."

"It could be," Breeta said. "But my father liked lots of things. He wasn't an educated man, you know. He said that all the education in the world wouldn't have made him a success, just hard work. He left school early to work with his father in the family business, before he ran away to sea. Despite what he said, though, I think he felt the lack of education keenly. That's why he wanted you to go back to school, Michael." Michael nodded.

"Da was exceptionally well read, though, self-taught. He'd been brought up on all the old stories, like the one Denny just told us, and he taught them to us, my sisters and me. In some ways, he believed the old stories. Oh, I don't mean he believed in magic or the Little People or anything, at least no more so than most Irishmen, but unlike some, he believed the ancient stories were, in fact, real stories about real events and real people, and when he wasn't at work, he was out trying to prove it. He found and read old manuscripts, studied old maps, located all the sites of the great epic battles. You can find them, too, if you look."

"I gather this isn't a point of view shared by everyone," Alex said.

"You're quite right about that," she laughed. "I remember studying the *Leabhar Gabala,* the *Book of Invasions*, at school. Amairgen's poem comes from that, incidentally, and the story Denny just told us. It's the story of the arrival of various people on Ireland's shores, starting with someone called Cessair. There were Partholanians, Nemedians, then the Tuatha dé, and eventually the so-called Sons of Mil, the Celts. I'd learned it at my father's knee, as they say." Her voice caught a little as she spoke.

"Anyway, the school had got in a professor of archaeology to talk to us about it. He said that the Mythological Cycle, the part of the *Leabhar Gabala* containing these very old stories, was just a collection of old fables, stories that were supposed to tell us something about the human condition, but not in any way true, and that they had been written down by monks in the twelfth century, not by poets like Amairgen at all. He even said there was no real archaeological evidence for all the invasions that the book tells us about. I was terribly disappointed, and I raced home to talk to Da about it. I can't have been more than ten years old at the time, and I still believed all the stories he'd told me to be absolutely true, like children believing in Santa Claus, I suppose.

"Da was absolutely furious. He said that for all his schooling, the professor was nothing but a bloody ijit. He said it was true that the stories had been written down by monks all right, but that these monks had worked hard to preserve the old stories and that the stories themselves were much, much older than that. He said maybe the old stories had been exaggerated a little over time, and given a lot of magic, but that once you stripped away these elements in the stories, you would have a record of real history remembered and passed down through the centuries as myths."

"Your father was what is sometimes called an annalist, I believe," Alex said. "Quite an honorable tradition in the study of ancient times, trying to prove an historical basis for the old myths."

"Yes, but my Da became obsessed with the idea of proving that professor wrong, partly I think, because of his lack of schooling—he was a little sensitive on that score—but also because he really did think the man was an ijit. My father believed there were successive invasions of various peoples, many of them probably different groups of Celts. And he set out to prove it, to track the evidence down."

"So how was he planning to do this?" I asked.

"Well for starters, he set out to find and identify the four great gifts of the gods," she said.

Michael just looked at her. "He was daft," he said.

"Maybe," she said. "But what about Lia Fail? It exists, doesn't it?"

"You are going to have to enlighten us a little," Alex said. "Who or what is Lia Fail? And what are the four great gifts of the gods?"

"The stories of the Tuatha dé Danaan tell of four

fabulous objects that were supposed to have been brought from the four cities from which the Tuatha dé came," she replied. "From Falias, one of those cities, is supposed to have come the Stone of Fal. The Stone of Fal was at Tara, seat of the High Kings of Ireland. If someone was to be that High King, he had to touch the stone. If it roared, then he was the rightful king. There really is a stone called Lia Fail at Tara to this day—I mean you can go there and see it. But most people feel that it is not the original. The real one was sent over to Scotland for use in a kingship ceremony there, and was eventually taken to Scone.

"The Stone of Scone!" Alex exclaimed. "That's the so-called Coronation Stone, isn't it, the one just recently returned from Westminster to Scotland? The one that was in the base of the British throne?"

"Exactly," she replied. "It was said that whoever had the Stone would rule Scotland, or Scotic, actually, to use an earlier term, by which we mean the Scots/Irish Milesians. That's why it's so important that it be returned to Scotland. The Scots never did take too well to the idea that the King or Queen of England was sitting on it.

"Now there are a lot of tales about that stone. Some say that the Stone in Westminster is not the real Stone of Scone, or Lia Fail, if we go back to its origins, just a plain old stone, and that the real one is hidden somewhere in Scotland. Some say it never left Ireland. What Da would say is that there was a real stone that played an important part in the choice of the High King of Ireland. He wouldn't go so far as to say it roared when touched by the chariot wheel of the true king, but he did believe there was an important stone.

"And he'd say the same thing about the other gifts, one of which was a magic cauldron belonging to the

Dagda, the father god, that came from the magic city of Murias. The Dagda's cauldron was supposedly never empty, no matter how many people came to eat. Now there is no question that there were Celtic cauldrons with ritual importance. There is one called the Gundestrup Cauldron, for example, a silver and gilt cauldron from Gundestrup in Denmark, which is thought to date to the first or second centuries B.C. It shows a horned or antlered deity of some kind, possibly Cernunnos. So Da would say that there really was a cult or ritual cauldron to be found in Ireland that could have been believed in those days to be the Dagda's cauldron, without its magical properties, of course."

"That's why he collected those iron cauldrons!" I said. "And the other two magical objects?"

"The Spear of Lugh, who was the Tuatha dé god referred to often as Lugh the Shining, or Lugh of the Long Arm. His spear was supposed to guarantee victory. Then there was the Sword of Nuada Argat-lam, Nuada Silver Hand in Denny's story, from which no one ever escaped."

"Ah," I said. "Your father's sword and spear collection!"

"Yes," she said. "He was looking for the cult or ritual spear and sword."

"Did he think he had found them?" Alex asked.

"No, he didn't. But he kept looking. It was his passion. There was one sword, the one on the desk, that he thought might be the one, the metal equivalent of the Stone of Scone. It dates to Iron Age Ireland, so who's to say?"

"So are you saying that the treasure might be one of these things? The cauldron or another sword or spear?"

"Maybe," she replied. "Or something else, of course. He studied the myths for clues all the time, read all the ancient documents he could lay his hands on. He was a little obsessed about it, there's no question, and sometimes as his daughter, I felt as if he was more interested in his search than in me. I found it intensely irritating after a while, to be called Banba, instead of Breeta."

"Who or what is Banba?" Jennifer asked.

"One-third of the triple goddess of the Tuatha dé Danaan: Banba, Fotla, and Eriu. All three were names of Ireland at some point in time, but Eriu, through an agreement with Amairgen, actually, won out in the end. Erin is a form of Eriu."

"So you and your sisters were named—nicknames, of sorts—after three goddesses."

She nodded. "It was nice at first, to be named for a goddess, but after a while, I thought it was merely a mark of my father's obsession with these mythological creatures. And who wants to be named after a goddess associated with the pig, which Banba was, particularly when you're the size I am? Anyway," she said, looking at her watch. "That's enough ancient Irish history for one night. I have to catch the bus back into Killarney."

"Why don't you stay at Second Chance?" Michael said.

"No thanks," she replied. "I'm not comfortable there anymore."

Michael had a "my place?" look in his eyes, which Breeta was ignoring.

"Speaking of Second Chance," I said, "if I were you, I'd get the tortoise, Vigs, out of there."

Breeta looked alarmed.

"I don't think your mother likes him," I said. Now that was an understatement. I hoped we weren't already too late, and the family wasn't slurping turtle soup even as we spoke.

"Michael!" she exclaimed. "Will you get Vigs out of there for me?"

"I will," he replied. "I'll take him to my place."

"Tonight!" she said.

"Yes, all right. Tonight," he agreed.

Alex and I walked them to the door. "Can I give you a lift?" I said.

"No, but thanks," she said.

"I'll walk you to the bus, Bree," Michael said.

She smiled at him. "Only if you promise me you'll go to the house and get Vigs afterwards," she said.

"I promise," he said. "I'll go tonight for certain. I'll creep in, so the family won't hear me, and spirit old Vigs away. I'm going to start looking for the treasure tomorrow," he called back. "First thing. It's my day off. Will you help us find it?"

I looked at Alex. He nodded. "Okay," I said. "Why not?"

"Do you promise?" Michael asked.

"Yes, I promise," I said.

He grinned. "Good. Let's get an early start. I'll be here at eight tomorrow morning. Okay?"

"Okay," Alex and I said in unison.

The street was slick with rain, but only a light drizzle was now falling. The air felt fresh and good after the heat and smoke of the pub. Several people were out on the street, their collars turned up against the damp. A few yards away, Fionuala was getting into her car, and idly, I wondered where her husband, soon to be ex, was. It was definitely, I decided, none of my business.

Alex and I stood watching Breeta and Michael until they were almost out of sight, he walking his bicycle with one hand, holding Breeta's hand with the other. It was the happiest I'd seen her, and him for that matter, and I couldn't bring myself to tell them that Amairgen's clues led just about nowhere, that the second clue, retrieved with such drama, contained the same old chicken scratches the first one did. It could wait until tomorrow.

"Eight o'clock tomorrow," he called back again, just as they were about to round a corner. "I'll be at your door at eight."

As I watched them disappear around the corner, I had this flash of insight the way you sometimes do. It was hard to tell with that layer of insulation about her, but I was pretty sure I knew who the all of us that Michael had room for were. It was Michael, Breeta and her as yet unborn child. Breeta Byrne was pregnant.

Chapter Seven

THE BEAUTY OF A PLANT

WE found Michael in his garden, among the roses, out of sight of the house. Eight o'clock had come and gone; then eight-thirty; then nine. He was lying facedown, and from the look of the tracks in the mud behind him, he had dragged himself a hundred agonizing yards before he died. There was not a mark on him that I could see. But if John Herlihy had not fallen forty feet onto a pile of rocks, perhaps there'd have been no mark on him either.

Better trained eyes than mine found the tiny tear in the fabric of his jeans, the puncture in the skin behind his knee. "Poison," they said. "If only someone had found him in time."

In his rigid hand, Michael held a torn piece of paper so tightly it was as if he'd wrestled the Devil himself for it. EONB, it said, and Second Cha. The ragged clue was marked as the seventh, 'The beauty o.' "

I remember two things about that horrible moment when we found him. One is the light. The sun, preternaturally bright, seemed to have sucked the color from all the flowers, the blood from the roses, the heart from the purple hydrangeas, the living breath from the ivy. The other was the sound: Breeta, beside me, making small animal noises, like a kitten being drowned or a child's pet strangled.

And then, some days later, I found myself in a churchyard. It was raining, a bone-chilling drizzle, as it damn well should have been. Michael's coffin, adorned with the flowers he had coaxed into life—a bunch of white roses, a spray or two of tiny orchids— was lowered into the ground. He was buried less than a hundred yards from where he was born. The priest spoke of dust and ashes. I could taste both of them in my mouth.

I looked about the churchyard. There were many among the mourners I did not recognize, townspeople, Michael's friends. Breeta was there, standing apart from the others. Her eyes were strangely opaque, and she twisted her handkerchief over and over. Sometimes her lips moved, but no sound came out. At some point, I edged over to try to comfort her, but she turned away.

My friends were there: Alex with a look of inconsolable sadness; Jennifer, ashen, realizing for the first time, perhaps, that people her age can die. Looking at her, I remembered the feeling of suffocating panic as I lost her for a moment in the cold sea. I looked at Rob who, as a policeman should know sudden death, but whose face barely hid his pain. I came to know as I stood there that it is not possible to be inured to the death of anyone, let alone someone so young, so fine, as Michael. I knew Rob was thinking of Jennifer too. Maeve Minogue was there, in uniform, her face solemn and sad, but also watchful.

Padraig Gilhooly stood way to the back, dark, enigmatic, and solitary. From time to time, he looked over toward Breeta, but made no move in her direction. Malachy, Kevin, and Denny clung to each other as if together they could outwit death.

On the other side of the churchyard was the rest of the Byrne family, all in black, protected from the rain by large black umbrellas that reminded me of black sails on death ships. Deirdre of the Sorrows stood with them, but alone. She looked as if her heart would break. I saw Margaret, who reminded me of nothing so much as a large black crow; Eithne, more tremulous than ever; Fionuala, a little startled somehow. Conail O'Connor was not among them nor anywhere to be seen. Sean McHugh was, though, looking bored, as if there from a sense of noblesse oblige alone, the lord of the manor at the funeral of his vassal.

As I looked across at him, I had a stirring of memory of that fateful morning, which was coming back to me slowly and in flashes, under the careful prodding of Rob and Garda Minogue: Sean McHugh, who appeared at the sound of our cries, tapping Michael's body with his foot. In my head, I knew he was trying to see if he could wake him. In my heart, I saw it as the most callous of gestures, one that ripped open McHugh's soul for all to see, a shrivelled and blackened shell.

I looked at the Byrne family across the great gulf that was Michael's grave and coffin, and I realized, that with the exception of Deirdre, I hated them. He'd asked what there was to lose, looking for the treasure, and now the answer was clear. I knew in that instant that if I could bring every single one of them down, I would. I came to terms with the fact that I was very, very angry. I would avenge him if I could. But even more than that, I had a suffocating sense of a creeping evil that threatened everyone I held most dear: Alex, who as one of the recipients of Byrne's largesse, was surely a potential victim; Jennifer, who might have drowned that day on the water, a careless casualty in a vicious game.

Then I remembered I had made a promise to Michael Davis. I told him I would help him find the treasure. I felt I would do anything to fulfill that promise, not just because I had made it, but because to find the treasure seemed the only way to put an end to the horror. But even as I thought this, I knew I had no idea where or how to start. All I had was a chant, an ancient spell, perhaps, recited by a Celt who might or might not have existed, and two clues the poem had led us to, clues that told me nothing, just scribbling, a cruel joke perhaps, of a bitter, dying man.

The priest was talking about God, and I concentrated on that, and on the ancient Celtic deities, the Dagda, Lugh the Shining, the triple goddess, Banba, Fotla, and Eriu. And I thought whoever or whatever is out there, I could use a little help.

Then the wind whipped the sea into whitecaps, and the rain swept in undulating sheets across the land, like a lace curtain in the breeze, and I had a horrible feeling that in looking for divine assistance I had blasphemed, and the gods were warning me with this rain. The service over, people headed for cover, some to the church, others to their cars to steal away. Denny left with some people I took to be his family. Rob walked Maeve to her car.

Alex, Malachy and Kevin, Jennifer and I ducked under some trees to wait it out, hoods pulled over our heads, shoulders hunched against the damp. It was inexpressibly dreary.

"Very bad day," I said to Kevin. It was all I could manage to say.

"The worst," he sadly agreed.

Then, just as suddenly as it began, it was over. The sun came out, and with it, not one, but two rainbows arched across the sky. It was breathtakingly beautiful, almost painfully so, the world's colors back again, huge drops of rain on the large leaves of a plant nearby. I thought of Amairgen's ray of sun and the beauty of a plant. I looked out across the little cemetery, the headstones worn until the names on them could barely be deciphered, the carved figures fading with time, now just a little clearer because of the rain. At one corner of the graveyard, just a few feet away, stood a single stone, a miniature and rough obelisk, about three or four feet high. Carved on one face at the top of it, I could see a Celtic cross. Below that a series of cuts, some straight, some angled, had been slashed into the stone along one edge. I turned away, but then looked back again. I knew my prayer had been answered. I saw that help had come. Alex followed my glance across the graveyard. "Good heavens!" he exclaimed.

"Ogham," Alex said, "an ancient Celtic script and the first known written language in Ireland. Named for Ogmios, sometimes called Oghma, the Celtic god of poetry, eloquence, and speech, and the supposed inventor of the script. It's thought to have originated in this part of Ireland and is apparently based on the names of trees. As I understand it, it's a linear script composed of groups of lines, up to five of them, either horizontal or angled from upper left to lower right, across a vertical spine or stemline. In the case of the standing stone we saw in the cemetery, the sharp edge on one of the front corners of the slab was the vertical stemline. The slashes, if you'll remember, went to either side of that edge of the stone.

"Now, each group of lines can be made to correspond to a letter in the Roman alphabet. Some groups of lines cross the vertical stem, others are restricted to either the right or left of it. The position of the lines relative to the vertical is important. Do you understand what I'm saying?"

"I do, and it's brilliant," Jennifer said.

"I think I do too," I said. "But just to clarify, are you saying that it makes a difference whether the lines are to the left or right of the stemline?"

"I am. For example, five horizontal lines to the right of the vertical make an 'n'; five horizontal lines to the left is a 'q.' A group of five horizontal cuts right across the stemline is an 'i.' Five diagonal lines across the stemline make an 'r.' It's not very sophisticated, I suppose, as written languages go, rather cumbersome in fact, and I think it was mainly used for commemorative purposes, inscriptions and the like, rather than as a daily, working language, but I should think it will work well enough for our purposes.

"Now, here are the letters," he said, pointing to a chart. "I got them from the local library. Let's get out the clues and see what we can see."

My hands were almost trembling with excitement as I got out Malachy and Kevin's slip of paper with Byrne's initials and home address at the top and carefully smoothed it for Alex's study.

"I think this is the most exciting thing I've ever done in my whole life," Jennifer sighed. "What does it say, Uncle Alex?"

"We'll have to see, won't we?" Alex replied. "Here we go. Four lines to the right of the vertical is . . . "—he paused and looked at his chart.—"an 's.' Then there's four lines that go straight across the spine which is," he paused again, "an 'e.' Then five to the right, an 'n.' Are you getting this all down, Lara?"

"I am," I replied, showing him the piece of paper on which I'd written SEN.

"All right then, let's go on. Two horizontal lines running across the stemline: an 'o.' Then three horizontals, to the left of the line which is a 't.' Another 's' is next, I believe, then another 'e,' then an 's.' No wait, it's a 'u,' another 'e,' then one to the left: an 'h.' "

And so it went until Alex had deciphered them all. There were lines to the left, lines to the right, horizontals, verticals, and diagonals. In the end, I looked at my piece of paper. S E N O T S E S E H T N O E B E S R U C A was what I had written. My heart sank.

"Do you think it's Gaelic?" I asked no one in particular.

"I'm not sure, but it's not Latin," Alex said. "That I do know. An anagram perhaps?"

Jennifer peered at it. "Senat seset nob es ruca," she exclaimed, or something like that. We looked at her.

"A curse be on these stones!"

Chapter Eight

A BOAR ENRAGED

As occupations go, service to the Byrne family fit into roughly the same category—particularly if you took into account the opportunity for a long and healthy retirement—as fiddle player on the *Titanic*, a fact not lost on Deirdre Flood. Deirdre was well on her way to the Bus Eireann pick-up point in Dingle Town that would take her to Tralee train station, and thence to the farthest point in Ireland she could contemplate, when I overtook her on the road. She was dragging along with her a large and dented suitcase and what looked to be a hatbox. It was a few days after Michael's funeral, and Deirdre was making a run for it.

She was reluctant to accept my offer of a lift into Dingle Town, but eventually the weight of her bag and the long stretch of road ahead won her over. "I've given my notice," she said, as we got under way, her eyes straight ahead, her hatbox clutched tightly on her lap. "There's nothing in the Will says I have to work there forever. I asked those solicitors, Mr. McCafferty and Mr. McGlynn, and they say I can leave whenever

I wish. I'm using my holidays as notice," she added defensively. "They can't say as I'm taking advantage, but I won't stay another day under that roof. The cook left too. They'll have to fend for themselves." I enjoyed a fleeting, but satisfying, image of Margaret Byrne in black Chanel suit and snakeskin pumps attempting to boil water.

"I don't blame you, Deirdre," I said. "I'd want to leave too. But what about the police? Do they know you're leaving? You know there's an investigation going on." I avoided the word murder in connection with the investigation. Deirdre looked rather skittish, and I wasn't sure she was up for it.

"I've told Ban Garda Minogue," she said. "She knows where she can find me."

"What time is your bus, Deirdre?" I asked, as we pulled into Dingle Town.

"Twenty of four," she replied.

"That's over an hour. Why don't we leave your bag in the car and have a nice cup of tea somewhere?"

She hesitated for a moment. She was quite obviously very nervous with anyone associated with the Byrne family in any way. "I suppose it wouldn't hurt," she said at last. "There's a lovely cream tea down the street."

The place was charming, a tearoom on one side of the entrance, a pub on the other. In the tearoom, the tables were set with Irish linen, china in a pretty green and cream pattern, and silver spoons, real silver, with a crest of some kind on the handle. Nicely executed watercolors of the surrounding countryside and harbor graced the walls. A pleasant-looking woman bustled about, with help from a young man I took to be her teenaged son, bringing large pots of tea, and plates of scones, with jam and thick cream. A lovely cream tea it was, and all terribly, well, English, although it would probably be worth my life to say so in such an Irish town. We took our place in a table by the window where we could watch the life on the street through lace curtains.

"Deirdre," I said, as she poured milk into her teacup and carefully buttered herself a scone. "A few days ago, when Alex Stewart and I were out at Second Chance, you were good enough to warn us to stay away from the place." I waited for a second or two, but she did not acknowledge that I'd said anything. A meticulous person was Deirdre. She made sure the butter covered every last bit of the surface of the scone.

"I know they aren't very nice people there, some of them, but what was it that you wanted to warn us about, Deirdre?" I went on.

"Just as you said. They aren't very nice people."

"But you said the place was cursed, Deirdre. That's quite a different thing from unpleasant people." She did not reply. "Please," I said. "Alex Stewart is a really good friend of mine, and although he never expected anything from Eamon Byrne, he got Rose Cottage. And now Michael's dead, and so is John Herlihy, and if Alex is in some danger, then I need to know what it is."

"I'm not entirely certain," she said reluctantly. "Maybe something happened a long time ago, before I gained employment there."

"How long ago was that?"

"Going on five years," she replied. "Since the last maid retired."

"So what do you think it was that happened?"

"Something bad," she said. "Somebody died, you'd have to tink, and since then, the place is cursed. You should stay away like I told you."

"Who would know about this, Deirdre? Are there other people who worked there who would remember? You mentioned a cook, the other maid."

"The cooks don't last long in that place," Deirdre snorted. "Not with that family! Never satisfied. Mrs. O'Shea stayed a year or more. That was the longest."

"But you stayed nearly five years, Deirdre. How was that?"

"I needed the money, why else? Kitty, the maid before me, she stayed a long, long time. And despite what they say, Mr. Byrne was not a bad employer. There was always a touch of sadness about him, but he was a generous man, giving me extra money at Christmas and my birthday, and telling me not to tell that woman, Mrs. Byrne. John, too, he liked. John had been there forever. They had the odd drop of drink together after the others had gone to bed."

"Where's Kitty now?" I asked.

"Don't know," she replied. "I never met her."

"And Michael? Did he get along well with Mr. Byrne?" I asked.

"Michael," her voice caught, and she paused for a minute before continuing. "Yes, Michael and Mr. Byrne got on too. When he was really ill, dying, he liked to watch Michael work out in the garden. Michael was sweet on Breeta, you know. Perhaps you noticed. He was not so good at hiding it. He was heartbroken when she left. She was a mere slip of a thing then, not fat at all, and really lovely. She looked so bad at the funeral," Deirdre said. "Very bad. Michael stayed because he liked Mr. Byrne, and because he was waiting for Breeta, hoping she'd come back. Do you think she'll recover? She looked—at the burial—a wee bit strange."

"Why did she leave, do you know?"

"It was over a young man. Breeta was seeing some-one in the village, and her father didn't like it. They had a terrible row, Mr. Byrne ranting, and Breeta yell-ing. Terrible, it was. Breeta left and wouldn't come back. I heard she'd broken up with her young man not long ago, but she didn't come back."

"Do you know who the young man was?"

"Paddy Gilhooly," she said. Funny how that name kept coming up again and again. Eamon Byrne had apparently liked him well enough to give him a boat, but not enough to let him date his daughter.

"Did you see Michael that night? The night he . . . " My voice trailed off at the sight of Deirdre's stricken face.

"I did not," she replied. "Why would I? He was off for the night. And he lives in the staff quarters down the road. I lived in the big house," she added. "On the top floor. Snug little spot. Mr. Byrne had it fixed up for me."

"I just wondered if he had gone back to the house for some reason. He was found in the garden, nearer the main house than his flat, so I thought he must have gone to the house." Of course he had, I thought. He'd promised Breeta he'd go right back for Vigs, and he was a man of his word.

"Not that I am aware," she said.

"Would he have a key to the main house, do you think? I mean, could he get in without waking any-one?"

"I suppose he must," she replied. "All the staff had keys. Not to the front door, mind you, but the service entrance around the back. But what are you getting at?"

"Nothing," I said. "It's just that I saw Michael at the pub before he died, and I got the impression he was going back to the house."

Deirdre looked at her watch. "It's time I was going," she said.

"I'll walk you back to the car for your bag. Where are you going? Have you some place to stay?"

She looked at me suspiciously. "It's okay, Deirdre," I said. "I'm not going to follow you, and you don't have to answer the question. I just wanted to know that you'll be all right."

"I'll be staying with my nephew in Dublin until I can find another position," she replied, finally. "I'll manage."

"I'm sure you'll do just fine," I said soothingly. She was rather prickly, and there was more I wanted to know. "Do they all live in that house? The daughters and their husbands, I mean?"

"Eithne and Mr. McHugh live in the house. Fionuala and Mr. O'Connor used to live there too—there's plenty of space in that big house—but they had a falling out with the rest of the family, at least Mr. McHugh and Mr. O'Connor seemed not to get along, and they moved to a smaller house, still on the property, but down the road a bit, not too far from the staff cottages. Well, she lives there still. Mr. O'Connor, I hear he's getting a flat in town now," she said, reaching for her handbag.

"I'd like to treat you to tea, Deirdre," I said, gesturing for her to put down her purse. "What did the family have a falling out over, do you know?"

Deirdre shrugged. "I didn't hear. Money, I expect, and the business. Mr. McHugh and Mr. O'Connor were running Byrne Enterprises between them while Mr. Eamon Byrne was ill, and they didn't get on too well. It was all right while Mr. Byrne was in charge: he made

them work together, but after . . . " Her voice trailed
off.

"And Conail and Fionuala? What happened to
them?"

"The usual, I expect," Deirdre replied primly. "She
was always one to be looking around, and he corrupted
with drink. Bone lazy as a result of it. The Irish curse,
you know. Alcohol. The English brought it on us."

The English got blamed for quite a few things
around here, I was beginning to notice. As I was getting my wallet to pay the bill, I looked toward the bar.
It looked nice, the walls deep blue, with lots of old
posters, nicely framed, advertising various types of
brew. Newcastle Brown Ale! one poster said. Courage!
said another. Apparently they drank English beer here,
their views of the English notwithstanding.

I looked at the sign for the British brew, and then
picked up one of the spoons and peered at the crest on
the handle. It was a boar, rather fierce-looking with two
bones crossed in its mouth. "What's the name of this
place, Deirdre?" I asked.

"Here or the bar?" she replied. "This is Brigid's Tea
Room: That's Brigid over there," she said pointing to
the woman who had brought the tea and who was now
at the cash. "The pub's called The Boar's Head Arms."

"Give me a minute," I said. I took a piece of paper
out of my bag and scribbled a note on it. I handed both
the money and the note to Brigid. She looked at it, and
then me.

"Come with me," she said finally. She picked up a
tray of tea and headed up a flight of stairs to the second
floor. This was obviously the living quarters for Brigid
and her family. An elderly woman sat in a large armchair in front of a television set. She looked up as we
entered the room and surveyed me suspiciously.

"Is everything all right?" she asked Brigid in a querulous voice.

"Just grand, Mother. Here's your tea now. How are you feeling?"

"As well as can be expected, at my age. Is it strawberry preserves?" the woman replied, poking at the food with a spoon. Apparently satisfied, she turned to me. She was very frail, her hands almost transparent and lined with blue veins, her hair absolutely white. Despite the warmth of the room, which I found uncomfortable, she was wrapped in a blanket, and she was almost dwarfed by the large chair in which she sat. But her eyes were bright, and I had the impression she was sharp as a tack.

"Who are you?" she demanded.

"My name is Lara," I said.

"She's come for Eamon's clue, Mother," Brigid said. "She has the password, 'the boar enraged.'"

"You're not from around here. How would you know about it?" the old woman asked suspiciously.

"A friend of mine received something from Eamon Byrne in his Will."

"Who is your friend, and what did he get?"

"His name is Alex Stewart, and he was left Rose Cottage."

The old woman looked surprised, and then peered at me intently. "Then he must have been a special friend of Eamon's."

"I suppose in some way he was," I agreed. "Alex saved Eamon's life long ago."

The woman just nodded. "He was a fine man, no matter what they say. He's been very good to us. Wasn't his fault what happened, you know."

"And what was that?" I asked, but Brigid returned from another room and handed me a piece of paper.

"None of your gossip now, Mother," she admonished her mother. "Pay her no mind," she said to me as she lead me to the door.

I'd have loved to ask more, but one thing about this place seemed clear. If there were secrets here, and there were enough hints they existed, people were not about to share them, at least with me.

I walked Deirdre back to the car, and got out her bag, and waited with her until the bus came. As she was about to board, she turned and handed me the hatbox. "For Breeta, when she's ready," she said.

She was almost on the bus when I thought of one more question. "Who gets Michael's and John's money now that they're gone, do you know?"

She paused, one foot up on the lower step, perplexed. "Now, that's a question, isn't it? I can't say as I recall. I was so pleased to be receiving something I didn't pay much heed to the rest of it." She shrugged and stepped up on to the bus. "I don't expect it's me."

As the bus pulled out, I opened the hatbox. Vigs was happily munching on a lettuce leaf inside.

"What am I going to do with you?" I asked him. The simple answer was give him to Breeta as Deirdre had suggested. There were two problems with that. In the first place, I wasn't sure this was the best idea. Michael had gone back to Second Chance to get Vigs at Breeta's request, and while neither she nor the tortoise could be blamed for what happened, the sight of the little creature might upset her. The second was that I didn't know where she was. Sheila, the innkeeper, had said Breeta had been seen around looking for work and a cheap place to stay, refusing, even under the circumstances, to move back home.

Rather fortuitously, or so I thought at the time, I caught sight of Breeta at a table of a small local eatery, and approached her, Vigs in his hatbox with me.

"May I join you for a moment?" I asked her. A few seconds went by before she nodded her assent and I sat down across from her and ordered a coffee.

Breeta went on eating, virtually ignoring me. She was obviously eating for two, a rather large platter of fish and chips in front of her, with bread on the side, and a large cola too.

"I'm so sorry about what happened, Breeta," I said. "Michael was a lovely young man. This has all been quite dreadful." Breeta concentrated on working on the meal in front of her. It was not so much eating, come to think of it, as stuffing food in her mouth. She barely chewed it. I had the feeling that, whether she was conscious of it or not, she was stuffing herself with food to keep churning emotions, grief and anger, from rising up and pouring out of her.

"Breeta," I went on undeterred, although the sight of all that greasy food making its way so rapidly into her mouth was making me slightly nauseated. "I was wondering, I mean, I'm very worried about what has happened, and as selfish as this sounds, what it might mean to Alex. First John, and then Michael. I'm so afraid that being involved in this Will may be very dangerous for everyone named. I'm sure your father never thought that such awful things would happen . . . "

"I hate him," she said vehemently. "Hate him!"

"But perhaps finding the treasure would put a stop to this," I went on after a few seconds pause after this outburst. "We, Alex and I and some friends, have found a number of clues already. I have them back at the hotel. If you would just have a look at them, I'm sure you could help us. You know so much about Celtic history and . . . "

"No!" she exclaimed. "Stop. Never. I will never forgive my father for this. My life . . . ruined." She looked as if she would cry, but then stuffed some more chips in her mouth.

"But Breeta, you need the money," I protested. "Please . . ." I reached over to touch her hand. She wrenched it away.

"Leave me alone," she said getting up from her chair. "Go away. This is all your fault. Why did you have to come here?" She almost ran to the cashier and then out the door. Stung, I let her go. After a few minutes of feeling awful, I picked up Vigs and trundled him back to the Inn, where he was greeted with real enthusiasm by Sheila and Aidan's three young children, and resignation on the part of Sheila herself. Then I headed for the bar, and ordered a drink: nothing wimpy like wine, this time—a single malt Irish on ice.

It was depressing to think that Breeta blamed me for what happened. I told myself it was ridiculous to feel guilty about everything, but found it almost impossible not to wonder if I had, however unwittingly, done something that had set off a chain of events. But if this was the case, then I had to do something to fix it. The question was, what? It was not lost on me that not everyone shared my enthusiasm for finding the treasure, but I could not think of what else to do. While there were dire hints about Byrne's past from time to time, the treasure remained the most logical place to start. I'd heard lots of tales about Byrne in the last few days, in this bar and around town. As Deirdre had said, he wasn't the most popular person in town, but there seemed to be a grudging admiration for his business acumen. He kept to himself, it seemed, was not an habitué of the bars the way many in town were. And the place being what it was, he was still regarded by the locals as a newcomer, despite the fact he'd arrived in the Dingle a newly married man many years before. But there wasn't a whiff of anything that would meet Deirdre's criteria for a curse. The more I thought about it, the more Deirdre sounded like a superstitious and perhaps not well-educated woman, and the more plausible the treasure as the key to the question about why Michael was killed: a clue had been found clutched in his dead hand, after all. In the end, I promised myself that I'd keep my eyes and ears open for more on Byrne, but concentrate on the treasure, though it was clear we were going to have to find it without Breeta's help.

Even without her, we were not doing so badly on that score. The first clues had been the easiest to find, all right around Second Chance. There was Alex's clue and Michael's, and then the one about the beauty of the plant, the one found clutched, at least part of it, in Michael's dead hand.

I'd assumed that one would be found in his garden, probably in the toolshed. When I got there, however, I discovered someone had gone looking ahead of me. At least, I thought that the only possible conclusion, because I couldn't believe that Michael, whom I'd watched meticulously tending his garden, would have left his domain in such a mess, with garden implements strewn everywhere, and broken pots and spilled soil in messy little heaps on the floor and worktable.

I was afraid that clue was lost to us, but then Rob saved the day, although he didn't know it. He'd stopped to admire a vase full of roses in the entranceway of the Inn with the words, "quite the most beautiful of flowers, don't you think?" and I was off to Rose Cottage moments later. It was a bit of a trek because I was determined not to cross the Byrne property and went overland from the main road. It was worth the scratches from the wild berry bushes and the scrapes from the rocks: once I got there, the clue was quickly located, wedged behind the door frame.

The next clues took us farther afield and had been quite a bit harder to find. The Dingle is a peninsula only about thirty miles long, and is often described as a finger that juts out into the sea, the farthest point west in Ireland. To me, though, the Dingle is not so much of a finger jutting out from a hand, but a primordial creature, mountains for its spine, its undulating torso slipping into the sea so that only the tip can be seen as the Blaskett Islands off shore, its head way down in the depths. In reality, it has four mountain areas, the Slieve Mish Mountains where the finger joins the hand, as it were, the Stradbally Mountains, Mount Brandon on the north side, and Mount Eagle to the southwest. In between are fabulously beautiful but isolated valleys, rocky gorges, and breathtaking vistas. Roads through the mountain passes rise up steep inclines, then drop precipitously to the coast, where there are dozens of little towns and hundreds of ancient sites. In other words, there were a lot of places to search.

Nonetheless, we were making progress. I wouldn't go so far as to say we'd fanned out across the countryside with military precision or anything, but while Rob cooperated with the Irish police in the murder investigation—at least that's what he called it—the rest of us, with a copy of the poem Alex had dug out of the local library, and Malachy and Kevin's knowledge of the area, had set out to find the rest of the clues.

Kevin, who turned out to be rather good at all this, figured out the hawk above the cliff. "Has to be Mount Eagle," he said. "Hawk, bird of prey, eagle. Cliff, mountain. Not perfect, but where else could it be?" Mount Eagle turned out to be a rather big place, a mountain that ran down to the edge of the sea near

Slea Head. Kevin lead our little ragtag bunch on a merry chase over the hilly terrain. We clambered over stone fences, dodging sheep and their poop and slogging through the mud, stopping whenever we came to the remains of some ancient structure. Dotted over the landscape were ruins of tiny stone beehive-shaped huts, where centuries ago people had not so much lived as taken shelter, "clocháns" Malachy called them. Many were just heaps of rubble, but others still stood as little masterpieces of engineering, carefully placed stones fitted together and angling up to a peak without benefit of mortar to form stone huts that had withstood centuries of weather, and various invasions.

"Eamon Byrne liked old places," Kevin said, as we looked about us, "so I think we should search them." We checked as many of them as we could, dodging through the low stone doorways and scanning the interior walls for any sign of a clue. We found nothing, but Malachy wouldn't give up. Eventually, we came upon the remains of an ancient stone fort right in the middle of a field. It was there, a tiny roll of paper wrapped in plastic and wedged between two stones. Malachy and Kevin were ecstatic.

Jennifer was an able assistant as well. She'd realized right away that ogham was read from right to left, or bottom to top, and saved us a lot of time. Who'd have thought that her thinking-outside-the-box class, and its rather irritating lessons on how to talk backwards, would have had such practical application?

She found one of the clues by herself. From the vantage point of her sailing lessons out on the bay, she'd spied a CD store on shore called Music of the Sea. As soon as she'd hit dry land again, she'd climbed up a fire escape to get level with the sign, and found the clue taped to its underside.

The clue at the Boar's Head Arms disturbed me a little. Seven clues had been handed out, for Alex, Michael, Margaret, Eithne, Fionuala, and Breeta Byrne, as well as Padraig Gilhooly. The Boar's Head clue was the eighth line of the poem. Either that meant that every line did not lead to a clue—and since we only had our own, we didn't know—or that we were expected to figure out the clues were from Amairgen's Song and look then for every line of the poem.

Even before the Boar's Head clue, we were still missing the stag of seven slaughters and the ray of the sun. It was difficult to know whether to keep looking for them, or to assume someone else had found them first. Other than the mess in the garden shed and our little set-to with Conail O'Connor, there had been no signs of anyone else looking for clues. Maybe Margaret Byrne had been quite sincere in saying the family wouldn't be participating, and Conail was the only renegade. Somehow, I doubted it, though. They'd shown themselves to be quite ruthless, certainly where Alex's inheritance of Rose Cottage was concerned, something else I still had to deal with. We should keep searching, I thought, looking about the bar. My eyes alighted on the painting over the fire, the scene which I found quite repulsive despite its quality, of a stag, its snout full of arrows, being set upon by a pack of hounds. Stag of seven slaughters, I breathed, counting the dogs. Seven, of course. Right under my nose.

Picking up my drink, I ambled over to the hearth in what I hoped was a nonchalant way, then stood for a minute or two with my back to the fire, drink in hand, that most Irish of poses. As Aidan entertained the lads at the bar with one of his stories, and all eyes seemed fixed on him, I pulled up the lower corner of the painting and took a quick peek behind. The clue was there, or at least it had been. All that was left of it was a corner of the paper still secured by the tape which had held it to the back of the painting. I quickly pulled it away. I would check it against the paper on which the clues we'd already found had been written, but there was little doubt my question had been answered and that at least one other person was, despite all protestations to the contrary, looking for the treasure just as we were. The question was who, and just how dangerous were they?

I went to the front desk to retrieve, from safekeeping, what we were calling the Master List, and added the Boar's Head clue to it, then studied it for a while. I took a fresh piece of paper, drew a line down the middle, and marked one column *Amairgen's Song* and the other *Ogham clues*, and looked at what we had.

AMAIRGEN'S SONG	OGHAM CLUES
I am the sea swell	May's sunrise by Tailte's Hill is seen
The furious wave	A curse be on these stones
The roar of the sea	Leinster's Hag to Eriu's Seat
A stag of seven slaughters	—
A hawk above the cliff	Aine's Mount to Macha's Stronghold
A ray of the sun	—
The beauty of a plant	Raise a cup to the stone
A boar enraged	Almu's white to Maeve's red

It was all rather baffling. The ogham clues didn't seem to have anything in common with the lines of the poem, other than that the clues in the poem had led to their discovery. Was there supposed to be a direct relationship? I didn't know. It seemed to me that it was possible that the first ogham clue referred to a real place. What of the rest? Almu's white to Maeve's red sounded like a board game to me, White Queen or something to Red whatever. I assumed that Maeve wasn't Garda Maeve Minogue, although I had absolutely no basis for thinking that. Maeve, I knew, had been an ancient Celtic queen.

Three of the ogham clues had a something-to-something-else pattern, again perhaps directions, but the trouble was I didn't know what, or where, any of these things were. Stones were big, that was certain. The clues irritated me: they were either coy or the product of someone who thought he knew a whole lot more than the rest of us. I felt I was being toyed with and by a dead man at that. But I did acknowledge, reluctantly, that had the circumstances been different, that is, had the family and the rest of us been working together amicably, this might have been fun. But whose fault was it they didn't?

A curse be on Eamon Byrne, I thought, rather uncharitably, which led me right back to what Deirdre had said and to the other hints about something bad in the past that no one would tell me. I understood their reticence. Really, why should they tell a total stranger, and one from far away, their worst secrets? This was the Dingle, after all, a wild and relatively remote place with its own ways. Even in Ireland, I suspected, it would be regarded as someplace different: the Gaeltacht, the Gaelic-speaking part of Ireland, a throwback in an all-too modern world. But it was frustrating nonetheless.

I decided that maybe we really would have to come at this several different ways. Malachy, Kevin, and Jennifer could search for more clues. Alex I'd send on another research project, to the local library, or wherever, to begin to identify the names in the ogham clues. Myself, I thought I'd do a little poking around in Eamon Byrne's past. After all, we had the time. We were stuck here for a while as the murder investigation marked its stately course. Currently, we were awaiting the possible exhumation of John Herlihy to check for poison in his system, an outcome I didn't doubt for a minute.

Rob, I thought, was perfectly happy to stay indefinitely. He'd managed to convince his superiors on the force back home to lend him to the local authorities for a while, a stroke of good fortune, according to Rob, as it meant he'd be paid while he was here. I rather thought he would consider it a stroke of good fortune for other reasons, but held my tongue. Jennifer was only too happy to be able to stay a little longer. While Rob had initially objected to her taking sailing lessons from Padraig Gilhooly, who he reasoned was part of a murder investigation, I'd persuaded him to lighten up a little, there being no evidence whatsoever to implicate Padraig. Several of Paddy's chums had attested to his presence at their favorite watering hole the afternoon the Will was being read and the evening Michael had died. His landlady—he had a flat in town—claimed to have heard him come in shortly after closing time, not to leave again till morning. In any event, Jennifer loved her sailing lessons, was beginning to make some friends in town, and had really blossomed, not nearly the shy and rather immature person I'd arrived with. Alex was his normal calm self.

The only problem for me was the shop, and I was starting to fret about it. Sarah didn't seem terribly perturbed when I told her my return had been delayed, saying that Clive was being very helpful. This development I found disturbing. What exactly was Clive, the rat, up to, I wondered. I decided I'd go up to the room before the others came back so I could phone my friend, and Clive's new partner, Moira, to assess the situation without having to admit I was worried. I hesitated at the bottom of the stairs, then turned back to put the Master List under lock and key once again at the front desk. I felt sort of silly doing this: carrying around my cash and credit cards, but locking up a piece of paper, but right from the start, I'd decided to be safe rather than sorry.

A good thing it was too. I opened the door to Jennifer's and my room, and my jaw dropped. If I needed confirmation that we weren't the only ones in this treasure hunt, I had it. The place was a shambles. The room had been thoroughly searched. The mattresses had been lifted and pushed against a wall, the carpet tossed in a heap in a corner; the drawers were all open and contents dumped; our suitcases had been lifted down from the shelf in the cupboard, opened and dropped as well. Even the bathroom had been searched. It looked as if every packet in my cosmetic bag had been opened.

Conail again, I wondered, or worse yet, Breeta? As much as I didn't like to think it, I had told her that very afternoon that we had several clues back at the Inn. At peak time in the bar, the residential part of the Inn was pretty much left untended. The front door of that part of the Inn was kept locked, but to someone who knew their way around the place, it would be easy enough to get in, through the kitchen, or the entrance off the bar. I'd given her plenty of time while I'd moped around the bar, licking my wounds after her accusations.

Shocked, I just stood there staring at the mess. Eventually I became conscious of footsteps coming up the stairs and two familiar voices.

"It's my money," Jennifer said. "You said so. You said I could do whatever I wanted with it."

"No daughter of mine," Rob began as they rounded the corner and stopped dead at the open door. Jennifer gasped.

Two thoughts came into my mind at that moment. One was that Rob was just being an old poop where Jennifer was concerned, and I was going to tell him so. The second was that it was time I saw a little more of Ireland.

We stood silently in the doorway for a moment or two.

"Ffuts ym gnihcuot mucs etah I," Jennifer said at last.

"Oot em," I agreed.

Chapter Nine

A SALMON IN A POOL

DEIRDRE almost dropped the tea tray when she saw me. And a shame it would have been too, as it would have fallen on an exquisite antique Aubusson carpet, and dashed to pieces some very fine porcelain cups. I suppose it might actually have cost her her job, the obsession of her new employer being what it was.

While nobody in these parts talks about it much, there was a period of time when Dublin was the second city of the British Empire, rivalling, and in some ways surpassing, London in grandeur and conspicuous consumption. London had its Thames, Dublin its Liffey, both cities taking advantage of strategic maritime positions to ensure a vibrant trade in goods from the far-flung reaches of the Empire, and in Dublin's case, a corresponding outflow of its magnificent craftsmanship, silver, porcelain, glass, and textiles, to grace stately English homes across the Irish sea.

In addition to bitter memories of repression and sectarian violence, that period left Dublin with some impressive public monuments—broad sweeping avenues, soaring bridges and architectural gems like the Four Courts, home of the Irish law courts since 1796, and the Custom House with its graceful arcades, columns and soaring dome—together with some glorious urban spaces like St. Stephen's Green, a perfect Georgian square surrounding a pleasant little park, where the offices of McCafferty & McGlynn, Solicitors, were to be found.

While Deirdre Flood might have thought that Dublin was sufficiently far away that she would never have to see any of us associated with Second Chance again, it was, in reality, only a few short hours' train ride from Tralee.

Jennifer had mentioned several times that she'd like to see Dublin, and I'd managed, quite easily, to persuade Rob to let me take her there for a couple of days' sight-seeing. This little excursion of ours worked well for a number of reasons, not the least of which was that we were all getting on each other's nerves. What no daughter of Rob's was to do, apparently, was to cut her hair, buy herself dark lipstick and black clothes— tights, turtleneck, and a short skirt that she wore with her trusty Dr Martens—and, horror of horrors, put a rhinestone stud in her nose. Telling Rob that almost every girl Jennifer's age had done something similar fell on deaf ears, and so I'd resorted to calling him an old poop to his face, as I'd promised myself that I would if he didn't listen to reason, a statement that, while true in my opinion, did not exactly endear me to him. A little space between us for a while seemed an awfully good idea.

The second reason was that the less-than-subtle search of our room had unnerved us all, although to be truthful, I was having more trouble dealing with scum

having touched my stuff than Jennifer was. She'd been
pacified by a new room and once-laundered clothes,
immediately taken care of by Aidan and Sheila, the
innkeepers, who had, if anything, been more upset than
we were. I, however, found myself surreptitiously making my way to a laundromat to wash everything for a
second time. A little space between me and whoever
had trashed our room at The Three Sisters Inn seemed
a good idea too.

I suspect Rob thought that keeping me away from the
Dingle, and the Byrne family treasure hunt and ensuing
murder investigation in particular, and his daughter
from Padraig Gilhooly's sailing classes, was also an excellent plan. He would therefore have been disappointed
to learn that my reason for going to Dublin was to pay a
visit to McCafferty and McGlynn, Tweedledum and
Tweedledee, and that after seeing Jennifer off at the
gates of Trinity College on a two-hour walking tour of
historic Dublin, I headed directly there.

Eamon Byrne had said the two solicitors, or legal
bookends as he'd referred to them, had become too
accustomed to the good life in St. Stephen's Green to
refuse him any request, and I could see that would be
easy enough to do.

Their offices were located in a town house on the
square right in the heart of the city. The exterior was
pure Georgian, white, with a cheerful red door flanked
by two columns, and crowned by a magnificent arched
fan light above. Similar town houses, each entrance just
a little bit distinctive, stretched out on either side, and
all around the square: doors in every color imaginable
from black to yellow to pink to lilac, some with similar
fan lights, others with sidelights. A brass knocker on
this one matched the discreet nameplate, C. B. Mc-
Cafferty and R. A. McGlynn, Solicitors.

The door opened into a foyer of black and white marble floor tiles, black urns and white walls, with lovely decorative rococo plasterwork on the ceiling. A bust, vaguely Roman looking, a Caesar, perhaps, occupied one corner. It was as if one had entered the town home of a wealthy Irishman in the middle of the eighteenth century, the only jarring note the receptionist's computer and telephone. Jarring or not, McCafferty and McGlynn were doing quite nicely, thank you, that much was clear.

Straight ahead of me was a staircase. For some reason, this reminded me that at one time in the royal courts of England and Europe, one's worth was reflected in the room in which one was received at court. The closer one came to the monarch's private chambers, the more important one was. I wondered if I'd make it up the stairs.

As it turned out, I got as far as the second of four floors, if I'd counted stories correctly as I'd approached from the street. Not that my progress there was entirely effortless. I had decided upon a surprise attack and came armed only with a letter from Alex, co-conspirator that he was, but no appointment.

"I know this is really presumptuous of me," I said to the receptionist, a young woman with perfect fingernails, which she obviously worked on most of the day. "I'm sure that Mr. McCafferty and Mr. McGlynn are both extremely busy, but I'm in Dublin quite unexpectedly and must soon be off back to Canada, and I was wondering whether there might be any chance I could have a few moments with one or the other of them. I have some questions about Mr. Alex Stewart's inheritance from the Eamon Byrne estate." I hoped I sounded suitably contrite for this serious breach of legal etiquette.

Up until the words "Eamon Byrne," she'd been regarding me with considerably less interest than her fingernails, but those, apparently, were the magic words. "Both Mr. McGlynn and Mr. McCafferty are with a client," she said in upper-crust vowels she obviously worked hard on. "I'm not sure when they'll be free."

"I'll wait," I said, plunking myself down on a very fine wing chair in the corner of the room. She looked at me for a moment or two and then reluctantly picked up the phone. What followed was one of those conversations in which the secretary pretends she is talking to an assistant when she is, in fact, talking to one of the lawyers. "There is a Ms. McClintoch here from Canada wishing to speak to Mr. McCafferty or Mr. McGlynn about Mr. Byrne's estate," she said. There was a pause. "No, she does not have an appointment." Another pause. "Yes," she said. "One of the solicitors will try to work you in," she said, hanging up the phone. "You may wait upstairs. You might want to have a look at this," she added, handing me an engraved card which listed McCafferty and McGlynn's fees for various services. They were, in a word, breathtaking.

After passing this first hurdle, I went upstairs to the library, an attractive room on the second floor, with walls of blue, stripped back to the original coat of paint, by the look of them, and lined with legal tomes by the yard. The centerpiece of the room was a marble fireplace that sported two carved rams heads, one on each side of the mantelpiece, and over it, a somewhat Italianate fresco of a country scene, probably dating to the early- to middle-eighteenth century. On the walls to either side of the fireplace, white plaster plaques depicted a blindfolded Justice, appropriately enough, robes flowing, scales in balance.

A large table had been placed in the middle of the room under an interesting chandelier with blue colored glass sprinkled through it to match the walls. It was here, I decided, that the lawyers or their assistants did their research, judging from the volumes in piles on the surface, seated in carved and intricately decorated armchairs that I believe are sometimes called Chinese Chippendale. Several choice mezzotint portraits had been hung on the walls, and placed about the room were some rather handsome pieces of furniture. Every piece was exquisite and chosen with impeccable taste or, to be more precise, taste very similar to mine.

A lovely period, Georgian, I thought. Some of the decorative touches were a trifle ornate for my taste, but overall the proportions were so pleasing, everything so elegant, I was quite enchanted.

My favorite object of all was the attractively worn Aubusson carpet. I like old carpets. They make me wonder about all the feet that have crossed them, the conversations that have taken place above them, the ghosts that still haunt them. This one was particularly fine in that regard, a worn patch where some heavy furniture had been placed for a long time, the hint of a well-travelled path, from one room to another perhaps.

Whoever had renovated and decorated the place had done so with meticulous attention to detail, a real sympathy for the Irish Georgian style, and a thoroughly lavish budget. I could only just imagine how much it would cost to accomplish the look. It was very impressive, and a little intimidating, and I decided this was intentional. If the fee schedule you were given upon entry to the building didn't deter you, then this room might prove an effective winnowing process for all but the spectacularly financially endowed or, like me, the profoundly stubborn. After a few minutes here, one would be either impressed and prepared to pay big for Tweedledum and Tweedledee's clearly exceptional services, or would have skulked away, convinced one couldn't afford them. I stayed the course, hoping I wouldn't have to take out a second mortgage on my house, or worse yet sell my half-interest in Greenhalgh & McClintoch, to pay the fees.

After several minutes of cooling my heels and being suitably cowed by the decor, I heard footsteps and voices coming down the stairs from above, someone more important than I, apparently, then a few minutes later, footsteps coming up the stairs, and Deirdre entered with the tea tray. We were both surprised to see each other.

"What are you doing here?" she gasped, cups rattling and the tray precariously balanced. I immediately remembered my promise in Dingle Town that I wouldn't follow her to Dublin. But how was I to know?

"I'm here to see one of the solicitors about Alex Stewart's inheritance," I said in my most soothing tones, reaching out to steady the tray. "It's lovely to see you again, Deirdre. I'm delighted to see that you've been able to find some employment right away. I hope everything is working out well for you."

"Yes, thank you," she said regaining her composure. "Would you like a cup of tea and a biscuit?" She poured tea from a silver tea service into two faintly iridescent cream-colored cups, Beleek most likely, mine clear, and another drowned in milk. Seconds later, the solicitor entered the room.

I rose from my chair. "Mr. . . ." I began. Which one was it? McCafferty or McGlynn, I wondered, frantically. Tweedledum or Tweedledee?

"Ms. McClintoch, I'm Charles McCafferty," he said,

extending his hand. "Thank you, Dcirdre. You may leave us. How may I be of service?" he said looking first at me and then at his watch. Was it my imagination, or could I hear a meter ticking away?

He was dressed just as formally as he had been that day at Second Chance, dark three-piece suit, white shirt with impeccably starched collar, silk tie and puff, this time in a classic maroon with a crest of some kind. I wondered what his partner was wearing, maroon tie with stripes perhaps? He smelled nice, though, a subtle cologne that made me think of fresh sea breezes blowing across fields of heather, and leather armchairs in front of roaring fires.

Get a grip, Lara, I told myself. "Thank you for seeing me on such short notice," I said, shaking his hand.

"A pleasure," he said graciously, gesturing me toward a chair, and sitting opposite me.

For several minutes, it was all business. We talked about Irish taxes, land ownership by foreign residents, the question of the right-of-way across Byrne's land, and so on, all things Alex might legitimately need to know. McCafferty made a few notes with his expensive but refined fountain pen, in a little notebook with gold-edged pages and a leather cover, and from time to time dispensed advice which, considering how much we'd have to pay for it, I hoped would be useful for Alex.

I had a rather delicate matter I wanted to discuss with him, and it took me a minute or two to work my way around to it. It was a subject on which Alex seemed surprisingly passive, but I was not about to give in. "The Byrne family has indicated that they may be contesting the Will in an effort to get Rose Cottage back," I said finally. "I don't want to put you in a bad position," I added, "and I know you have represented Mr. Byrne's interests for some time, but whose side would you be on, in that regard? And if not ours, could you recommend another solicitor? We don't know anyone here, of course."

"The heirs would sue the estate, and as executor of that estate, I would be obliged to defend it," he said. "We would enlist the services of a barrister, of course, to represent us in court. I sincerely hope it will not come to that, however. I think that would be quite unfortunate. And so, yes, I would be on your side, to use your terminology."

"Thank you," I said, rising from my seat. "By the way, what happens to the money that would have been paid to John Herlihy and Michael Davis?"

"Unfortunately, Mr. Stewart does not benefit," he said.

"I assumed that," I persisted, "but who does?" This was, after all, one of the things I'd come to Dublin to learn.

"Essentially, the money reverts to the family and is allocated amongst them. There's a very complicated formula," he added, giving me a don't-worry-your-pretty-little-head-about-it look. I believe he was actually flirting with me.

I wanted to say, "try me," but instead took a different approach and flirted right back. "Your offices are just wonderful. Georgian, isn't it?" I said looking about me. "Did you restore the place yourself?" My words were quite sincere, although my motives were not. On the assumption that he must be very proud of the decor, I was hoping to soften him up in order to angle my way around to a number of other questions I had.

Charles perked up immediately. "Yes," he replied. "My partner, Ryan McGlynn, and I found this house in terrible disrepair. Shocking, really, it was so badly damaged. We've been working at it for years now. We found some skilled craftsmen, and we've been doing it a little at a time, acquiring the furniture piece by piece. The original paint, you know," he added.

"I thought it must be," I said, giving him what I hoped was my most attentive look. "The carpet is my favorite," I added. "Aubusson, isn't it?"

"Yes. Mine too," he agreed. "There is something about carpets, isn't there? I like to think about the people who walked on them over the years."

I was quite nonplussed. The law offices of Mc-Cafferty and McGlynn were just about the last place I'd expect to find a kindred spirit. It made me see him in a whole new light, and I momentarily forgot what I'd come to Dublin to find out, and instead found myself trying to recollect whether or not he was wearing a wedding ring. He wasn't. It's not conclusive, of course, but a good start.

"Do you use all four floors as offices?" I asked.

"Three," he said. "Ryan and I have our offices on the next floor up. We meet with our clients either in our offices or here. Ryan has a flat on the fourth floor. I live in Ballsbridge," he added. I had no idea where that was, but I assumed I was supposed to be impressed.

"With your spouse and family?" I asked. Admittedly, subtlety is not my long suit.

"Regrettably, I have neither," he replied, with a slight smile.

"Nor I," I said. We held each other's glance a little longer than necessary. He was very attractive in many ways, with a faint hint of gray at the temples, and a nice build, about my age, or a little younger.

"Tell me about this piece," I said, breaking away and pointing to a piece of furniture against one wall. I knew perfectly well what it was, this being my business after all, a rather handsome writing cabinet dating to about the mid-1700s, I'd have said, but I didn't want the conversation to end. I'll admit I enjoy a little flirtation from time to time. It is, after all, in the right circumstances, perfectly harmless and rather pleasurable to let someone know you find them attractive, and to enjoy their admiration in return. It was all very formal, of course. I was Ms. McClintoch, he Mr. McCafferty, but it made it all the more fun, somehow.

I told him I owned an antiques shop in Toronto.

"Do you indeed!" he exclaimed. "Then please permit me to give you a little tour. Everything here is authentic to the time, the real thing where possible," he said, gesturing toward the chairs and sliding his hand across the fabric in a way I found quite suggestive. He had nice hands, I noticed. He then pointed out each object in the room and gave a little of its history, where he'd found it, what great family had owned it, what it cost him. I tried to look impressed, which was not difficult, because frankly, I was. When I wasn't making eye contact with him, and enjoying the way he touched everything, I was mentally launching a new line in the shop—Irish Georgian—complete with accompanying design service to make sure our clients got the look just right. It was a good, no a great, idea: Irish anything was in style, thanks to some pseudo-Celtic dancers and singers very much in vogue. I was a little unsure how to get the look of the original paint, but I knew someone who could do it, if I could bring myself to ask him: Clive, who'd been my first employee, a designer, before I made the mistake of marrying him. That problem aside, I thought I had a sure-fire winner, although some of the sums McCafferty mentioned as purchase prices were daunting.

If I could find fault with McCafferty's offices at all,

it was that it was all too perfect. People who decorate like this don't just sweat the details, they are obsessed by them. I found myself longing for a jarring note, an object out of place or out of time, so he'd seem more human to me, somehow. There wasn't one. I have customers like this, whose requirement for authenticity is absolute, and who, in many ways, keep me in business. Personally I prefer a little more relaxed approach, more mixing of complementary styles. Moira, whose taste in decorating is best described as eclectic—she changes the decor in her salon cum spa about every six months, often with my help, making her not only my best friend, but the shop's best advertisement—would call the offices of McCafferty and McGlynn the product of a diseased mind. Maybe he'd become too set in his ways as a bachelor, I thought.

Needless to say, I did not voice my opinion in this regard. "You've done a wonderful job restoring the place," I said. "You are obviously successful at everything you do. You have your pick of clients," I went on. "People like Eamon Byrne. I am most grateful you took time out of your busy schedule to see me."

"I'm delighted to have been of assistance," he said, self-consciously straightening his lovely tie. He was enjoying every minute of this, just as I was.

"And very kind of you to give Deirdre Flood employment," I said. "I was delighted to see that she'd landed on her feet."

"Not at all," he replied. "Dreadful business, those deaths. The poor dear was quite terrified. I'm glad I could help her out, under the circumstances."

"He must have been a challenging client, Eamon Byrne, I mean," I said, prattling on, "judging from that video. Not the easiest man in the world to get along with. I never met him, of course, but Alex Stewart knew him a number of years ago, when he was in the merchant marine. Did you know him long?"

"No," he replied, rather tersely. I waited for further clarification, saying nothing, but just looking at him. It's an old reporter's trick, I'm told, leaving a long enough silence that the interrogated person feels compelled to fill it. Finally he said, "We took over from his former solicitor about five years ago."

Too bad, I thought: not long enough to know about an old family curse. "What business was he in? Byrne Enterprises, I mean."

"Many things. It was a group of several different businesses. Land holdings, originally. He owned large tracts of boglands. Very profitable."

"Are bogs profitable?" I said. I was genuinely surprised.

"Oh, yes," he replied. "Quite. Peat is a major source of fuel here in Ireland. There is a huge commercial operation, of course: Bord na Mona. But there are smaller, private ones as well. Eamon Byrne leased out parcels of bog property for three months at a time. Renters cut as much peat as they can for fuel, and take it away to heat their homes, then Byrne rented the property out again to the next person. He had huge land holdings, so the supply was never exhausted, and there was a very nice, steady income. He used that to branch out into other businesses. Import/export for one. Medical supplies, for another. All very successful."

"Mr. Byrne didn't seem to have much confidence in the ability of his sons-in-law to run the business successfully," I said, hoping that now that McCafferty's guard was down, he'd prove to be someone who enjoyed being in the know and telling everyone about it.

"No," he replied. "And with good reason. The two of them don't get along, and aren't very good businessmen. It was fine while Eamon Byrne was running the businesses, but when he became ill, well, things deteriorated right away. Too bad, of course, but there is nothing we can do about it. Amazing how they can make such a bollocks of it. Forgive my language, please. It upsets me to see what they're doing. The peat business practically runs itself; and still they can't seem to make a go of it."

"I heard Fionuala and Connor split up," I said, conspiratorially. There's nothing like discussing other people's relationships when you're toying with the idea of getting into one yourself.

"I heard that too," he said. He actually giggled as he said it. I gathered he was in some way rather enjoying the family's tale of woe.

"What do you think that will mean? Who do you think will take over the management of the company?"

"I'm not sure," he replied, "but it will be interesting to see, won't it?"

"Extraordinary thing, that treasure hunt, isn't it?" I said. I may have been enjoying the flirtation, but I wasn't so far gone that I had entirely forgotten what I'd come for. Not yet, anyway.

"Yes," he said, suddenly solemn. "You noticed, I'm sure, that Byrne said we didn't approve of it. We stayed in, not because, as Byrne said, we wanted his money, but because we felt we had to bring a modicum of good sense to the whole process."

"So what did you have to do? Do you know what all the clues are?"

"We did not," McCafferty averred, looking at me with some suspicion. He wasn't that far gone, either. "Byrne asked us to distribute the envelopes to his heirs on his demise, that is all."

"And you didn't take a peek?" I asked, adopting what I hoped was a playful tone.

"Absolutely not," he said, looking offended. "They were sealed when we got them."

"I'm glad to hear that," I said. "It seems a little dangerous to know the clues. Michael Davis was found with part of one clue in his hand. I'm thinking it wouldn't be too much of a stretch to assume that whoever had that clue was his killer."

"The police have already asked us that question," McCafferty replied. "Unfortunately, we were unable to help them." He was watching me very carefully now.

"Something struck me as a bit odd about it," I went on, as if oblivious to his glance. "I mean, who hid the second set of clues? Not Eamon Byrne surely. He was very ill. He couldn't possibly have climbed up Mount Eagle to the ring fort, neither could he have climbed down to the cove and out to the boat to place the first clue."

"Perhaps he did it some time ago, when he was well," McCafferty said. I noticed he didn't seem surprised by my reference to the ring fort and the boat, nor by the reference to a second set of clues.

"But Deirdre here told me he had suddenly fallen ill, very ill. Why would he have been out placing the clues that would be given to people when he died, when he was quite well and not expecting to die soon? There would be too much danger they'd be lost, wouldn't there, especially the ones outside?"

"I don't really know," McCafferty replied. If I had struck a chord with him, it didn't show. "It doesn't really matter who hid them, does it?" he continued. "As long as the family works together to find the treasure as Byrne wished."

"But it does matter," I said. "I think that whoever

placed them might well have looked at them. They weren't sealed, just stuck in plastic. And I think that person might have inadvertently placed their name on a death list. You will be careful now, won't you, Mr. McCafferty?" I said looking him right in the eye.

"Charles, please," he said. "Of course, I will be careful," he said, placing his hand on my arm.

It was the first time since the initial handshake that he'd touched me. I suddenly felt as if I was falling into something I might not be able to control. "My," I exclaimed, looking at my watch. "I really must be going. I have to meet a young friend of mine who's on a tour of historic Dublin. I mustn't keep her waiting. I've really enjoyed the tour of your offices, though."

"I have enjoyed it as well," he said as we descended the stairs to the front door. "I hope you'll come and visit us another time. Perhaps our paths will cross again. I have to be at Second Chance from time to time to assist the family with various matters."

"Perhaps we will." I smiled. So much for my intention to call this one off.

"Good," he said. "If I needed to find you for some reason, the legal challenge to the Will, for example?"

"The Three Sisters Inn in town."

"I know the place," he said, as we descended the steps to the main floor.

Deirdre and Tweedledee, Ryan McGlynn, were in the foyer, a fact that brought our flirtation, or was it seduction, to a close. As I had predicted, they were dressed very much alike once again. I searched the two men's faces for some family similarity, but the resemblance seemed to stop at their age, which was about the same, their clothes and demeanor. McGlynn was a little heavier, not quite in such good trim as Charles, and more relaxed in outlook. He was smoothly seeing a stately dowager out the door, telling her not to worry, that everything would be taken care of. She looked pathetically grateful, considering what she was going to have to pay to be able to stop worrying.

"We've met, have we not?" he said, turning his charm on me. "Ms . . . ?"

"McClintoch," McCafferty said. "Ms. McClintoch is here to see to details about her friend's inheritance from Eamon Byrne's estate."

"Of course, Second Chance," he said, shaking my hand.

"I must compliment you on your offices," I said. "Mr. McCafferty has been showing me around."

"They are grand, aren't they?" McGlynn responded. "All Charles's doing. He's the connoisseur. I just go along with whatever he suggests."

"Ryan is rather more interested in good food," McCafferty smiled.

"Food," McGlynn agreed, patting his stomach, "and wine." He gave me a wink. Neither of these gentlemen, it seemed, were short at all on charm.

The good-natured jousting came to an end as the front door opened, and Fionuala Byrne O'Connor walked in. She did not look pleased to see me. But then Deirdre didn't looked pleased to see her either, adopting her scared rabbit look the moment she set eyes on Fionuala.

"What's she doing here?" Fionuala demanded to know, looking at me. It was the second time since I'd arrived that question had been asked. Deirdre, however, assumed Fionuala was asking about her, and her mouth moved soundlessly a couple of times. I knew Fionuala meant me.

"Now you know we can't answer that," Ryan McGlynn said in a soothing tone. "Allow me to take your coat, Mrs. O'Connor, won't you, and then we'll go upstairs." I turned away from her and busied myself with paying the bill, a feat that required a fair number of travellers checks to accomplish. I could feel her eyes boring into my back.

"Charles," Fionuala said in a breathless voice, having established to her satisfaction that I was on the way out. "I really need your help with something."

"I'll do whatever I can, of course," he replied, in the same familiar tone of voice he'd adopted with me just a few moments earlier. I felt a twinge, just a twinge, of jealousy.

"Won't you come upstairs?" he continued, taking Fionuala's arm and then directing her up the stairs ahead of him. When she was almost to the top, he turned to me for one last time, and leaning close enough that I had the full benefit of the marvelous cologne, said, sotto voce, "Tell Mr. Stewart that I pride myself on writing airtight Wills." Then he hastened up the stairs after Fionuala. I headed out the door.

I still had a few minutes to kill before I was to meet Jennifer, and was very glad of it. I felt off balance somehow. I actually found myself wondering what it would be like to live in Irish Georgian splendor, and where exactly Ballsbridge was. It annoyed me that I felt this way. I like to think that by and large I have a very firm grip on reality, but I felt myself losing my hold on it. The strange thing was that although there seemed to be some mutual attraction there, I wasn't sure how far it went. Indeed, the sexual energy was, I thought, more on my part than his, that his passion was directed elsewhere. At Fionuala, perhaps? I could hardly bear to think it. I decided that while it had been fun, and I was pleased to think he would be on our side if we ended up in court with the Byrnes, this was a dead-end relationship, and anyway, I was happier when I was on my own. I told myself to forget him.

I resolutely turned my attention to thinking about what I had learned about the Byrne family and the treasure hunt, admittedly not that much, and certainly nowhere near what I had hoped. I still didn't know for certain who had hidden the clues; nor did I know for certain that it mattered, although I had a feeling it did. It couldn't have been one of the participants who had received a clue: they would simply have looked at them all before hiding them. After all, I would have. That let out the family members, Padraig Gilhooly, Michael himself, and Alex.

Was it John Herlihy? Could have been, I suppose, either him or Deirdre, which might explain why she was always looking so terrified. Malachy or Kevin? They had known Eamon Byrne; they'd told me as much. But I couldn't see them being so deceptive in their dealings with us, somehow. Their excitement at finding the clues seemed absolutely genuine to me. Denny didn't seem to be any more likely than his two pals. And so, unless it was a complete stranger, that left McCafferty and McGlynn as the most likely candidates for the job.

The next obvious question was, who had hidden the treasure itself, whatever it was? Eamon Byrne in earlier, healthier times was one possibility. Perhaps he had found it a long time ago and hidden it then. I had a vague recollection that hoards of treasure had been found in the bogs of Ireland—I'd have to do some research on that score—and so he, big landowner that he was, might have found something and left it hidden. But if it had required hiding at the same time as the clues, the big question was who had hid it, and was it still there, temptation being the powerful motivator that it is.

I arrived at the gates of Trinity College several minutes before the tour was due back, and could see no sign of Jennifer. I decided to walk a little farther, to get Charles McCafferty out of my system and soon found myself passing a statue of a woman with a wheelbarrow that I could only assume was Molly Malone of cockles and mussels alive alive-o fame, and then on into Grafton Street, a busy shopping street closed to cars for several hours of the day. At every corner, there was something else to see, nice old buildings, lots of store windows, and flower sellers with huge pails of really spectacular blooms, most notably lilies in white and pink, their heady scent lingering in the air as I strolled by.

Partway along the street I found myself in front of Bewley's Oriental Cafe, a landmark three-story building, and an establishment famous for its coffees and teas for almost a century and a half, apparently. I stood back to admire the facade and noted through the reflection on the glass, a couple seated at a table in the window up on the second floor. It was kind of sweet, the way they had their heads together, holding hands on the table. As I watched he leaned over and planted a kiss on her lips, and for a second or two I could see them both clearly.

Rob is going to kill me, was all I could think.

"Not you too," Jennifer wailed. "I'm eighteen! Lots of girls my age are married already. With kids," she added.

"How old is he?" I demanded. "Thirty-five? Thirty-six?"

Jennifer bit her lip. "That's twice as old as you are,"

I huffed. "Padraig Gilhooly is way, way too old for you."

"He's sophisticated," she argued. "Not like those stupid boys at school." Sophisticated was not a word I would have associated with Padraig Gilhooly, but I suppose it's all relative. Certainly, he would have to be more worldly than the boys her age at home, which was a real worry. Also, I didn't think his relative sophistication was the issue here. While age eighteen was a dim memory for me, I remembered enough to know that Gilhooly's dark hair, blue eyes, and fair skin, to say nothing of his brooding manner, would be powerful attractions. How far had this gone?

"I hope you haven't done something you will regret, Jennifer," I said. My, I sounded like an old prune, but I couldn't stop myself. Maybe I shouldn't have called Rob a poop.

"Paddy's a gentleman," she sniffed. I hoped that meant what I thought it did. That had been some kiss he'd planted on her in the upstairs window of Bewley's, and she hadn't appeared even remotely reluctant. I wasn't sure gentlemanly was going to last for long.

"Don't tell Dad, okay?" she said beseechingly. It was tempting to agree, I'll admit, but I knew I couldn't.

"I'm sorry I didn't tell you, that I lied about going on the walking tour and everything. It's just that Dad is so weird about the guys who ask me out." She snuffled. I sighed. Neither of us, when it came right down to it, had been honest with the other when it came to our motives for the trip to Dublin. And, let's face it, it was true what she said about her father. He was really nuts where his daughter and boys were concerned. She was a very sensible young woman, and was being more truthful than I was prepared to be. But Paddy Gilhooly! Twice her age!

"I asked Paddy about *Lost Causes*," she said. "I didn't want to date someone who drove his boat like that. He left his boat in for repairs while he went into Cork to see his lawyer. They, the boatworks people, left it outside their place with the keys in it, so that Paddy could pick it up after hours when he got back, because he'd need it really early the next day. Someone had chartered his boat to go fishing for an hour or two right about dawn. The boatworks closes at four. So anyone could have taken it and then just put it back where they'd found it."

"That's reassuring," I said. "Did he tell you why he's feuding with the Byrne family and why they kept him out of the Will?"

"He hasn't told me yet," she replied. "I asked him about the family, but he just got mad, so I dropped it. I told him about the treasure hunt, though," she said after a pause. "And how well we're doing with the clues and everything."

Bad idea, I thought, but predictable, I suppose, under the circumstances.

"Anyway," she said triumphantly. "He told me his clue. A salmon in a pool. He says that now that I've explained to him how the clues work, he thinks he can find the one that goes with his clue when we get back. He'll bring it to us to decipher the ogham because he doesn't know how to do it. I knew I could convince him to help."

You'd think after my performance not even an hour earlier, I'd consider Jennifer a woman after my own heart. I didn't. In fact, I was aghast. "You mean to tell me you held his hand and let him kiss you to get his clue!"

Jennifer looked wounded. "That's disgusting!" she

exclaimed. At least she and I agreed on something in this conversation.

"The thing is," she went on. "I think I'm in love with him."

Yes, Rob was going to kill me. But he'd torture me first.

Chapter Ten

A LAKE IN A PLAIN

Y OU *were asking me about the gifts of the gods. Let me tell you about Lugh. There's many a fine tale about that one, sometimes called Samildanach for his many talents, of which I'm planning to tell you more, or Lamfada, Long arm, for his prowess with spear and sling. 'Tis Lugh we are celebrating, whether we remember it or not, at the August harvest festival of Lughnasa.*

'Twas Lugh who convinced Nuada Argat-lam, king of the Tuatha dé Danaan, to throw off the yoke of the oppressors, those Fomorians, demons that they were, who were exacting great hardship on the Tuatha dé, so much so that even the great Dagda was doing service for them. But first Lugh had to get into Nuada's royal court, a mighty feat in itself.

But to go back to his beginnings: Lugh was part Fomorian, believe it or not. His mother was Eithne, daughter of Balor of the Evil Eye, a vile giant who was king of the Fomorians. Balor got his name because one glance of his eye would kill you dead on the spot. Now

Balor was living up in the north of Ireland on Tory Island, and he kept Eithne locked up in a tower because of a prophecy that he would be killed by his grandson. Balor, you can understand, was determined there wouldn't be one. But Kian of the Tuatha dé held a grudge against Balor and, dressed as a woman, got into Eithne's tower. Just what you might expect happened: Eithne bore triplets. The dreadful Balor had them thrown over a cliff to be drowned.

But one didn't die and grew up to be a man, quite unlike any other, a god really, of formidable strength and talents: Lugh Lamfada. Lugh presented himself at the court of Nuada Argat-lam, Nuada Silver Arm, and asked to be in service to the king. The doorkeeper wouldn't let him in. "I'm a carpenter," says Lugh. "We already have one of those," says the doorkeeper. "I'm a smith," says Lugh. "We've one of those already too." And so it went, weaver, poet, harper, man of science, and many more. And to each the doorkeeper said, "We have one of those."

"But do you have one who is all of these?" Lugh countered at last, and Nuada let him in. And a good thing it was, too, for it was Lugh as much as anyone led the victory against the Formorians.

As for the gifts of the gods: Lugh had one of them, the spear from the magic city of Gorias, a spear against which no battle was ever won.

Second Chance went up for sale. There were no unseemly signs stuck into the beautifully manicured lawns, which were, quite frankly, beginning to show the lack of Michael's attention. Instead, there was a discreet notice in the local paper suggesting interested parties direct their enquiries to McCafferty and McGlynn, Solicitors, St. Stephen's Green, Dublin.

Eamon Byrne's body was barely cold—it was not two months since he'd been buried—and already his family's fortunes were on the downward spiral he had predicted just before his demise. One of his businesses, a distribution company, had posted a significant loss, and I got the impression from the news reports that investors were leaving the Byrne empire in droves.

The buzz in town was that Margaret Byrne would not be replacing either John Herlihy or Michael, at least not full time. A part-time gardener was being sought to keep up the grounds until the house could be sold. They were also looking for a housekeeper/cook to come in for a few hours a day to keep the household in order. Needless to say, with the rumors swirling around about what had happened to John and Michael, no one was lining up for the job.

Breeta had found employment, however, although the position was far beneath the capabilites of the young woman who had recited "Song of Amairgen" in a bar not that long ago. I suppose that, all alone, with a baby on the way and no inheritance, she took what she could get, in this case, a job as a waitress in a restaurant in Dingle Town. I had tried to track her down after our initial conversation after the funeral, without success. She'd given up her flat in Killarney and left no forwarding address. I'd seen her a couple of times on the streets of Dingle Town since then, but she'd crossed the street to avoid me.

At last I caught sight of her through the window of the cafe, and had gone in and sat down at a table. She was the only one there, and I figured she'd have to say something to me. I was wrong. She stood at my table, pushed a lank piece of hair out of her eyes, and just looked at me, pen poised over her order pad.

"Hello, Breeta," I said. "I've been looking for you,

hoping to talk to you again." She said nothing. The silence between us lengthened. "I was wondering if we could get together, after you get off work, perhaps, for a chat." Still nothing.

"Tea with lemon," I said finally. "And perhaps a cheese sandwich."

She turned without a word and walked away, returning a few minutes later with my order, which she placed in front of me with what seemed to be a deafening clatter.

"I'm very sorry that what I said last time upset you so much," I said. I meant that, too, although I still wasn't sure if she'd been the person to trash our room or not. She said she wasn't looking for the treasure. Maybe. But if that really were the case, perhaps she was actively trying to stop the rest of us from looking. In any event, she turned away without a word.

"If I can help you in any way . . . " I said helplessly to her retreating back. I looked down at the tea and sandwiches, and realized I couldn't eat a bite under the circumstances. I left some money on the table and walked away.

Despite all the gossip in town about the cause of the two deaths, and my personal apprehension, the second autopsy on John Herlihy's body had not turned up any poison and had merely confirmed what we already knew: that John Herlihy was a drinker of serious proportions. Michael had been killed by an overdose of heroin, bad heroin, and there being no other indications he'd used drugs before, let alone been an addict, this was still being investigated as murder.

I hadn't yet told Rob about Jennifer and Gilhooly, although I still intended to do so, despite Jennifer's pleading. I told her I'd give her a couple of days to break it to him herself, but it was difficult for her to find a quiet and private time with him to do so. Rob was spending a great deal of his time with the gardai, or at least one of them, trying to solve Michael's murder, and he wasn't around much in the evenings either. He'd taken to smoking, something he'd told me he'd given up when Jennifer was born. The men-sex-smoking thing being what it is, I assumed his relationship with Maeve had moved to a more intimate plane, but perhaps he took it up again in self-defense—so many people in Ireland had the habit and the restaurants and pubs were filled with smoke most of the time. We didn't discuss it, although I gave him many a disapproving look on the few occasions he lit up in my presence.

Occasionally, he'd stop by and have a bite to eat with Jennifer and me at the Inn, but the place was invariably crowded, and when I tried to leave them alone together, it just didn't work out. I'd come back after hiding out in my room for several minutes to find Aidan telling Rob and Jennifer a joke, or Malachy and Kevin would have sat down at the table and ordered a beer. Rob was very distracted and would occasionally rouse himself from the private world he was inhabiting to ask me how I was doing and ask Jennifer how her sailing lessons were going, but that was about it. I'd never seen him like this, and was occasionally tempted to shock him back to reality by telling him Jennifer might well be learning more than how to sail with Paddy Gilhooly, but somehow it just didn't seem fair.

Alex had taken himself off to stay at Rose Cottage for a few days. He said he wanted to try the place out before he decided what he wanted to do about it, but I figured that as much as anything he just wanted to get a good night's sleep without Rob creeping in and out at odd hours. The idea of Alex staying alone at Rose

Cottage—I couldn't go with him and leave Jennifer alone all night, that much was certain—caused a frenzy of anxiety for me. I told myself that it was because I was worried about his health, and his proximity to Second Chance, and the possibility of a murderer there. He told me not to fuss. The compromise was he had to take my cell phone and meet me for a pub lunch, usually splendid fish and chips and a pint of Guinness for him, Kilkenny for me, almost every day.

Jennifer, needless to say, was consumed by her sailing lessons, and all that these entailed.

All of which meant that I was left on my own, feeling generally out of sorts. I felt abandoned somehow, bereft, with everyone else involved in something different—Rob with his Maeve, Jennifer with her Paddy, Alex with his Rose—none of which included me. In the end, I concluded I was just not myself, for reasons I could only explain as the aftermath of finding two bodies and being so far away from home.

So I did what I always do when I am in the thrall of feelings that I consider beneath my dignity: I threw myself into my work, or at least I tried to. I called Sarah a couple of times to see how things were going, but she sounded remarkably calm about my extended stay in Ireland, a fact I had trouble believing. I could only assume that this tranquility on her part meant that Clive had taken over control of the store, a thought that I translated into visions of returning eventually to find the place cold and dark, with Clive's shop across the road a mecca of bright lights for antiques enthusiasts everywhere. After a couple of nights of waking up in a cold sweat, I broke down and called Moira.

"Everything's fine," she said, to my question about how things in general were. I was working my way around to subject of the shop gradually.

"Sarah must be exhausted by now looking after the place by herself," I said, testing the waters.

"No, I don't think so," she said matter-of-factly. "She seems to be getting along all right. Clive has found her a co-op student, someone studying merchandising at the community college, to help her out a couple of hours a day after class. Sarah says the kid's terrific."

Kid, I thought. Knowing Clive this would be some nubile young thing who liked to sit on older men's knees. Moira had better keep her eye on him.

"And Ben thinks this is the best thing that's happened to him since he started the course," she continued. Ben, I thought, in amazement. So, no nubile young thing. What was the catch? Maybe Ben cost a fortune. Maybe Clive was bankrupting me.

"He's cheap too," Moira went on. "The school picks up half his wages as part of the course."

Much to my surprise, even after several more pointed questions, I could find nothing to fault with Clive's activities. I didn't know whether I was relieved or disappointed. "That's great," was what I said.

"Clive has an idea he'd like to discuss with you when you get back," Moira said. "A little joint promotion idea he's come up with. I won't tell you about it, because he'll want to. I think it's a terrific idea, though."

"Oh, I don't know . . ." I said. There was a pause in the conversation.

"Lara," Moira said. "We have never discussed this business, Clive and I, I mean. I know it's been difficult for you, and I've never felt that you wanted to talk about it, which I really feel badly about, because until Clive and I got together, you and I had always been able to discuss everything. And maybe a transatlantic call isn't the right time, but Clive is really trying hard. He knows how much your friendship means to me. I've told him. I've told him that I've been through a lot of men in the time you and I have been friends, and that I intend for us to be friends forever. I've really been hoping that despite your nasty divorce, the two of you could get along."

I kind of doubted that Clive and I could ever really get along, but Moira's friendship meant as much to me as it apparently did to her, and I figured I'd better try. "I'm sure we can," I said.

"Great!" she said happily. "Now tell me what's happening over there."

So I told her, about the family, the Will, about Second Chance and its gardens, the treasure hunt, and finally, the murders.

"Am I understanding this right?" Moira asked. "It's the servants that are getting offed, not the family members? Isn't this a bit odd?"

"It is," I agreed.

"Did the servants have clues?"

"Michael Davis did. John Herlihy didn't. Neither did Deirdre Flood, though she's still among the living."

"Why give it to only one of them? Was Michael the only non-family member that got a clue?"

"Paddy Gilhooly, also a non-family member, got one. His connection with the family, at least the only one I've come across, is that he dated Breeta Byrne, the youngest daughter, and that the family objected and Breeta left home. She's not dating him anymore. Deirdre was a relatively recent arrival in the household, less than five years, she said, so it would make sense she wouldn't get one. It's a bit surprising about Herlihy, though, because I got the impression he'd been with the family forever. Michael had been there for a while, but not much longer than Deirdre. I'd have expected that Herlihy would have got one, although he got a sizable amount of money from the Will. Deirdre got some too, although not as much. Michael got something somewhere in between, if I remember correctly, plus some extra money if he went back to school. Which he won't be doing," I added sadly.

"Are you sure this is about the treasure, then?" Moira asked. "I mean, if Herlihy didn't get a clue, maybe it's about something entirely different."

"That's a good question," I replied. "But it's the only thing I can think of. This treasure, if it exists, is supposed to be worth something. And what else could it be?"

"I don't know," she replied. "Don't they say the motive is almost always money or passion? The treasure is the only money angle, I suppose."

"Well, the money that John and Michael got reverts to the family, according to their solicitor, but I can't imagine it's enough to kill for."

"So what about the passion motive? A family secret or something. A horrible secret from Byrne's past. Am I overdoing this, do you think?" she laughed. "All right then, a grudge of some sort. A former gardener, say, a psycho, who was fired by Herlihy for killing the orchids and who got back at Herlihy and his replacement. A little farfetched, I admit. But what about this Gilhooly fellow? Maybe he thought he was going to marry a fortune, and then was disappointed. But then," she said, answering her own question, "he wouldn't kill the staff for that, now would he? It's a mystery, all right."

"It is," I agreed. "There are hints, from time to time, of something in Byrne's past, but it must have been a very long time ago, if at all, because he's been here for at least thirty years, and no one around here seems to know anything specific. But I have another problem I could use your advice on, Moira, since you mention Gilhooly," I added, then told her about Jennifer's escapades.

"Aieee!" she exclaimed. "Thirty-five or -six? This is bad. I think you had better tell Rob," she said after a minute's contemplation. "If you leave it too long, he'll think you're a party to this whole thing, that you've been hiding it from him, or worse, maybe even helping them get together. I'd give Jennifer about five minutes more to tell him, if I were you, and then, if she doesn't, you do it!"

"You're right, as usual, Moira," I said. "I've been intending to do it. It's just that Rob has a new friend, a police officer by the name of Maeve Minogue. I think it's serious, and he isn't spending much time with Jennifer and me."

"What!" Moira exclaimed. "Are you telling me Rob has a girlfriend over there?"

"Yes," I said.

"Oh," Moira said. I could hear disappointment in her voice.

"Moira!" I said. I knew what that tone meant.

"I know," she said. "I sort of had him in mind for you. He's kind of cute, isn't he? Steady job. Steady kind of guy, in fact. I thought he'd be good for you. And you for him," she added loyally. "He can be a bit of a tight ass, and you'd lighten him up. I thought you two would be perfect together, in fact."

I laughed. Moira is always trying to fix me up with somebody. What are your women friends for, I suppose.

"Don't laugh. What about Jennifer? You like her, too, don't you? Don't you think they make a nice package deal?"

"I like Jennifer very much. In fact, I'm surprised how much I'm enjoying her company, and Rob's a lovely guy," I said. "But he and I would drive each other crazy. Do drive each other crazy, and we're just friends. I'd give up on him if I were you."

"We'll see," she replied, in a tone I'd come to recognize as only a temporary retreat. "In the meantime, be careful. Don't go near that awful family."

"Okay," I replied, and I meant it. I'd made up my mind to give up on this treasure thing, at least for a while, and get back to business. Nobody had died in a while, after all, and there had been no more threatening incidents. Maybe Moira was right, and it was about something else entirely. "I'm going to have a look around for some antiques while I'm here. I might as well do something useful until they let us go home, which I sincerely hope will be soon."

"Good," she said. "Let us know when you're flying back. We'll pick you up at the airport."

"Thanks," I said, but knew I wouldn't. Being picked up at the airport by Clive was more than I could manage, friendship with Moira notwithstanding, but I knew I'd have to try harder. "Tell Clive how much I appreciate what he's doing for Sarah and the store, and that I can't wait to hear his idea for the promotion," I said, gritting my teeth.

"I will," she said, sounding pleased.

When I'd hung up, I resolutely turned to execute my decision to tend to business right away. I called my shipper in Toronto, Dave Thomson, and asked for names of contacts I could use to send stuff home if I found anything. Then I called my bank and had them fax a letter of introduction to the Inn. Next, I made enquiries of the proprietors about places to look for furniture of the antique variety, old houses up for sale

and so on, and armed with a couple of leads, headed
out in the car to see what I could find. I spent a pleasant
enough afternoon and was rewarded with a couple of
great purchases a terrific dining room suite, early
1800s, and a beautiful silver tea service that I was so
in love with, I thought I might keep for myself if it
didn't sell soon after I put it out for sale, within
minutes, say. After making arrangements to have them
picked up and taken to a shipper in Waterford, I went
back to the Inn feeling altogether pleased with myself,
promising myself a nice glass of wine as a reward, and
to do the same thing again the next day.

My intentions were good, but my actions were
thwarted.

I may have wanted to give up on the treasure hunt
and go back to my shopkeeping, but there was renewed
enthusiasm for the quest in other quarters, as I learned
the minute I got back to the Inn. Gilhooly had been
good as his word, and had gone off to find the clue
that went with salmon in a pool. Translated from ogham, it said simply Axis Mundi, presumably the center
point around which the world turned. Very helpful, I'm
sure, but Gilhooly and Jennifer were fired with enthusiasm for finding the rest of the clues, and had enlisted
the support of Malachy and Kevin to do so. It was quite
clear by this point that we didn't need the rest of the
family's clues: we just had to find the clues that went
with the lines of Amairgen's song and decipher the
ogham. By the end of that one day, while I was out
antiquing, the intrepid foursome, who must have been
a sight, the two old guys, the blond Canadian in her
pink and purple Take No Prisoners jacket, and the local
sailor, twice her age, had found not only Axis Mundi,
but the clue that went with a flame of valor. The clues
now looked like this.

AMAIRGEN'S SONG	OGHAM CLUES
I am the sea-swell	May's sunrise by Tailte's Hill is seen
The furious wave	A curse be on these stones.
The roar of the sea	Leinster's Hag to Eriu's Seat
A stag of seven slaughters	—
A hawk above the cliff	Aine's Mount to Macha's Stronghold
A ray of the sun	—
The beauty of a plant	Raise a cup to the stone
A boar enraged	Almu's white to Maeve's red
A salmon in a pool	Axis Mundi
A lake in a plain	—
A flame of valor	—

It was still all rather baffling, and the clues were not my only source of bewilderment. Strangely enough, Deirdre had come back and asked for her old position at Second Chance, only a few days after I'd seen her in Dublin. According to the gossip in the bar, Margaret Byrne had leapt at the opportunity to take her back, there being no one else in town who would stoop so low. Townspeople said Deirdre hadn't liked Dublin, noisy and dirty as it was, and the pay was poor, even worse than the notorious Margaret was prepared to shell out, and some said Margaret couldn't afford to pay Deirdre what she'd been paid before, a rumor I sincerely hoped wasn't true. I did know that I had had the unfortunate experience of overhearing a shopkeeper tell Eithne that she could be extended no more credit until the outstanding bill was paid, an encounter that brought cheeks pink with embarrassment to both of us. I could understand that Deirdre might prefer the lovely Dingle to Dublin, but I was surprised, nonetheless. I'd thought Deirdre would never even consider returning to these parts, so terrified she had been by the murders of her colleagues.

I'd have liked to ask her about it, but she wasn't talking. At least she wasn't talking to me, but she was in good company in that regard, joining a small but growing group of people who regarded me as the local version of Typhoid Mary. When I saw her the next day on the street in town, doing some shopping, like Breeta, Deirdre hurriedly crossed the street when she saw me coming toward her. I waved, but she gave me her frightened rabbit look and disappeared quickly into a laneway. By the time I got over to where I'd seen her disappear, she was gone, lost in the maze of tiny streets. I supposed it was my surprise appearance at McCafferty and McGlynn that had made her so afraid of me, but I would have thought that, weighed against the happenings at Second Chance, on balance, I would be seen to be the lesser of two evils. Apparently not.

If Deirdre had nothing to say to me, however, she had plenty to tell the gardai.

Chapter Eleven
A FLAME OF VALOR

W HAT Deirdre had to say to the gardai put Conail O'Connor in jail. Or rather, to be more precise, Conail's reaction to what Deirdre had to say got him in trouble. Conail, hot-headed at the best of times, I'd warrant, was brought to the brink by his split with Fionuala and the constant ribbing he was subjected to, some of it friendly, some of it not, on the subject of his little encounter with Alex. His being hauled in for questioning had resulted in a physical altercation in the garda station that left one police officer with a bloody nose and Conail in handcuffs.

Conail was being led off to a cell, as I went into the station to talk to Rob.

"Piss off, will you?" he said as an officer took his arm. "I was looking for my wife," he bellowed over his shoulder as he was taken away. "I know she was there. Flirting with every man she came across. Somebody will have seen me."

"Seen him where?" I asked Rob as he led me to his little corner of the station. They'd given him a desk in the middle of a busy room, opposite an engaging young officer who gallantly gave up his chair and went searching for another when Rob and I arrived.

"Town," Rob replied. "Deirdre has told us this morning that she saw Conail O'Connor at Second Chance late the night Michael Davis died. After pub closing time. He says he was looking for his wife, but in town, not at Second Chance."

"Well, we all saw him in town at one point, didn't we, when he made that scene in the bar. But I talked to Deirdre before she went off to Dublin, and she didn't say a word about it. Why is Deirdre saying this now? Why not before?"

"Something about loyalty to the family, didn't want to get any of them in trouble when she was sure Conail hadn't really done anything wrong et cetera, et cetera. I can see why you refer to her as Deirdre of the Sorrows, by the way. Sad little lady. I see her kind of face from time to time, usually on the victims. They have an expression on their faces that seems to say that they know life will disappoint them, that something bad will happen to them. And the funny thing is, it does. I don't know whether they're victims because they look like victims, that they invite it in some way, or they look that way because of things that have happened to them already. Either way, I never quite know what to do or say to people like that." He paused for a moment. "Anyway, that's the reason I asked you to come down here, to try to confirm times again. I know we've been through this before, but in light of Deirdre's statement, we're going to have to go through it all again."

He looked tired. Well he might, of course, chasing criminals all day and doing the horizontal two-step with Ban Garda Maeve all night.

"How are you, anyway?" he said, smiling at me.

"It's ages since we had a chance to talk."

"Fine," I said. "I'm using my time here to find some stock for the store. Figure I might as well do something useful while I wait."

"Good," he said. I knew what he was thinking. He wanted to believe me, but wasn't sure whether he could or not. But he liked the idea of what I'd said. He thought it would keep me out of trouble. "Are you really?" he said suspiciously.

"Absolutely," I replied. I took a photo of the dining room set the seller had given me out of my bag and laid it out in front of him. "See? Lovely, isn't it? I found a beautiful silver tea service, too."

"Great," he said, handing the photo back to me. We seemed to be having trouble talking about anything other than police work, I realized. We used to talk all the time. This was not so good.

"Well," he said. "Down to business. Let's go over that evening again. Michael and Breeta left together?"

"Yes. She had to catch the last bus into Killarney. Michael was going to walk her to the bus stop, then he'd promised her he'd go back to Second Chance to get Vigs."

"The turtle," Rob said.

"Tortoise, actually, but yes."

"Method of transportation?"

"He was walking her to the bus, but he had his bicycle, so he would have used that to get to the house. She would confirm this, I'm sure."

"She has, more or less. Sullen young woman, isn't she? Has she said anything to you?"

"Not a word," I said. "Literally. She's not speaking to me."

"She's not saying much to anybody, I gather. Okay," he sighed. "The last bus was at ten-thirty. Breeta was

on it: the driver remembers her. He thinks Michael was
at the stop, which makes sense. He would have waited
with her until the bus came. Then he bicycles to Second
Chance. That would take at least twenty minutes. Bren-
dan here," he said gesturing to the officer at the desk
next to him, who smiled, "strapping young man that he
is, did the route and timed it. Let's say he got there
about eleven. Now Conail was in and out of various
pubs all evening, although he has difficulty accounting
for his time beginning around ten or ten-thirty. He says
he ran into Fionuala, and they had another argument,
a loud one, I gather. Several people say they heard a
man and a woman shouting at each other out in the
street. That may account for a few minutes, but that's
all. What do you figure Michael did?"

"I think he did what he said he would do. He went
back to Second Chance to get Vigs. He could let himself in at the back door. The staff had keys to the staff
entrance. It was late . . ."

"Not all that late, but the family, that is Sean, Eithne,
and Margaret claim to have gone to bed very early, and
didn't hear a thing. Deirdre has a room up in the attic,
so she probably wouldn't have heard anything. She
claims she didn't. She does say, though, that she saw
Conail creeping around outside the house. She looked
out the window, apparently. It was raining a little, so
it might have been difficult to see in the dark, but she
says she recognized his walk and his shape. Conail is
adamant that he went nowhere near the place."

"So Michael would have gone looking for Vigs.
Deirdre had Vigs, though. She gave him to me when
she went to Dublin. That may mean Michael didn't find
Vigs, that he never made it into the house, or that he
did and took him outside. Did Deirdre say where she
found Vigs?"

"In the house, she says."

"So Michael could have run into Conail before he got into the house. And then what? Conail stabs him with a hypodermic?"

"Conail doesn't seem to have a drug problem, just an alcohol and temper problem," Rob replied. "These Irish do seem to like their drink, don't they? Almost a stereotype, some of them. But I don't know. Conail insists he didn't see Michael that evening at all. Too busy yelling at his wife to have seen Michael in the bar at the Inn, apparently. The question is, even if he did, why kill him? Just because he'd had a very bad day? It wasn't Michael's fault Conail's wife ditched him, although I suppose she could have been flirting with him. She was flashing a fair amount of leg around that evening, chest too, if I remember correctly."

I smiled to myself. I'd thought he was so besotted with Maeve that he hadn't noticed Fionuala, but apparently he had.

"And it wasn't Michael who flattened him out at Malachy and Kevin's place: It was our very own Alex." He grinned. "Sure wish I'd been there to see that. So what would he kill Michael for?"

"For a clue?" I said. "Michael had a clue in his hand, part of one at least."

"We've looked into the clues, of course, talked to those lawyers, McCafferty and McGlynn, one of them anyway. I can't seem to tell them apart," he said, checking his notes. "McCafferty it was. He says they had nothing to do with hiding the second set of clues and didn't know who did. Nor did they know which line of the poem went in each of the envelopes. I suppose we have to believe him, being a fellow member of the justice system and all that."

"Did you find out what clues everyone had? That would be important, wouldn't it?"

"Of course I did," Rob said. "I'm a seasoned crime investigator, remember? Conail and Fionuala got one about," he stopped and looked at his file again, "a ray of the sun. Conail showed it to me, or rather he threw it at me. Margaret claims to have destroyed hers, without looking at it, so it could be anything; Eithne and Sean got the clue about the stag of seven slaughters; Padraig Gilhooly got . . ."

"Salmon in a pool," I interjected. "Michael got the furious wave, Alex, the sea-swell. The trouble is there are more clues than people, or original envelopes if you will. The beauty of the plant might have been Breeta's clue, the one stolen from the safe at Second Chance. Michael must have found it—maybe he wrestled Conail for it. Michael was awfully fond of Breeta, and he'd not want anyone else to get her clue."

"Wrestled Conail or somebody else," he replied. "Could be. Or maybe he just found it in the house somewhere. A lot of speculation isn't there? We'll keep seeing what we can get from Conail. Ban Garda Minogue is interrogating him now." I noticed he always referred to her as Minogue in my presence and never Maeve. "We haven't got enough evidence to hold him for the murder—at this point it's her word against his—but fortunately perhaps, he's given us another reason to keep him here. Garda Murphy might not agree it's fortuitous, of course. His nose is being looked at right now. Broken, most likely, and swelling up something fierce. By the way," he said, "can you decipher this?" He handed me a sheet of paper, one that I'd come to recognize, with Eamon Byrne's initials and Second Chance at the top.

"Conail's clue?"

"Yup. He gave it to us. Said it was a worthless piece of junk. Jennifer told me you'd all been able to decipher any that turned up, ogham or something I think she said."

"It is. Alex is really the expert. He broke the code, so to speak. I recognize some of the letters now, but I'd have to have my cheat sheet. It's in a safety-deposit box at the Inn. Make me a copy, and I'll go right back there, do it and call you back."

"Thanks," he smiled. "That will save us some time. I already have a copy, so here it is. I'd like the rest of the clues, too, if you don't mind, although I gather they don't say much. Don't say anything about Deirdre's accusations, will you? We don't want to reveal our source to the family, most especially to Conail himself. We've just told him that an unspecified someone passing by saw him hanging around there. How's Jennifer doing, by the way? She's all right, isn't she? I haven't seen her much lately, but she seems happy."

The question I'd been dreading. I looked about me. There was one garda, Rob's deskmate, working just a few feet away, two others well within earshot. Somehow, I didn't think this was the time to tell him his daughter thought she was in love with an Irish sailor twice her age. "She's okay," I said. "But I think she misses you and your fatherly guidance." There, that was a big hint. "You should try and spend some time with her, just the two of you, so you can talk."

"Yes," he replied. "I should, and I will. I'm sure she's getting plenty of guidance from you, though. Just like you're guiding me, right now." He smiled. "Thanks for the advice."

I got up to leave. If he thought I was giving his daughter guidance, he wasn't going to be too pleased with the result.

"Since I'm dispensing advice right now, I have some more for you. Get some sleep," I said as I headed out the door. I heard him chuckle, but didn't look around.

Conail and Fionuala's clue, the ray of the sun, was Grianan Ailech to Granard down the line of the noonday sun. No more helpful than any of the rest. I wrote them all down on a piece of paper and dropped them off at the garda station for Rob on the way to my next buying expedition. I'd heard there was an auction at a town on the other side of the Dingle Peninsula called Ballyferriter. I stopped off for a bite of lunch at a little wine bar on the main street of town and found, to my surprise, Jennifer and Gilhooly, Malachy and Kevin. I smiled at her and the two brothers, and glared at Gilhooly.

"How'd you get all the way over here?" I asked them.

"Paddy borrowed a van," Jennifer said, gesturing toward the window. A dilapidated van sat outside.

"We've found another clue," Jennifer said. "I made a copy of Uncle Alex's ogham table and brought it along."

"It's a mystery," Malachy said. Jennifer handed me the paper.

"All seen and seeing ring of fire," I read. "Which line of the poem did this one come from?"

"A flame of valor," Malachy replied. "And we've found another one, the one that goes with he who clears the mountain paths. Kev here had the idea that would refer to Mt. Brandon, named after St. Brandon, so we hiked all the way up the path to a cairn, and found it there."

"That's great," I said.

"Not entirely," Malachy said. "Tere's a small problem with it, you see. 'Twas hidden the same way as the others, and it has Byrne's initials on it and everything."

"But?"

"But it's blank! Here, take a look."

I looked. The now familiar paper was there, but it was, as Malachy said, quite blank.

"What does this mean?" Jennifer asked no one in particular. "The paper doesn't look as if it's ever been wet, or anything. Like the ink might have washed away."

"How should I know?" I replied. "Unless . . ." They all looked at me.

"There have been more of the second set of clues than the first. I mean, we've found ogham clues for lines of the poem no one was given. Presumably, we were supposed, with the clues we got, to figure out it was from 'Song of Amairgen,' and go and find all the lines of the poem, not just the ones we had." I stopped there, and they all waited. "So," I hesitated. "So I don't know."

"So, this means that when we get this far, there are no more clues," Jennifer said. "Isn't that what you're thinking?"

"I guess so. We're still missing some lines before this. We would have to try and find them, to see if there are any ogham clues that go with them, and maybe one or two lines after this one to see if they are blank too. Then we'd know."

"The lines from this one, the one about the mountain paths," Malachy said, looking at the copy of the poem Jennifer had brought with her, "are slightly different in structure. Instead of I am something or other, they start with he who: he who clears the mountain paths, he who describes the passage of the moon and so on. So maybe we have come to the end of the clues. Maybe we need to find the missing ones before that. We're missing the one about the stag of seven battles and the ray of the sun, aren't we?"

"Not anymore," I said. "We now have ray of the sun, which is," I paused to hold up my notes.

"Grianan Ailech to Granard down the line of the noonday sun," Jennifer read aloud. "Where did you find this one?"

"The garda station," I replied. "It's a long story." I felt vaguely guilty about handing over the clue I got from Rob. But I'd given him all the ones we had so far, hadn't I?

"Did you get a chance to talk to Dad?" Jennifer asked. She looked a little lonely in a way, I thought, and missing him. She was wondering whether I'd told him about her and Paddy.

"Only briefly," I said. "There were a lot of people around." She looked relieved. "Don't tell him I told you about Conail's clue," I added.

"Maybe we could do a deal here," she said, a mischievous smile slowly appearing on her face.

"And maybe we couldn't," I said, although I found myself beginning to smile too. "Just don't tell him."

"What did she say?" Kevin asked.

"She said don't tell Rob she told us the clue," Malachy said directly into Kevin's ear.

"Not that, the clue," Kevin shouted. "What was the clue?"

"Grianan Ailech to Granard down the line of the noonday sun," Malachy shouted back. A couple of other diners looked our way.

"I know Granard," Kevin said. "It's a town, County Longford, I believe. I don't know about this ring of fire thing, but Granard's a real place."

"This is the first real place name we've had," Paddy

said. "Maybe it's hidden in Granard. Maybe we should go there. I'll see if I can keep the van for another day or two. We could leave tonight."

Jennifer doing an overnighter with this guy? I didn't think so.

"Hold on a sec," I said. "There are a lot of other clues we still haven't found. Why don't we just concentrate on finding them all, and then see what we've got."

Jennifer looked disappointed. "I guess you're right," she sighed. "But I just want to get going and find this thing, whatever it is."

"That's a good point," I said. "Eamon Byrne said the clues were about what it was, as well as where it was. Maybe the Granard clue is a what, not a where. Without the what, even if we knew where, we wouldn't know what to look for. I mean is it bigger than a breadbox? Animal, vegetable, mineral?"

"I think it's gold," Malachy said. "The bogs. Eamon Byrne was in the turf business, peat. They've found all sorts of treasures hidden in the bogs, stashes of gold and everything. The Celts apparently hid stuff in the bogs, or maybe they threw it in as an offering or something. Roman coins, Viking treasures, gold torcs. Those are the metal collars the Celts wore around their necks," he said to Jennifer. "In battle that was all they wore, that and their swords and shields. Starkers, they were, when they were fighting. Must have been something to see." He roared with laughter and slapped his knee. "Denny has some good stories about those battles," he said. "We'll get him to tell them soon. That's if you're up to helping him to a whiskey or three, Lara," he added.

"I am," I replied. I had to laugh too. I loved these three old guys.

"So what's left in the way of lines of the poem?" Paddy asked. "The stag of seven slaughters, I know, but what else?"

"Let's see," I said, looking at my notes. "Lake in a plain, a piercing spear waging war, and a god that fashions heroes for a lord, whatever that is."

"Kevin has an idea for one of those," Jennifer said. "We were going there after lunch. Some observatory, or something."

"Oratory," Malachy corrected her. "The Gallarus Oratory. Kevin thinks that would be the place for lake in a plain. Religious place, very ancient. Yer man Eamon Byrne's kind of place. 'Tis a bit obscure to be sure. The clues we've left are getting harder. But Kev sees it this way. There are no lakes in plains around here. They're all in the mountain valleys. So he tinks 'tis the Gallarus Oratory, on account of it's in the shape of an overturned boat, and it's resting on one of the few flat areas there are. So if we're done here, let's get going."

The Gallarus Oratory was an extraordinary structure, very old, and set in a windswept plain with a view over to the water far away and three hills that looked like curling waves whose motion had been caught and frozen in some cataclysmic event in earth's early history. "The three sisters," Malachy said, following my glance. "That's what they're called. Now come look at the oratory."

It was made without mortar, just thousands and thousands of stones carefully placed to create a tiny early Christian church, maybe twenty feet by sixteen, its sides tapering up to form a corbelled arch roof and ceiling. It did indeed look a little like an upturned boat, its keel in the air. There was only one small window and one low door facing each other at either end.

I touched the walls inside. "A beauty, isn't it?" Malachy said. "No mortar, but it's still watertight, after a thousand years! More. It is supposed to date to the eighth century. It's the same construction as those clocháns we saw on the slope of Mount Eagle, except they were round, and this is a rectangle. A beauty," he repeated.

We heard a shout outside and hurried to find Jennifer and Paddy waving a piece of paper that had been folded and wedged until it was about an inch square.

"Found it around the back, between the stones," Paddy said.

"Hurry up, open it!" Jennifer exclaimed. "I've got the alphabet."

The two of them unfolded the paper as quickly as they could, but not fast enough for the others who crowded around.

"Is there anything on it?" Kevin asked, trying to peer over Paddy's shoulder.

"There is!" Jennifer crowed. "But it's too windy here. We'll have to translate it later. What about the hero one, what could that be."

"Now let's think about that," Malachy said, as we headed back to the van. "What do you say to the god that fashions heroes for a lord, Kev? Any of your brilliant ideas on this one?"

"Did you say hero?" Kev yelled.

"I did," Malachy said.

"Well, who's the greatest hero of the west of Ireland?" he said.

"Grand idea, Kev!" Malachy said.

"Okay," I said. "I give up. Who is the greatest hero of the west of Ireland?"

Kevin and Malachy looked horrified at my ignorance. Paddy merely smiled and opened up the van.

"Why Fionn MacCumhail!" Malachy said, saying

something that sounded like Finn McCool. "Head of the Fianna, wasn't he? The greatest warriors ever. And, as it turns out, Fionn fought one of his greatest battles right here in Dingle. Can you get this thing moving any faster this time, now Paddy? And do you tink it's up to the climb?" he said, giving a tire a little kick.

"We'll go as fast as it will take us, Malachy," Paddy said. "Fast as it will go. Now hop in. Will you be following behind, Ms. McClintoch?"

"Where are we going?"

"Two possibles. Fionn MacCumhail's table, which is a dolmen in the Slieve Mish Mountains, or some sites around Ventry, where an epic battle was fought by MacCumhail. The dolmen will be a bit of a climb, and I may have to be the one to do it. If that's the case, I won't be doing it today," he said, squinting into the sun, now low.

"Then let's pause here for a moment," I said. "What about the other one, the one about the piercing spear waging war?"

Kevin scratched his head. "This one's got me puzzled," he said. "But I'll keep thinking."

"I'd think the piercing spear might very well be in Eamon's own study," I said. "It was filled with swords and spears and stuff. It could be Margaret's clue—she claims she destroyed hers without looking at it—and if so, Eamon might have wanted to make it easy for her to find. The first one was right on the property, at least down in the little cove. Maybe this one is there, too. If it is, she's probably found it already, unless she really meant it about not looking for any of them."

"How would we get that one?" Jennifer asked. "We'd have to get into the house to do it."

"Tere's no way I'm going into that fecking place," Paddy said.

"Me neither," Malachy said.

"Nor I," Kevin agreed.

"I was just passing by on my way to Rose Cottage," I said, handing Margaret Byrne my card at the door of Second Chance. For a moment, she stared at it. "This is my assistant, Jennifer, by the way. Jennifer, this is Mrs. Byrne. I'm sorry to trouble you, and I'm not sure whether you were aware or not, but as you can see, I am the co-proprietor of an antiques and design shop in Toronto called Greenhalgh & McClintoch. I have noticed that your home is up for sale, and it occurred to me that you might be thinking of selling some of the contents. I'm particularly interested in some of your husband's maps, which I saw the other day, if there are any that are not being given to Trinity College. I have a client who is a map collector and several of them are quite good. If those are not available," I went on, "I'd be most grateful if you could show us anything that you're thinking of selling."

"We have not yet decided what we will be selling," Margaret said reluctantly. "We will, of course, be getting rid of some things. We are thinking of moving to cozier quarters," she said, "and won't have the space, you understand."

"Of course," I agreed. Perhaps, I thought, the family really was as broke as everyone in town was saying. "I do hope you will decide before I leave for Canada, which I think will be very soon. By the way," I said, taking an envelope from my bag and handing it to her. "A letter of reference from my bank."

Margaret looked at it for a moment. "Come in," she said at last.

"Will you be looking for another place around

here?" I asked, brightly attempting to make conversation.

"I doubt it," Margaret said. "I think I'd like to go back where I was born. It's in Connemara. Do you know it?"

"I don't," I replied, "although I've heard Connemara's spectacular. That's close to Galway, isn't it?"

"It is," she replied. "Absolutely beautiful. I think I might like to go back."

"Is that where you met your husband?" I asked. She nodded.

"Did you meet him after he'd been to sea, after he knew Alex?"

"Before that," she said. "We were engaged, but he went off to sea. I became engaged to another man, but then Eamon returned, and I was swept off my feet again." For a moment, she sounded sad, almost wistful, and I began to feel horribly guilty. This treasure hunt occasionally felt a little like a parlor game, and it was easy to forget that these were real people, with real feelings. It was only by concentrating on the task at hand and reminding myself that finding the treasure might be the key not only to Alex's future, but also an end to the violence, that I was able to carry on. Then she turned abruptly. "Here," she said. "My husband's study.

"The people from Trinity College have been here as you can see," she said, pointing to glass cabinets stripped bare, darker red marks showing where the weapons had rested against the velvet. "They have not left much. Are you interested in oils? These were my father's. Quite good, I believe." Not too sentimental, that woman, but perhaps she was just being pragmatic.

"Lovely, aren't they, Jennifer?" I said. Jennifer nodded vigorously. In truth, there was only one oil there that had any value beyond the sentimental, in my opinion, so I made a note of that one. While Margaret stood watching us, we carefully looked everything over, lifting objects from time to time, moving others slightly to look under them. At last I found what I wanted; at least I was reasonably sure I had. I went to the glass doors and looked outside. "Lovely day, isn't it?" I said before turning away. I was rather overusing lovely, it occurred to me, but perhaps it was because I was nervous.

My presence in the window was the signal for Alex, now hidden behind the potting shed, and who if found could claim to be crossing the property to get to Rose Cottage, to use my cell phone to call the house. The telephone rang three times. There was one in the room, but Margaret ignored it. A few moments later, Deirdre hove into view. Once again, she seemed surprised to see me. "It's for you, Madam," she said, ignoring me.

"Excuse me for a moment," Margaret said. I was elated. I was banking on the fact that Margaret would not take a call in my presence. The trouble was, Deirdre stayed put.

Jennifer walked up to her. "Sorry, but would it be all right if I used the bathroom?" she asked. Deirdre looked startled and hesitated for a moment, and I thought all was lost.

"Oh, you mean the toilet," she said finally. "Yes, please follow me." Quickly I lifted the glass case, now empty, where once Byrne's favorite spearhead, the one he attributed to Lugh Lamfada, had rested. I pulled the piece of paper out quickly, and by the time Margaret returned, I was standing looking out over the grounds once again.

"They hung up," Margaret said.

"How annoying," I said. "Ah, here's Jennifer." I

looked around a little more, extracted a promise that she'd call me if she decided to sell the old Oriental carpets in the room, then offered more than it was worth for the painting, paid cash, and told her I'd send someone around to pick it up later, if that was satisfactory. Apparently it was.

A few minutes later, Jennifer and I were sitting in Rose Cottage with the others, clue in one hand, ogham alphabet in the other, Jennifer regaling them with the story of our adventure. By the time she was through with her tale, Margaret Byrne was only microseconds away from discovering what we were after, and Deirdre about to call the police.

The story was better, or more edifying at least, than the clue: "Umbilicus Hiberniae, the sacred center" it said. Not very helpful, but there was one more clue to go, if my theory was correct. Then we'd see what there was to see.

Alex had gone down to the pier and brought back some wonderful fish, determined to prepare a meal for us all, his first dinner party, he said, in his new home. It was somewhat daunting with no electricity, but Paddy got the fire roaring, Jennifer and I lit candles and set the table, and we had a rather jolly time of it in his cozy little cottage. There was the fish, cooked in a pan over the fire, potatoes hot from the coals and slathered in Irish butter, and lots of fresh vegetables followed by strawberries in thick Irish cream. It was a bit strained at first, between Paddy and me, although I could find nothing to fault in his manner that night, no matter how I tried. He was solicitous to Jennifer, kind to Malachy and Kevin, helpful to Alex, and generally stayed out of my way, calling me Ms. McClintoch when called upon to address me. He had the casual charm of the Irish that was quite disarming, when the conversation and the companionship drew him out of his normal reticence, and finally I decided a truce was in order. "We didn't get off to a very good start the other day," I said to him as we were setting out the food on the table.

"We didn't," he agreed.

"I thought you'd run us down in the water. It was your boat, I think," I added carefully.

"Could have been," he said. "Do you still think I was at the helm?"

"No," I replied. "Malachy and Kevin said you wouldn't do such a thing, and that's good enough for me."

He smiled. "They're grand old boys, aren't they? And no, it wasn't me, although I regret to say it may have been my boat. There were a few extra knots showing on her than there should have been for its just being in the boatworks. The boys at the works took her out to see she was going all right, after they'd worked on her, but not as far as all that."

"Who do you think might have taken it?"

"Conail," he replied.

"Why?"

"Kind of hotheaded thing he might do. Get us both at one time, if you see what I mean: scares you off the hunt and gets me in trouble at the same time. They're a bad bunch up there at Second Chance," he added. "Treated me rough, they did. Tink they're better than everybody else, but they're not. Except Eamon. He was a fine one. Took me in, made me feel like one of the family. Treated all of us right—Michael and John and me. Not her, though. Margaret. A bad piece of work, she is. Treated me like dirt. Conail too, and Sean. The two sisters, they went along with it."

"Only two of them?"

"Not Breeta," he said softly. "Not her. She's a fine one, like her Da."

"You should call me Lara," I said.

"Should that be Aunt Lara?" he smiled.

"No, it shouldn't," I replied. Don't push your luck, I thought.

Late in the evening, well fed and warmed by the conviviality, we left Alex ensconced in his cottage and picked our way carefully overland to the main road, not wishing to run into Sean McHugh and his rifle at night, and thence back to town. I dropped Malachy and Kevin off before going on to the friend of Paddy's from whom he'd borrowed the van. He took off from there on his motorbike, and I took Jennifer back to the Inn.

There was an envelope waiting for me on my return. In it was a note. *I came to see you,* it said. *I will come back on my day off. Day after tomorrow, 11 o'clock. Please wait for me. There is something I have to tell you. Very important. D. Flood.*

Chapter Twelve

A PIERCING SPEAR WAGING WAR

REGRETTABLY, the Byrne family followed through on their threat to take legal action to get Rose Cottage away from Alex.

"Lara," the smooth voice said. "Charles, here." I could almost smell his cologne over the telephone lines, and I confess my heart did a little dance, all my good intentions to the contrary. "I'm afraid I have bad news. Despite my efforts to persuade them to the contrary, the Byrne family has engaged the services of another solicitor and are suing Eamon Byrne's estate for Rose Cottage. They're claiming, as I suspected they might, that Eamon was *non compos mentis* due to the spread of the cancer to his brain. We will need to get together to discuss how to proceed. Ryan and I will be driving down your way later today. Do you think you could get in touch with Mr. Stewart for me, and the four of us might meet for an hour or two late this afternoon?"

I thought we could. As irritated as I was by this development, I decided that seeing Charles again would go some distance toward making me feel better.

We met in the lounge of the Inn, sitting at a large table so that Charles and Ryan could spread their notes about. The two of them were in lawyer uniform again, three-piece suits and all, which turned more than a few heads of the rest of the clientele in this rather more casual setting.

"Now, Mr. Stewart," Ryan said, smiling rather engagingly. "You really mustn't worry about this. I can assure you the family has no case. We have copies of earlier versions of Eamon Byrne's Will, some of them dating back several years, and you were named in all of them. So their case, the idea that Eamon was not quite right at the end, if you see what I mean, will simply not hold water. We are hopeful, I think," he said, looking toward Charles who nodded, "that the court will find this action merely capricious and refuse to even hear it."

"I don't know," Alex said. "I've been thinking a great deal while I've been out at Rose Cottage. It's a lovely place, but . . ."

"Of course it is," Ryan interrupted. "A wonderful place. And Eamon Byrne wanted you to have it."

"I know," Alex said, "but I don't need it, and I'm beginning to think—I mean all the rumors in the village—that the Byrne family might . . ."

"Hardly," I interjected. "They still have Second Chance, and while they may have to sell it, they're not exactly in the poorhouse. What could you get for a place like that these days, anyway? More money than you and I will ever see, I'm sure. And they still have control of Byrne Enterprises, even if it isn't doing as well as it should."

"But if it means that much to them," he protested.

"Oh, no, Alex," I exclaimed. "Don't do this. You

know you love the place. I saw you the other night, cooking over the fire. It's the best you've looked in a long time. The place is good for you: the sea air, the quiet away from the city."

"But my friends, my life, are in Toronto," he said. "You know that as much as I do. What would I do if I couldn't come into the shop every day? You think I'm doing you a favor, but I'm not. I hated retirement five minutes into it. I need the activity, the sense of being needed."

"Well, let's just say that we both benefit from having you in the shop. I'm glad to hear it, but that's not the issue, Alex," I said. "If you don't want to use it, you can always sell it, or rent it out for some extra income, get yourself a little cottage closer to home or whatever, but as Ryan says, Eamon Byrne really wanted you to have the cottage, and those people have no business being so entirely selfish. You saved his life, Alex, and he wanted to repay you in some way."

"Did you now?" Charles said turning to Alex. "I've often wondered. Tell us about it."

Alex gave him a delicately edited version of Eamon's story, telling him that Eamon had fallen off the pier in Singapore.

"Singapore!" Ryan exclaimed. "I love that place. I had the best sweet and sour soup in the world in a little dive not far from the Raffles Hotel. And the dim sum!" I smiled, remembering Charles's description of Ryan as a gourmand. I looked over at Charles, and he was smiling too.

"I know exactly where you found it!" Alex said, and the two were off on a culinary tour of Singapore, then Hong Kong, then Shanghai. Charles listened with real interest, and soon he and Alex too were trading stories of places they'd been, and adventures they'd had.

Charles, it seemed, had not been to the manor born, as it were, and had worked very hard to put himself through law school. There was a determination under that cultured exterior that I found quite attractive.

After several minutes of armchair travel, Charles gently steered the talk back to the subject at hand. "Now, Mr. Stewart," Charles said. "As enjoyable as this conversation is, we'll need to get your direction on the lawsuit. We will accede to your wishes, of course. If you do not wish to keep Rose Cottage, then we will simply not contest the suit. But Eamon Byrne felt quite strongly that you should have it. To that I can personally attest. I had no idea why he felt that strongly, of course, not having heard the story, but I discussed the Will with him at some length, and there is absolutely no doubt in my mind as to his intentions. And he was quite lucid, I can assure you."

"Would you be defending the Will, then?" Alex asked. He obviously liked the two solicitors, and was coming around, much to my delight. I couldn't stand the idea of the family taking the cottage away from him.

"We'll be the defendants, yes, but we will hire legal counsel to represent us, a barrister for the court work," Charles said.

"Won't that be expensive?" Alex asked.

"It will, most likely, if the case proceeds to court, which as Ryan has mentioned, we think may not happen. But you don't need to concern yourself with that. Normally, the costs would come out of the estate, not from you."

"All right then," Alex said. "If you think so, Lara?"

"I do, Alex," I said. "I think the Byrne family is just being mean, that's all. They couldn't possibly be as desperate as they look."

"Are you with us, then?" Ryan asked.

"I suppose I am," Alex said. " I really do like that little place."

"Excellent!" Charles exclaimed. "Now, Ryan, I think you have something to do out at Second Chance before we head back to Dublin?"

"I do, yes. It's one of the anomalies of this particular situation," he said, looking at me, "that while the family is suing the estate, and therefore us as executors, we continue to represent Mrs. O'Connor in some personal matters. Are you coming with me, Charles?"

Charles glanced at me. There was a slight question mark in his look.

"Perhaps not," he replied. "Perhaps . . . a drink?" he said looking at me. "Ms. McClintoch, Mr. Stewart?"

"Sure," I said. How nice, I thought.

Charles went to the bar for drinks for the three of us, and we chatted for a while, until we were interrupted by Malachy. "There you are!" he exclaimed, looking at Alex. "We've been looking all over for you. Don't you remember we're to get together at Tommy Fitzgerald's pub?"

"My goodness!" Alex exclaimed. "I had no idea it was this late. Will you excuse me, Lara? Charles?"

"Of course," we said in unison.

"I'll see he gets home," Malachy said. "Don't worry."

Charles smiled at me. "Could we have something to eat together, do you think? It's a long drive back to Dublin. There's a very good fish restaurant right down the street. I always try to have some seafood when I'm here. It's so fresh. What do you think?"

I thought it was a very good idea, and I said so, and a few minutes later we were sitting at a table in the window, as a waiter brought a blackboard over with the day's catch listed.

"Champagne, I think," Charles said. "To start. A little celebration of Mr. Stewart's decision."

Charles McCafferty was the kind of man I and my women friends tend to make fun of, with old world manners, rushing ahead to open doors, and choosing our food for us, as if we couldn't do it for ourselves. For some reason, though, I found it all rather relaxing, not having to think too much about anything, and just enjoying the very fine food and wine that he picked. Ryan might have been the gourmand of the two, but Charles was no slouch in knowing what was good to eat around the place. He also gave me his undivided attention, something I found very flattering. I'll flay myself tomorrow, I told myself, to make up for this serious lapse in feminist ideology, but tonight, I think I'll just sit back and enjoy it. I reminded him about the shop, though, lest he think I was merely one of those ladies who lunch.

"I do recall that," he said. "I enjoyed showing you through our offices immensely. Do you specialize in any particular period?"

I told him all about the place, my favorite subject, after all. It was fun to talk about it. It reminded me of my early conversations with Clive, when we were still dating, before we married and everything turned sour. It was pleasant to share an interest with someone, to be able to discuss everything in such detail with someone who was as enthusiastic about the subject as I was. I still felt a little confused about him, though. I couldn't tell whether he was really interested in me or not. Nor could I decide if he was my kind of guy or not. We'd flirt a little, then back off, both of us, I suppose, a little ambivalent on the idea of a new romance. I had such a bad track record where men were concerned, that the idea of starting a new relationship with someone, particularly someone so far from home, was daunting to say the least. I wondered if he felt the same.

I did find him attractive, though, no doubt about it. I found myself wishing I'd had an arrangement of some kind with Jennifer, of the college dorm variety, where a ribbon tied to the door handle meant Do Not Enter. However, if we had that arrangement, I suppose it would have to cut both ways, and I wasn't about to condone an intimate relationship between Jennifer and Paddy.

At some point in the conversation, I had the feeling I was being watched, not that this was unusual on this particular occasion. Charles had a commanding presence and was rather better dressed than anyone else in the place. And the bottle of champagne chilling in the ice bucket had drawn more than a casual glance. This was different somehow. I looked about me, and there, by the bar, was Rob. He had the strangest expression on his face, part nonchalance, part . . . what? Jealousy? It couldn't be! I looked again. Maybe, I thought. Well, good. I smiled at Rob and then leaned forward toward Charles, who reached across and grasped my fingers. I locked my hand with his. Rob turned back to the bar and ordered another drink. Where was Maeve, I wondered.

No matter how the evening might have ended had we been alone, that particular option didn't present itself. Just as we were finishing our coffee, Ryan appeared. "Ah, there you are," he said. "Thought I might find you here. What did you have? Sea bass? Sorry I missed it. I had some awful Irish stew kind of thing out at Second Chance. Margaret made it. I hope she finds a cook soon. Dinner there is not what it once was.

And that Deirdre! Kept dropping everything and clattered about. It's a relief she left us, Charles. She'd be dumping tea in our clients' laps more often than not."

"Why did she leave you?" I asked. "The way she was going on about Second Chance the day she left, I thought she'd never come back."

"God knows," Ryan replies. "I certainly don't. But she did us a favor."

"I think she didn't like Dublin," Charles replied.

"What's not to like?" Ryan said. "Speaking of which, what do you say? Is it time to head back there, Charles?"

"Regrettably, yes," Charles said, kissing my hand. I looked up to see Rob staring at me again. "Perhaps some other time, though?"

"That would be lovely," I said. "And thank you for helping Alex, and for a very pleasant evening." The two men went outside to a waiting Mercedes and soon pulled away, Ryan at the wheel. Both waved and smiled at me as they left. When I looked around again, Rob was gone.

The mention of Deirdre reminded me that I was to see her the next day. Something very important, she'd said. It was a little irritating, I'd have to say. I'd planned another day of antique hunting to get some more stuff for the store. But I resolved I'd wait for her, nonetheless. Maybe she really would have something interesting to say.

Sometime after midnight, the phone in our room rang. It was Charles, back in Dublin. "I just called to say good night," he said in that lovely Irish lilt of his. "It's late, I know, but I wanted to hear your voice again. I had a wonderful evening, although it was far too short."

"I did as well," I replied. Despite the fact that I'd

told myself he wasn't my type at all, I found I was pleased that he'd called.

"We'll see each other again. That's one of the benefits of being sued by the Byrne family," he chuckled.

"Till then," I said, hanging up.

"Who was that?" Jennifer said drowsily.

"Charles McCafferty," I replied. "Go back to sleep."

"Dad said you were having dinner with one of those lawyers," she said. "I think he's jealous."

"I'd think he'd be too busy with Maeve to be jealous of me," I said tartly.

"I like you better than Maeve," she said.

"I didn't know this was a contest," I said. "Now go back to sleep!"

The next day, Deirdre didn't show up. After waiting for a couple of hours, I called Second Chance.

"Is Deirdre there?" I asked. It was Sean, I thought, who answered the telephone.

"Who's this?" he asked suspiciously.

"It doesn't matter who this is," I replied. The man irritated me no end. "It's Deirdre I wish to speak to."

"It's that Canadian woman, isn't it?" he demanded. "The friend of that fellow who's taken Rose Cottage from us."

"He's not taking it from you. Your father-in-law left it to him," I said. "Now is Deirdre there or isn't she?"

"No, she's not," he replied.

"Do you know where she is? She was supposed to meet me," I went on. I thought I probably shouldn't have said that. It would set him off and maybe get her in trouble.

"It's her day off. She can do whatever she pleases. I have no idea where she is. Now don't call this place again!" he said, slamming the phone down.

I waited another hour or two, then headed out to an

auction. Irritating woman, I thought. Irritating family, too. I wondered what Deirdre might have to tell me that was so important. The father of Breeta's child, perhaps? Interesting, no doubt, but did it matter? And if not that, what?

Chapter Thirteen

A GOD THAT FASHIONS HEROES FOR A LORD

NUADA, *now there's a man, both a man and a god. There's the ting with the Tuatha dé Danaan, you know. They were gods in some ways, but they had the struggles of the rest of us, and they could die, too. All of them died in the end, and later all their magic too, when St. Padraig came, cursing the old gods. The three goddesses in one, Banba, Fotla, Eriu, they died, and their kings, too.*

But Nuada, as I'm saying, was a very fine god. He was king of the Tuatha dé and fought in both battles of Mag Tuired, aided by his sword from whom no one could escape once it was drawn, a magic sword from the city of Findias, one of the four great gifts of the gods. In the first battle, he defeated the Fir Bolg, banishing them west to Connacht and the Aran Islands. But in that battle, Nuada lost his hand, and because any king of the Tuatha dé had to be perfect, he could no longer be king. Diancecht the healer made him a silver hand that worked as well as his own, but still it wouldn't do for him to be king.

And so Nuada had to watch as the new king Bres, called the beautiful, destroyed the kingdom. Because while Bres might be beautiful to look at, he was part Fomorian, son of the Fomorian king Elatha and Eri of the Tuatha dé, and he was not beautiful on the inside, if you catch my meaning. He was miserly with his people and demanded they pay tribute to him and to the Fomorians, to the point that even the great Dagda became a builder of raths, and Oghma was reduced to carrying fuel for the oppressors.

And Nuada watched all this. A bitter time it must have been for him, with the gods in terrible servitude. But then his hand was restored, through the spells of Miach, Diancecht's son, who some say obtained Nuada's own mutilated hand, others say took a swineherd's arm, and reattached it to Nuada's arm. Skin grew, the joints and muscles joined again. And once more, Nuada could be king.

And so he held a royal banquet, and who should come to the door but Lugh Lamfada, Lugh of the Long Arm, who persuaded Nuada to lead his people in battle once again, this time against the worst of foes, the evil Fomorians. Nuada turned his kingship over to Lugh, and this time the Tuatha dé were victorious, the victory of light and life over darkness, and the Morrigan, the crow, proclaimed the victory so that it could be heard throughout the country.

I liked Nuada the best—he seems so human, despite the magic, the weight of the oppression of his people on his shoulders, while he watched, helplessly, because he was maimed and couldn't be king. He died at the hands of Balor the Fomorian at the second great battle of Mag Tuired. I was with him, you know. I watched the magic die.

*Yes, I liked Nuada best. Yer man, Eamon Byrne, he
did too.*

Deirdre's body washed up on the shore, not far from
Second Chance. She never made it back to The Three
Sisters Inn for her appointment with me, or if she did,
no one there saw her. Whatever she'd wanted to tell
me had gone with her to her grave.

Fortunately, I was not the one to find the body. That
sad task fell to Paddy Gilhooly, who was out in his
boat early that morning, and saw something suspicious
nearer to shore.

"Can't blame Conail O'Connor for this one," Rob
sighed, "seeing as how we have him under lock and
key. I suppose we'll have to let him go. We can't hold
him forever for having battered a garda's nose. Not that
we wouldn't like to, but it can't be done."

"And the rest of the family?"

"Eithne, Sean, and Margaret have, as usual, provided
each other with an alibi. All at home all night together.
Way too cozy, if you ask me. Fionuala is being coy,
but I think we'll find she was with some guy, married,
no doubt, who will eventually come in here looking
furtive and asking us to promise we won't tell his wife.
Now, Gilhooly, I haven't yet talked to. He may have
found the body, but that doesn't automatically mean
he's innocent, although I understand he's pretty upset
by what happened. He's still hugging the porcelain
bowl after the shock of finding her, I gather, according
to Garda Minogue. We'll have to see what he has to
say for himself a little later.

"I'm supposed to check on Alex, by the way, since
he's on the list of people who got something out of
the Will. I doubt he'll have anyone to confirm his
whereabouts, seeing he's staying up there all alone.

And no," he said looking at my startled face, "I do not think Alex did it. I'm taking this note of Deirdre's, you understand. Any idea what she might have wanted to tell you?"

I shook my head.

"When did she die?" I asked.

"Sometime in the night, or very early morning. Several people saw her at dinnertime, including one of those lawyer types. Those two drove back together to Dublin—I've talked to them." I was tempted to tell him that Charles had called me at midnight from Dublin, to confirm his whereabouts, but I decided that was unnecessary, and I was just being uncharitable.

"The family said she went to bed at the usual time," Rob went on, "but sometime in the night she must have crept out, to what? See someone, I guess. Who, I have no idea.

"God, she had a rough life," he said, riffling papers in the file. "Looks to me like years of really poor working conditions. Second Chance, for all its faults, must have seemed like paradise. No wonder she came back. She worked for several years in a dry cleaners before she went there," he said, pulling out a piece of paper. "In the back, too, with all those chemicals. Perhaps that's why she looked so morose. Well, if you think of anything I should know, call me."

I walked back to the Inn from the garda station, thinking about Deirdre. Despite the morbid events of the last few hours, the town looked rather gay, with posters and banners strung everywhere proclaiming the music festival, set to begin in less than a week. Everyone in town was talking about it and obviously looking forward to it. I found it impossible to get into the spirit, however. I could not shake an overwhelming feeling of helplessness in the face of terrible events. I just couldn't make any sense of what had happened: another staff person killed, another individual, who hadn't even been given one of the clues, had met a horrible death.

I kept thinking about my conversation with Moira, when she'd said that it would be either money or passion that had led to it all. If that were the case, there seemed to be only two possibilities for me to explore: the treasure or Eamon Byrne's past. I hadn't found the treasure nor knew yet what it was. There was also a lot about Eamon Byrne I didn't know. But I did know he was always looking for the four great gifts of the gods. I headed down to the pier. Denny sat there talking away to a post.

"Denny," I said softly, then more loudly. "Denny!"

He looked slightly baffled for a moment. "Lara," he said finally. "It's you."

"I brought you a bottle of whiskey, Denny," I said. "And I need to hear some of your stories."

"Which one would you like?" he asked, looking pleased.

"All of them, Denny," I said. "I want to hear all Eamon Byrne's favorite stories, the ones about the gods and the great battles, the arrival of Amairgen on Ireland's shores. And I want to hear about the lost child again, the story of the Kerryman and the child stolen by the fairies," I added on impulse. "The one that was Eamon Byrne's favorite. Start anywhere you like."

And he did. Eamon Byrne's favorite stories, as I suspected, were the legends about the four great gifts of the gods. So he told me about the Dagda's cauldron, how it was never empty, no matter how much you ate, or how many came to dinner. He told me about Lia Fail, the Stone of Destiny, the one that roared when the true king of Ireland touched it, and which was now

either lost or in Edinburgh; he told me about Lugh
Lamfada, Lugh Long Arm, holder of the magic spear
no battle was ever won against, and how he killed his
grandfather, the Fomorian, Balor of the Evil Eye, after
entering the royal court and persuading the king to
throw off the yoke of oppression of the Fomorians.
And lastly he told me about his own favorite hero, and
Eamon's too, Nuada Silver Hand, Nuada Argat-lam,
holder of the fourth gift of the gods, a magic sword,
and king of the Tuatha dé Danaan, those godlike people
who, after the arrival of the Celts, were banished to the
sidhe, the fairy mounds. And for good measure, he told
me the story of the arrival of Amairgen and the Sons
of Mil, the coming of the Celts to Ireland.

And then he told me about the lost child, the child
stolen by the fairies, the child whose father had made
a pact with the devil to get, only to lose him. It had a
happy ending, what with the man finding the son just
before his death and their being reconciled, which for
some reason didn't ring true. It sounded like one of
those stories that started out true, but over time got all
mixed up as time went by and it got repeated. But it
was Eamon Byrne's favorite. It had brought a tear to
his eye, and he was not a man to cry lightly—I could
only assume—and as such it bore some looking in to.
It confirmed for me that Eamon Byrne had a past that
was not an open book. He'd moved here from Galway
with Margaret, after spending a miserable time at sea,
if Alex's story was anything to go by. Whatever had
happened to make him up and run away like that, from
the woman who later became his wife? I decided I
needed to know much more about Eamon Byrne's past.
But who would tell me? Certainly not Breeta. She was
still assiduously avoiding me. And maybe she didn't

know. Maybe none of them did. Perhaps it was the kind of thing you never told your family.

I took out the list of the clues and looked at it again.

AMAIRGEN'S SONG	OGHAM CLUES
I am the sea-swell (Alex)	May's sunrise by Tailte's Hill is seen
A furious wave (Michael)	A curse be on these stones
The roar of the sea	Leinster's Hag to Eriu's Seat
A stag of seven slaughters (Eithne/Sean)	Clue still missing
A hawk above the cliff	Aine's Mount to Macha's Stronghold
A ray of the sun (Conail/Fionula)	Grianan Ailech to Granard down the line of the noonday sun
Beauty of a plant (Breeta?)	Raise a cup to the stone
A boar enraged	Almu's white to Maeve's red
Salmon in a pool (Paddy)	Axis Mundi
Lake in a plain	Due east, Partholan turned to die
A flame of valor	All seen and seeing eye of fire
Piercing spear (Margaret?)	Umbilicus Hiberniae, the sacred center
God who fashions heroes	Clue still missing

Did it matter, I wondered, who had had which clue? I'd thought so, at first. Whoever owned the clue found in dead Michael's hand would be the number one suspect in his death. It was probably either Margaret's or Breeta's, although I was beginning to wonder whether, despite their general unpleasantness, I'd put either down for it.

Money and passion, I thought. I was willing to bet it was more often money than love at the root of these kinds of situations. That brought me right back to the treasure, and so I would start with the where and what of that. Maybe the who would follow.

"I've looked up all the references," Alex said. "I've checked the names and wherever I could, I associated them with a place. Actually, it was relatively easy to do."

"Okay, well, here's the map of Ireland," I said, unfolding it and spreading it out on the floor of Rose Cottage. "I say we ignore 'Song of Amairgen' from now on and forget who had which clue. Let's concentrate on the second column of clues, which if my guess is right, should lead us to the treasure. Let's go! Take them one at a time, from the top. May's sunrise by Tailtiu's Hill is seen."

"Tailtiu was an ancient goddess, sometimes referred to as goddess of the corn. Her hill is said to have been a royal residence in the dim past, and it's here," Alex said pointing to a spot on the map on the east side of Ireland, near Drogheda. "I don't understand the sunrise reference, however, although May could refer to the ancient feast of Beltaine on May 1. There were three other festivals: Imbolc on February 1; Lughnasa, August 1; and Samhain on November 1, although there are no other references to them that I can see."

"Never mind. Let's just keeping going. Found it, Jennifer? Yes? Okay, circle it. Next?"

"Next is a curse be on these stones. Haven't a clue on that one, but the one after that is Leinster's Hag to Eriu's Seat. There's a mountain in Leinster province called Sliab na Caillighe, or Mountain of the Hag. That's one. Eriu, we all know, is one part of the triple goddess of Ireland. Her seat, if that is what we want to call it, is said to be right here in the Dingle peninsula, in the Slieve Mish Mountains. Jennifer, Sliab or Slieve na Caillighe is not far from Tara and the Hill of Tailte."

"Got them!" she exclaimed. "Both circled. The mountains in the Dingle too."

"Right. Next?"

"I'll skip the ones I don't know and just give you the ones I do," Alex said. "I mean, frankly, I have no idea where the Umbilicus Hiberniae might be. Hibernia is an old name for Ireland, and umbilicus, well, I have this thought that it might be like the Greek concept of omphalmos, the navel of Greek civilization at Delphi. I don't know what the Irish equivalent could be. However, Aine's Mount to Macha's Stronghold I can locate: both ancient goddesses. The old word for Mount is *cnoc*, now spelled *Knock*. There's a place called Knockainy in Munster, which was a sacred center in that province a long time ago, sacred to the goddess Aine, so Knockainy, or Cnoc Aine, Aine's Mount. Macha was also a goddess, a horse goddess, apparently. Macha's Stronghold would surely be Emain Macha, now called Navan Fort, in Ulster. Close to Armagh, Jennifer."

"Got them both," she said after a few minutes.

"Grianan Ailech to Granard, down the line of the noonday sun. Grianan Ailech is the supposed home of the Dagda, one of the gods of the Tuatha dé Danaan. I think it's way to the north, Jennifer."

She checked the map index. "Grianan Ailech, yes, right at the top. Granard," she paused, "almost directly south, 'round about the middle of Ireland. Okay, marked them both."

"Almu's white to Maeve's Red. You were right about Maeve, Lara. Queen and goddess of Connacht. Very powerful woman. Her capital was at Rathcroghan. Almu was another goddess, referred to as 'the White.' Her home was on Knockaulin, that word *knock* or *cnoc* again, now the Hill of Allen, then the seat of the Kings of Leinster."

We waited until Jennifer had found them and marked their place.

"Due east, Partholan turned to die," I said. "I remember Partholan from Denny's story of the Battle of Mag Tuired. He was one of the early invaders of Ireland, wasn't he? He and his people perished mysteriously, if I recall. Plague or something."

"That's right. The Book of Invasions of Ireland tells of several different peoples who came to Ireland in the dim past. Partholan was one of the first and is said to come from the west, from out in the Atlantic somewhere, by some accounts. He and his followers did battle with the Fomorians, those primitive creatures who were later defeated by the Tuatha dé Danaan. Partholan is supposed to have driven these Fomorians north into the sea. But then they were afflicted by a plague of some kind. The place Partholan and his people are supposed to have gone to die is the Plain of Elta Edar, supposedly the first area to be settled in Ireland. It is just about due east of the Seat of the High Kings at Tara, north of where Dublin is today."

"I've got Tara," Jennifer said. "I'll mark the area east of that and north of Dublin."

"That's it," Alex said. "The others, I either can't figure out, or they refer to the object itself rather than the location, or something. One's like 'all seen and seeing fire eye,' for example. I could find no reference to such a thing in the books I've read. The same for the cursed stones and the cup lifted to the stone."

The three of us looked at the map. We had Jennifer's little circles all over the place, north, south, east and west.

"Do you think we have to go to all these places?" Jennifer wailed. "It would take us months. They're all over the country. Northern Ireland, even!"

"There must be something else here," I said at last. "First we are given clues that are lines from a poem. Then, we find these clues lead to other clues, all in ogham. At least some of these clues lead to other locations, but they're all over the map, literally. The object can't be in all these places, surely. We've circled ten spots, for heaven's sake. We can't be doing this right. I mean, is Jennifer right? Does this mean we have to travel all over the country looking for yet another set of clues? I don't believe it can be this complicated. Surely, Eamon wanted his family to find the treasure, not spend their lives in idle search."

"Maybe it's join the dots," Jennifer said. "But how?" She took a pencil and joined them. All we got was a somewhat smaller area of Ireland. "We could crisscross the dots in some way, but I don't see any pattern, do you?"

"No," Alex and I agreed. I had a feeling we could look at this map for a long time before a pattern would emerge. I studied the list of clues one more time. If I'd learned anything while I was here, it was that the Irish

possessed a particularly rich mythology, with more stories, almost, than anyone could imagine. Eamon Byrne
had picked only a few of them, but the ones he'd chosen were supposed to lead to a treasure.

"You know," I said, after a minute. "A lot of these
are something to something else, from one ancient sacred site to another, if you get what I mean. What if
we joined up these from-to's and see what we get. For
example, the Grianan Ailech to Granard clue also says
down the line of the noonday sun. Wouldn't that give
us a north/south axis?"

"I believe it would," Alex said. "And the clue about
Tailte's Hill talks about a May sunrise. When I think
about it, in May, the sun would rise right about here,"
he said pointing slightly north-east.

"However would you know that, Uncle Alex?" Jennifer interrupted.

"Years at sea, my dear. Now, we could join the Hill
of Tailte and the sun line."

"Not just join them, draw a line right through and
across the map. And do the same with Partholan's
plain. The clue says due east, Partholan turned to die.
You said the plain where he died is east of Tara. Draw
a line right through those two and then on across the
map. That should give us an east/west axis," I said.

"Some of the others link the ancient political or sacred centers of the four provinces of Ireland. If wc join
these circles, like Hill of Allen in Leinster to the capital
of Connacht at Rathcroghan, and Knockainy in Munster to Emain Macha, Navan Fort, that is, we would
get a big 'X' across the country," Alex said.

"And across the north/south and east/west axes," I
said.

"Maybe they all intersect," Jennifer said, as she

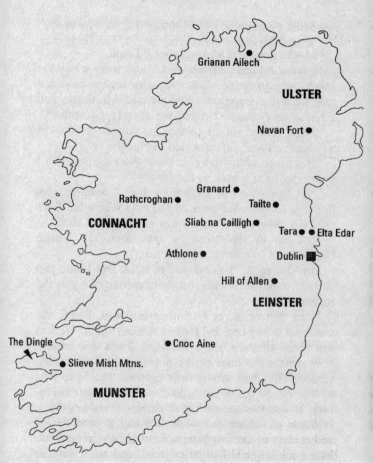

grabbed a piece of paper to give herself a straight edge to trace along.

They didn't intersect, not exactly anyway, but the lines did cross the north/south axis at approximately the same area, more less in the center of the country. We all peered at the map.

"Maybe I need reading glasses," I said.

"I have bifocals," Alex said, "and there's nothing much there to speak of. A couple of reasonable-sized towns nearby: Longford, Athlone, and Mullingar, and a few country roads. Do you see anything, Jennifer?"

"Nope. There are no ancient monument symbols in this area, either," Jennifer said dubiously.

"Not much of anything, in fact," Alex agreed. "So I guess maybe it's back to the library."

"But there must be something there," Jennifer said, pointing to the small area on the map where the lines crossed. "Maybe we should just go there and look."

"It's not all that small an area, Jennifer," I said. "We'd have to narrow it down first."

She shrugged. "I guess you're right. But I hate just sitting around here while maybe someone else gets the treasure."

Later that night, as I climbed into bed, I took the clues out of my bag and looked at them again. We had just about all there were, I decided. I was also reasonably certain the lines of the poem could now be discarded. They had served their purpose, that is to lead to the second set of clues, and were no longer necessary. It was this second set of clues, the ogham clues, that told us where and what. We had a general idea where the treasure might be hidden, although there was still a lot of ground to be covered, and we'd have to narrow it down. The question remained: what was it? What were we looking for?

I stared long and hard at it. I'm a firm believer in the subconscious, and its ability to analyze information and come to a conclusion. Whenever I have a problem I cannot seem to solve, or a decision that seems too difficult to make—open a shop or take a job, get married or not, leave Clive or stay and tough it out—these choices, I leave to my subconscious. This involves thinking over the pros and cons before going to sleep, and telling myself to make a decision. Sometimes I dream about it, sometimes I don't. I almost always awake with the decision made. I'm not going to say that the decisions are always the right ones, only that they are right for me at the time.

So when I awoke the next morning, I was pretty sure I knew what we were looking for, despite the missing clues, even if I hadn't figured out exactly where. The clues were in ogham, after all.

Chapter Fourteen

HE WHO CLEARS THE MOUNTAIN PATHS

EITHNE Byrne was born forty-five, forty-five and Irish. I have a theory, one not supported by so much as a particle of scientific evidence, that some people come into the world with a particular age stamped all over them. These are the people who seem so much older than the rest of us when we're young, but seen again after many years, a high school reunion for instance, look exactly the way they did in school. Eithne Byrne was one of these. Not that there's anything wrong with forty-five—I'm perilously close to it myself—but I realized when I got a chance to talk to her one on one, she was actually much younger, almost ten years in fact, than I'd initially thought that first time I'd seen her at Second Chance, and later when she was playing acolyte to her mother over tea.

She was also born Irish, with green eyes, slightly reddish hair, frizzed by the constant moisture, glowing skin, and a certain charming loquaciousness brought out by a few sips of sherry. She even dressed Irish, if there is such a thing, in a blouse with a lace collar, a short boxy wool jacket in dark green, and a long, pleated green skirt to match.

Her sister Fionuala, on the other hand, was the party girl, talkative, charming, and a flirt. She wore bright colors, in this case, a red suit, the jacket done up, but with no blouse under it, revealing a fair amount of lightly freckled skin and cleavage, the short tight skirt constantly riding up to show off more than a little leg.

I met both of them over a drink in the bar at the Inn. It was at their invitation, a fact that took me somewhat by surprise. It was the first time I'd seen them alone, that is, outside their family home, without their mother hovering nearby. Despite my inclination to think ill of them, I had to admit I saw nothing to fault. On this occasion, they both seemed to me very nice people, intelligent if a little naive, in Eithne's case, rather more good-hearted than I expected in Fionuala's. I could see that the two of them and Breeta, in addition to being closer in age than I'd thought, were more alike in personality as well.

"We've decided to open a shop," Fionuala said, the bolder of the two. "And we heard that you own one, an antiques shop, I believe, in Canada. We thought, we were hoping, you might give us some advice."

"I'd be delighted to. What kind of shop were you thinking of?"

"Antiques, like you," Eithne said. "There are lots of tourists in the Dingle every summer. And there are all of Da's things, the ones that didn't go to Trinity College, that is, maps and prints and books. Is it difficult to open a shop?"

"A little," I said. "Well, no, it's not difficult to open one. It's staying open that requires some luck, energy, and . . ." I hesitated, thinking about the rumors in town about their fiscal state. "Cash, frankly."

"Does it cost a lot?" Eithne asked.

"A fair amount. You're fortunate to have some items to begin with, that you don't have to purchase, I mean. But it takes a lot of merchandise to open a shop, more than you'd think. I expect you'd have to build up some inventory even with your father's things."

"How much does it cost?" Fionuala said. Talking about money didn't seem to bother her at all.

"That depends," I said, "on what you've got to start with and what you want to do."

"Well, there's the furniture in the house," Fionuala said. "It's quite good, I believe. And we won't need all of it. We're moving."

"We don't need all that room," Eithne added, with more than a touch of steel in her voice. I wondered just how bad the situation at Second Chance was.

"And how exactly do you go about setting up shop?" she went on as the waiter, at a sign from me, set second rounds in front of us.

It was becoming clear to me that working for a living had never been on either Eithne or Fionuala Byrne's life plan, but I told them what I had done anyway, about how I'd started out as a wholesaler to other stores, importing objects I'd picked up in my travels and warehousing them in the north end of Toronto, and how finally, with some money in the bank, I'd launched my business. I didn't tell them how I'd married my first employee and had been forced to sell the store when we divorced. They might have found that part of the story way too discouraging, particularly with husbands like Sean and Conail.

"But why don't you try working in someone else's antiques shop for a while?" I concluded. "You could learn about keeping the books, ordering supplies, advertising, and promotion and so on. Or why," I said, suddenly having a brainwave, "why don't you go and work in one of your father's businesses, the import/export one, for example? You could arrange that, couldn't you?"

Eithne bit her lip, and looked over at Fionuala. "Good advice, I'm sure. I'm not certain, though, how much longer there'll be a Byrne Enterprises. Mr. McCafferty has been helping my mother with all the family affairs, since my father died, and I believe we may have to close down the company. It's not doing very well. That's why I'm thinking that I'll have to do something, and I don't really know what else to do. I learned quite a bit about antiquities from Da, so I thought . . ." Her voice trailed off.

"But I thought your father was very successful," I said. "How could this be?"

"I don't know," she replied. "I haven't had anything to do with the business. Perhaps I should have, but Sean, my husband, works there, and he doesn't like the idea of a working wife. Thinks it's beneath him. He blames Conail, my brother-in-law. He says Conail hasn't been managing the peat business at all well, and it was always the part of the business that helped fund the newer and riskier ventures, the cash cow, I think Sean calls it."

"And Conail says it's Sean who's making a mess of it," Fionuala interjected. "Not that I care what he thinks anymore."

"It's a terrible thing to say, I know, sounding glad your sister's marriage is on the rocks," Eithne said, looking over at Fionuala. "But perhaps . . ." She couldn't finish these painful sentences, it seemed. She was like her mother in that.

"What she's trying to say is that now that Conail is gone, maybe we can be friends again," Fionuala said.

"We were inseparable once, the three of us, Breeta, Eithne, and I. Just like the triple goddess we were named after, our nicknames that is, Banba, Fotla, and Eriu. Breeta never did like being named after a pig goddess, though," she laughed.

"Banba wasn't just a pig goddess," Eithne protested. "She was the goddess who controlled the line between the underworld and the sky. Maybe we could go and see Breeta together," she said sadly, looking over at Fionuala. "Maybe if she could see the two of us, it would help get us all back together again. She's not speaking to us," she added. Me neither, I thought.

"Of course we'll go," Fionuala said. "She'll come around. We're family."

"I think I'd like to have an antiques shop," Eithne said suddenly, as if now she'd started talking, she wasn't able to stop. "I'm not just looking into this because of the money, and the business problems. It's something I often thought of doing, but there hasn't seemed to be an opportunity. Sean would never approve. Now perhaps I can."

I could hardly fault her for wanting to go into the antiques business, so for the next half hour or so, I told them exactly what they would need to do to get started. Eithne, the organized one, got a notepad out of her purse, and wrote everything down, asking some rather intelligent questions as we went along.

"Thank you," she said at last. "You've been just grand. Especially since our family hasn't been very nice to you and to your friend, Mr. Stewart. We hope he enjoys Rose Cottage, we really do. My father told us about Mr. Stewart many times, how he pulled him from the water when Da fell in and might have drowned." Fell in, was it? I thought. That's not the way I heard it, but a quite understandable editorial change, a father's tale for his daughters, when I thought about it. And it sounded as if the lawsuit was off.

"You didn't see any of us at our best, you know," Fionuala said. "Our Da, he wasn't really the way you saw him, on the video, I mean. The cancer, it had spread from his lung to his brain. He was actually a lot of fun. And Mother and my sister and I, well, Mr. McCafferty had just told us about the financial problems of the estate. We couldn't believe it. Everything seemed to be fine when my father was alive. We were in shock, I think, with Da's death and this news. I suppose we resented the idea of anybody else getting anything from the estate.

"And Sean. He looks like a terrible snob, I know, but he's quite good-hearted, under it all. It's just that the more worried he gets, the more standoffish he gets too. I know he seems cold and heartless to an outsider, but that's only because he's been terribly worried about Byrne Enterprises and what will happen to all of us, wouldn't you agree, Eithne?" Eithne apparently did.

"Do you mind if I ask you a question or two? Well, three, actually," I asked them. "Make that four." I was on a roll now, and they didn't seem to mind.

"Ask away." Eithne hiccoughed. She was on drink number three. "Lovely sherry." She giggled.

"Is the family looking for the treasure or not?"

"No," Eithne said. "Mother wouldn't stand for it. She wants to remember my father as he was, not the man on that videotape. I still do what my mother tells me," she added ruefully. "Sean isn't either, I think I can say with some assurance. He doesn't believe there really is a treasure. He thinks my father was too far gone, mentally that is, when he made the videotape, that the clues were just a mean joke from someone who didn't know what they were doing anymore."

"Neither am I," Fionuala added. "Breeta, I can't speak for, although I don't think she is. She couldn't anyway, come to think about it. Mother took Bree's clue out of the safe in Da's office and tore it up, along with her own. Mother is a very determined woman," Fionuala added.

"Are you telling me there was no robbery?" I asked.

"Of course there wasn't," Fionuala replied. "Mother went off on the most awful tear. She tore the pages out of Da's diary and burned them, along with two of his maps. She was afraid there'd be something in the diary she wouldn't want to know, and the maps might have something on them that would encourage the rest of us to go after the treasure. We didn't call the police, or anything, so it wasn't so terrible a thing to do, was it?"

"No," I replied. As long as you didn't burn one of those rare old maps, I thought. Although, come to think of it, the diary burning could be seen in another light. Perhaps Margaret really was trying to protect herself from painful things her dying husband might have written, or there were things she wouldn't want others, Garda Minogue and Rob, for example, to read.

"Anyway," Fionuala went on, "The only one I can think of who might be still looking is Conail. He's really angry at Sean, and now with this split with me, he might be doing it to spite the family. He told me, yelled at me actually, when I told him to get out, that he'd find the treasure first."

"Someone trashed our room at the Inn," I said. It was a statement, not a question, but I was still hoping for an explanation. "And tried to swamp us in a boat."

The sisters exchanged meaningful glances. "That might be Conail," Fionuala sighed. "Just his style, I'm afraid. Never one to tread lightly in any respect. It was what I liked about him once. Sorry to hear that, though. And he doesn't have a boat, you know."

"But he does know how to handle a boat," Eithne added. "Do you have another question?"

"How about Padraig Gilhooly?"

"Paddy, looking for the treasure? I don't know," Eithne said, misunderstanding my question. "Oh, you mean, how does he fit in the family? Or do we think he'd trash your room and swamp you in a boat?"

I nodded. "All of the above. And where he came from, too."

"I can't imagine he'd do anything like trash your room and swamp you out on the water. He's actually quite nice, despite his rather sullen looks. I'm not sure where he came from, though, do you, Nuala?" Fionuala shook her head.

"Da just kind of adopted Paddy. He did that sort of thing. He liked giving people a chance. He helped him buy his boat and set him up in the charter business. Paddy almost lived at Second Chance for a while. But then he imposed on our hospitality," Eithne giggled. "That's the way Mother put it. He started going out with Breeta, more than going out, if you see what I mean, right in the house, too." She blushed.

Fionuala laughed. "Scandalous!" she said.

"Mother was furious, said Paddy wasn't good enough for Breeta, and threw him out of the house. That made Breeta really angry. She didn't blame Mother for some reason. We're all a little afraid of her. She blamed Da and his money, which was silly, but Breeta saw it to be the root of the problem with Paddy, Mother thinking we were too good for him. They had a fight. I've never seen Da so angry. I think it was in a way because Breeta was his favorite, and she really adored Da. I think it works that way sometimes, the more you love each other, the worse the fight. Anyway, Breeta left. I heard she's not going with Paddy anymore, so it was hardly worth it," she said.

"That's what your father meant then about Paddy being considered a member of the family. He wouldn't have minded if Breeta had married him?"

"Yes, I think so," Eithne said. "That's all he meant. He never said anything about our boyfriends. I don't think he liked either Sean or Conail very much, but he didn't object to our marrying them."

"Your father went on about how the family was always squabbling. How he wanted the treasure hunt to bring you all together. Is this a squabbling family?"

"Not always, in fact, not until recently, do you think, Nuala? We were actually quite close, particularly the three of us sisters. But I suppose near the end of his life it was. The cancer brought out the worst in Da, accentuated his least positive features, in a way. He was difficult to deal with. Sean and Conail started fighting over what was happening to the business, each blaming the other. Breeta, of course, walked out. Paddy blamed the family for what happened with him and Breeta. Nuala and I were always very close, but with our husbands fighting and everything, it was hard. Also, I'm a little like my mother, I'm afraid, and so when things get a little rough, I withdraw, get a little snappy, frankly. It hasn't been too great, lately.

"Was that all the questions?" she said hesitantly.

"Not quite," I replied. "Tell me about Deirdre."

"I don't know what to say. It's terrible, isn't it? She was such a little mouse, and to have something like that happen to her—I can hardly think about it."

"Was she with you long?"

"Five years, I'd say, Nuala?"

"About that," Fionuala agreed. "She came after Kitty

had her stroke and had to retire. So, yes, about five years."

"She wasn't the greatest help when she first came," Eithne said. "It took a while for her to learn the ropes, so to speak. And she was always spilling stuff and breaking things, usually Mother's little glass ornaments or the good china. It drove Mother crazy." She giggled a little, and Fionuala joined in with a hearty laugh. "We shouldn't laugh, I know, but it was rather funny. I'll remember her that way, but with fondness. We got used to having her around, breaking china or not, and we were so grateful she came back to us. She felt like family. I told her, a couple of days before she died, that she wasn't to worry, that I'd look after her. I'm the eldest, and I know that I'm going to have to take charge of things: Mother's way too upset. And I will. I'll get this antiques business going somehow, and find us a smaller place to stay, and see about getting Breeta back with us again. She'll have the baby, of course. Do you think it's Michael's? Or Paddy's? It doesn't matter. We'll help her look after it. I would have looked after Deirdre too, and I wanted her to know that."

"Oh, Eithne, aren't you the serious one?" Fionuala sighed. "She's always been like this," she added, turning to me, "even when we were little. I'm taking you to the music festival, Eithne, since that dry stick of a husband of yours probably won't. Maybe Mother will come too. We'll hear some music, have a few drinks, maybe even dance a little and find a new man or two for Mother and me. You too, if you want one."

Eithne laughed out loud. "Rich would be good," she said.

"Essential," Fionuala agreed. "I know what I have to do," she added, twirling a piece of hair around her finger and batting her eyelashes outrageously. The three of us laughed so hard, the tears were running down our cheeks.

But then suddenly, Eithne's tears became real ones. "What do you think happened to us, Nuala?" she sobbed. "We all got along well once, didn't we? I know Da was sick and wasn't himself, but what happened to the rest of us? Especially you and Banba and I: The three of us used to be inseparable."

"You think too much, Eithne," Fionuala said, putting her arm around her sister's shoulder. "Things happen in families, that's all. We will get through this, and you're not going to have to deal with this family business all alone. We're going to stick together in this mess, so don't you fret about it."

I had to admire their determination. The woman who had frowned when her mother frowned, nodded when her mother said anything, stood up when her mother did, had revealed herself to have some backbone in the face of three murders and what was beginning to sound like insolvency. And her sister had shown that no matter how shallow she might appear, she was essentially good-hearted and a no-nonsense kind of person, and she would do what she had to do as well.

"I'm sure you'll both be fine," I said. "And if you need any more information at all, please write or call me," I said, handing them each a business card. "I have e-mail, too."

They both smiled, Eithne wiping away her tears. They had lovely eyes, and friendly smiles. "Thank you. You may very well hear from us," Fionuala said.

It occurred to me with some surprise, as I watched the two of them walk arm in arm down the street, that I wouldn't mind if I did.

Chapter Fifteen

HE WHO DESCRIBES THE MOON'S
ADVANCE

"I want to know about the stolen child, the real one, I mean," I said to Malachy.

"That's just one of Denny's stories," he replied. "You shouldn't pay much heed to them. He's not quite right in the head, you know, although I am still proud to call him my friend. He thinks he was there, way back then, when all the battles were fought. The magic ones, between the Tuatha dé Danaan and the Fir Bolg and the Fomorians. As far back as that."

"Then I want to know all about the Byrne family," I said. "Where they came from, what they did before they got here, everything. There must be someone who would know."

"Kitty McCarthy," he said. "Although she's getting on a bit. She was with them when they came here, many years ago. The housekeeper and nanny for the children. Denny's sister."

"Where do I find her?"

"The pub," he replied.

"She lives in a pub?" I said.

"Not in a pub," he said, laughing. "Over a pub. Over the Boar's Arms and Brigid's place. The tearoom. Brigid's Kitty's stepdaughter, Denny's niece."

I made my way along the main street, and into the door that separated the bar and the tearoom, and then quickly up the stairs. I knocked on the door where I had first met Kitty McCarthy. Brigid answered.

"I'd like to talk to your mother," I said to her.

"Whatever for?" she asked, perplexed.

"About the Byrne family," I replied.

"She'll not want to be talking about that," Brigid replied.

"People are dying, Brigid."

"I've noticed," she said tartly. "People who worked there, too. So my mother won't be talking to you, or anybody else on that subject."

"Who is it, dear?" a quavering voice inquired.

"Nobody, Mother," she called back in to the room.

"It's me, Mrs. McCarthy, Lara. The person who was here for Eamon Byrne's clue." Brigid glared at me. "I want to talk to you about the Byrne family."

"Come in, then," Kitty replied. "I like to have visitors."

"Mother!" Brigid exclaimed. "We decided you wouldn't speak to anyone about the Byrne family. It's dangerous, remember."

"I'm practically dead already, in case you hadn't noticed, Brigid, so let the young lady in," Kitty said. She had a tone to be reckoned with. I expect she used it to good effect with the Byrne girls.

"Thank you," I said to Kitty, as she gestured to a seat on the sofa next to her chair. Brigid sat across from us, her face rigid with anxiety.

"I'm sorry," I said to Brigid, "but there are too many people dying. I feel that if I could just understand what is happening to this family, if the police knew, then maybe the killing would stop."

"What do you want to know?" Kitty asked, her hands trembling as she held the blanket around her, but her eyes still bright and intelligent.

"I want you to start at the beginning, when you first met the Byrne family, and I want to know why Deirdre thought the family cursed."

"All right," she said. "From the beginning. I was housekeeper to Eamon Byrne's father, Michael, known as Mick. Mick was a widower, his wife had died when the children were young, and he needed someone like me to look after his home."

"Was it around here?"

"Oh, no, farther north, near Galway. The children were almost grown up when I went there. Eamon was in his early twenties, and Rose, the daughter, was about eighteen."

"Rose Cottage!" I exclaimed. "I've always wondered why it would be called Rose Cottage when there aren't any roses around."

The old woman nodded. "Rose Cottage was named for her. Eamon doted on his little sister."

"Where is she now?"

"Dead. Long gone and buried," she said sadly, shaking her head.

"Go on," I said.

"There was very bad blood between Mick Byrne, and another man by the name of Mac Roth, Oengus Mac Roth, a landowner up farther north, by Sligo. Had been for years, generations even. We Irish can hold a grudge for a very long time. I'm not even sure what was at the basis of it. Sometimes, it doesn't matter what started it really. It just takes on a life of its own. Even those involved can't recall why it all began. Probably an argument over some sheep or something like that, way back many years, or generations, before. Perhaps it was over a dun cow."

She hesitated for a moment, and then laughed a little. "That was by way of a little joke. There's a very ancient tale in Ireland called the *Tain bo Culainge*, *The Cattle Raid of Cooley*. It tells the story of a huge war between the forces of Connacht, led by Queen Maeve and her king Ailill, and the forces of Ulster, with their hero Cuchulainn. It all started with a disagreement over a dun cow. But you understand what I mean, don't you? In any event, the two men were rivals, and their families were too, although as far as I know, they never had a chance to meet. At least not right away."

The old woman coughed a little, and her daughter brought her some tea. "Here, Mother," she said. "You mustn't talk too much." I thought she had tears in her eyes.

"I want to talk, dear," she said, waving her away. "I've been wanting to talk about this for years. I promised Eamon Byrne I never would, but I don't suppose it matters much anymore.

"Mick Byrne had big plans for his son and daughter. Eamon was already working with him in the family business—peat, I think it was at the time. Rose, he planned to marry to a widower in the area, a middle-aged man by the name of MacCallum, who had great landholdings near those of Mick Byrne."

"A strategic alliance, was it?" I asked.

"I suppose you could call it that," Kitty replied. "Between them, the two families would control much of the land in the area." She paused for a moment, taking a sip of tea before proceeding. "But Rose loved another, a young man she'd met at a dance. And his name was . . ." she started to choke a little.

"Mac Roth," I said taking the teacup from her and trying to steady her hand. "Don't tell me it was Mac Roth."

She nodded. "Owen Mac Roth. Son of her father's sworn enemy. She didn't tell anyone about it, except I think for me. She was so happy with her young man, and he was a looker, eyes so blue you could see the sea in them, a very lovely young man. And she was a beauty, too, let me tell you. But it wasn't to be.

"Eamon found out about Rose's lover, told his father, and Mick forbade her to see Owen ever again. But she did, and . . ." here the old woman paused and wiped a tear from her eye, "and with my help. She was so much in love, you see, and begged me to help her. I never could really say no to her, nor Eamon either for that matter. But Eamon found out again, and told his father, and this time, Rose was sent away to Dublin. I wasn't told exactly where: I suppose they thought I might tell Owen, and perhaps I might. The terrible thing was, Rose was pregnant with Owen's child. She was sent away to have the baby—the family said she was finishing her schooling in Dublin. And she was forced to give up the child the minute it was born. She told me she wasn't even allowed to hold it, not once, not even for a minute. She was told her baby was sick and had died, but she never believed it. It had all been arranged by Mick."

"The lost child," I said. "So the Byrnes and the Mac Roths were the local equivalent of the Montagues and the Capulets, were they? Did it end just as badly?"

She smiled slightly. "I suppose you could put it that way, like Romeo and Juliet, but this is Ireland, not Verona. This is more like the old tale of Deirdriu and Naisiu. You don't know the Tain, but do you know the story of Deirdriu?"

"Deirdre of the Sorrows," I replied. "Yes, that one I do. Deirdriu was to marry an old man, a king, I think, I can't remember his name . . ."

"Conchobar," Kitty said.

"Conchobar. But she loved a strapping young man by the name of Naisiu. They ran away together, but Conchobar and his men tracked them down, and Naisiu was killed, I think. Is that what happened to Owen?"

"Go on," she said, "with the story."

"Deirdre was being given to someone else by Conchobar, and she was on a wagon or something, I can't quite recall all the details, but she dashed her head against a rock and died rather than be with either of these two awful men. Did I get it right?"

"More or less," she replied. "Well, Mick Byrne insisted the wedding between Rose and MacCallum go ahead, and that nothing ever be said about the baby— MacCallum was never to know. Eamon was supposed to be driving Rose over to see MacCallum the night before the wedding. He called her to come out of her room, but there was no reply." Kitty stopped for a moment, and tears started to pour down her cheeks. "Eamon went in after her, but she was dead when he found her. She'd hanged herself." Kitty crossed herself.

"She killed herself rather than marry MacCallum!" I exclaimed.

"She was very depressed, over the loss of her child, and all. Owen, I thought he would die with sorrow. I told him about the baby. I don't know whether I should have or not, but I did. He became a wild man. He looked everywhere for that child, his and Rose's, but he couldn't find a trace. It was very difficult in those days, to track down a child put up for adoption. More difficult than now, and Mick had seen to it there would be no evidence of the child. Owen took to drinking, lost his job."

"Where is he now?"

"I don't know. I moved away. For all I know he's still looking for his child."

"And Eamon? What did he do after all this?"

"He disappeared for about a year, ran away to sea. He came to hate his father, almost as much as he hated himself. I thought I'd never see him again, but after Mick died, shortly after that, a bitter man, Eamon came back, married Margaret, who'd been his sweetheart before all this happened, and set up here in the Dingle. He asked me to come and look after his household, and I did. Denny joined me a few years later. I met Brigid's father here, and little Brigid, long after I thought I could be so happy, and have made this place my home. I felt sorry for Eamon, you know, and he wasn't a bad man. I liked looking after his daughters, even though I couldn't see what he'd found to like in Margaret, and sometimes late in the evening, when his wife had retired, he'd ask me to sit by the fire in his room, the red one, and he'd talk to me about Rose. He had loved her, you know. And in his own way he had tried to do the best for her. When his mother was dying—he was just a little tyke and Rose just a toddler—she made him promise he'd take care of his little sister, never do anything to hurt her. And I suppose he tried. I think he thought he had broken a sacred promise to his mother." She paused for a moment. "Do you know what a geis is?" The word sounded like gaysh. I shook my head.

"It is sort of like a tabu. In the old stories, people are held to a geis: there is something they mustn't do, or perhaps something they must do without fail, an obligation if you see what I mean, and if they did it, or forgot to, as the case may be, broke the geis, that is, it usually meant their death. Eamon Byrne thought he had broken a geis, in hurting his sister. He was good to us, though, wasn't he, Brigid? He gave us the money for Brigid to start up the tearoom, and my son-in-law the pub." Brigid nodded. "And he did try to look for Rose's baby. I know he did. But the authorities said that there was no way to do this, that he wasn't the father, and in any event, the name would be revealed only if the child wished it. Died in his prime, did Eamon. He can't have been sixty. And I know he would have wished to find the child before he died.

"Strange, though," she went on. "About Deirdriu and Naisiu, I mean. In this story, the tragic one was Rose. It's Owen's sister who's called Deirdre."

I could see Kitty was tiring, and Brigid was begging me with her eyes to go. "I'll leave," I said, "And thank you."

"Thank you for listening," she said. "I feel better for telling you."

As I turned to go, I asked one more question. "The baby," I said. "Was it?"

"A little boy," Kitty said. "Rose said it was a beautiful, healthy little boy."

Maybe it was a coincidence, maybe it wasn't. There must be at least a million Deirdres in Ireland, and Deirdre had had a rather spinsterish way about her, the look of a woman never married, but one can never assume too much. "Was Deirdre Flood ever married, do you know?" I asked Rob.

"I believe she was," he replied.

"And do you know her maiden name?"

"I think I saw it on the file, but I don't think I can recall it. Why?"

"I don't suppose it was Mac Roth. Deirdre Mac Roth."

"I think perhaps it was."

So Deirdre Flood was the hidden Mac Roth in the Byrne household, the poison asp in the fruit basket, the bald face of revenge behind the mask of servitude.

"How ever would you know that?" Rob said, watching my face.

I told him. "So you're saying you think this blood feud is still going on, and that a Mac Roth, Deirdre, insinuated herself into the Byrne household . . . to do what?" Rob said. "She had ample opportunity, surely, over the five years she's been there, to do whatever she wanted. Are you saying she murdered Michael? Why?"

"I don't know what I'm saying," I replied. "Probably not that she killed Michael. Is there any indication she killed herself?"

"No. It looks as if she was strangled first, then thrown into the sea. The autopsy will tell us for sure. It's nigh on impossible to strangle yourself, and while she could have thrown herself over a cliff, she could hardly have done both. My guess is she was strangled first. There'll likely be no water in the lungs."

"Well, what if it was Owen? What if he's given up looking for the child and has turned his attention to taking revenge on the Byrne family?"

"And to exact this revenge, he kills the hired help? One of whom is his sister, I might add? Are you trying to say that having to do your own housework is punishment enough? Surely not!"

I glared at him. These policemen with their gallows humor. "I'd still like to know where Owen Mac Roth has been for the last thirty-five years," I muttered.

Rob just looked at me. "I'll check it out," he said at last.

"Please do," I said. I didn't care how ridiculous it sounded. My money was on Owen ·Mac Roth.

Chapter Sixteen

THE PLACE WHERE THE SUN SETS

"ABOUT Owen Mac Roth," Rob said the next day. "He spent twenty-five of the last thirty years in jail. Joined the IRA and bombed somebody, got caught, and got a life sentence."

"But he's out now, right?" I said.

"He got out," Rob agreed. "Five years ago. And promptly got himself killed in a drunken barroom brawl. Artery cut by a broken whiskey bottle. Bled to death before the paramedics could get to him. I'd say we could cross Owen Mac Roth off our list of suspects now, couldn't we? Any other theories you'd like to explore?" I was finding his tone irritating, and was about to say so.

"It was a good idea, though," he added. "And worth checking into. Maybe you should have gone to police academy instead of taking up such a risky profession as retail," he smiled. That's the thing about Rob: Just when I'm about to claw his eyes out, he says something funny and nice.

So much, though, for my theory about Owen Mac

Roth. I thought about it for some time. The point was, while I had come away that first day at Second Chance with a very poor opinion of the Byrne family, I was no longer sure I'd been right. Eithne Byrne was a very nice person; Fionuala and Breeta were too, despite appearances to the contrary. And Eamon Byrne had been a very sick man. Once long ago, he had made a mistake. A very bad mistake, no doubt about it, with tragic consequences, but a mistake nevertheless. And now the family was paying for it. I didn't believe in curses, or broken geise, any more than I believed in the fairies. Instead, I was sure that some malignant force was pulling the strings off stage, bringing the family to ruin. I just didn't know who this malignant force might be yet. It wasn't Owen Mac Roth. That much was certain. And it could hardly be Deirdre, although somehow she had to be part of it. So whom did that leave?

When I thought about it, there was something patently wrong with Deirdre that went beyond the fact that she was a Mac Roth. She wasn't a maid, either. Eithne and Fionuala had laughed about how she kept spilling everything and breaking their mother's ornaments. I'd thought at the time she might be either paying Margaret back for her ill humor, or was just nervous in her presence, something it was easy enough to understand. But Rob had said she'd worked for years in a dry cleaning establishment. Bent on revenge, perhaps, she'd infiltrated Second Chance. But how had she managed to snag the position with absolutely no qualifications that I could see?

I picked up the telephone and called Second Chance. Anticipating Margaret, I was relieved when Eithne answered.

"I'm sorry to be a pest, Eithne, but I have a couple more questions. Do you mind?"

"Not at all," she replied. I'd been afraid when the sherry wore off, she'd regret her candor, but she still sounded very nice and friendly.

"It's about Deirdre again. Where did she come from, do you know?"

"Not really," she replied. "As I told you, she came when Kitty McCarthy, our old housekeeper retired. I do remember we had trouble finding a replacement. We were heartbroken when Kitty left. She was getting on, of course, but we didn't seem to notice, at least I didn't. She'd been with us since I was a little girl. She was a hard act to follow, I suppose. We advertised, of course, in town, but my mother," she paused and then lowered her voice. "Well, my mother isn't the easiest person in the world to get along with. She has a warm heart under it all, really she has, but it's not what people see, and no one in town wanted the job. So we advertised a little farther afield and found Deirdre."

"Did she come with references?"

"I suppose she must have. Mother looked after all that."

"So you don't know who gave her a reference?"

"No. I suppose we could ask Mother."

"Would you mind? I know it would help the police in their investigation, tracing something of her life before she came to Second Chance." It wasn't entirely a lie. If they knew enough to ask, then the answer would be helpful to them, I was sure.

"All right. Wait a minute. Mother!" I heard her call.

She was back on the line in a minute or two. "Sorry for the delay," she said. "Mother's trying to cook. Terrible scene. She says our solicitors, McCafferty and McGlynn, helped us find Deirdre."

"Thank you. One last question," I said. "Does the name Mac Roth mean anything to you?"

"It's a good Irish name," she said after a short pause. "But other than that, no, I don't think so. Should it?"

"I don't know," I replied. "Perhaps. I really don't know."

I hung up and dialed again.

"McCafferty and McGlynn," the officious voice said.

"May I speak to Charles McCafferty?" I said.

"Who may I tell him is calling?" she said.

"Lara McClintoch," I replied.

"I'm sorry Mr. McCafferty is out of the office," she replied. "May I take a message?"

"I'm assisting the police in their investigations at Second Chance," I replied. "Either put Mr. McCafferty on the line, or the police will have to call." This was patently untrue, but I was beyond caring. Furthermore, brush-offs by imperious secretaries bring out the worst in me.

"Really, he isn't here," she replied. Then why did you ask who I was, I was tempted to say.

"Mr. McGlynn, then," I said.

I thought she was going to hang up, but in a few seconds McGlynn came on the line. "Ms. McClintoch," he said smoothly, although I could hear a hint of irritation in his voice. Apparently, he didn't like it when his receptionist was bullied by people like me. "How nice to hear from you again. How may I be of assistance this time?"

"I'm making inquiries about Deirdre Flood," I replied. "Margaret Byrne was telling me that you provided a reference for Deirdre and . . ."

"I do not believe that is the case," he interrupted. "I did not know Deirdre personally." His tone implied that he wouldn't have anything to do with a lowlife like Deirdre. "I do recall that Margaret, Mrs. Byrne, asked us to assist her in finding someone. This is not, you will understand, the kind of thing we would normally do as their solicitors." I got the distinct impression Ryan McGlynn considered this little task very much beneath him. "I would have thought Mrs. Byrne could have dealt with an employment agency," he continued. "But she insisted, for some reason I do not understand. We had just snagged, I mean we had just secured, the Byrne account, and of course, wished to do anything we could to help out."

"Did that include checking references?" I said.

"I'm sure it would have," he replied.

"She was a dry cleaner," I said.

"I beg your pardon?"

"She had worked for years in a dry cleaning establishment, you know, throwing clothes into large machines filled with cleaning fluid, then taking them out again and putting them on hangers. What was it about this kind of work that you thought qualified her to be a maid at the home of one of your best clients?"

"Well . . . I don't really know what you are talking about. What are you implying?" he blustered. "Of course we would have checked references."

"So who gave her a reference?" I asked.

"I would hardly recall five years later, now would I?" he said. "And even if I did, and if what you say about her background is true, which I'm not aware that it is, who is to say she didn't falsify her experience and provide bogus references?"

"I'd have thought you'd make a more thorough check than that, for such a good client," I said. "But perhaps you could check your files?"

"I very much doubt we would have kept such information in our files," he replied. "I am certain, however, that we would have taken the utmost care in selecting someone for the Byrne residence."

"Would you mind checking the file just in case?" I said.

"I do mind," he replied. "The information would be confidential in any event."

"Okay," I replied. "I'll let the police here know. If they really need the answer, they can get a warrant. But you know all that, of course."

"Stay on the line," he said icily.

A few minutes later, Ms. Officious was back on the line. "Mr. McGlynn has asked me to let you know that Deirdre Flood gave as a reference a training school called Domestic Help International. The letter says she passed her courses with distinction."

"Dated when?"

"March 1, 1990," she replied.

"And this is a well-known institution, is it, this Domestic Help International?" It had a rather generic sort of name. Just the same, I knew I'd never heard of it. Apparently she hadn't either.

"Well, I don't know," she replied. "I don't think I've heard of it, but I wouldn't. I graduated from secretarial college, of course."

"Of course," I replied. "Good for you." I was tempted to ask her if they had special classes in imperious demeanor at her college, a subject at which she would no doubt have excelled.

"It must be a reputable place, though," she went on, apparently not noticing my particular tone. "It's located in Merrion Square."

"That's good, is it?" I asked. I actually knew that Merrion Square was a posh part of Dublin, but I wasn't about to say so. I wanted her to tell me all she knew.

"Merrion Square? Of course it is. One of the finest addresses in Dublin. Very close to St. Stephen's Green," she added.

"And does it have a fine phone number too?" I asked.

"There's no phone number on the letter," she replied.

"Thanks for your help," I said as I hung up. "And give my regards to Ryan and Charles, won't you?"

I checked with Dublin information, but the prestigious Domestic Help International didn't appear to have managed to get itself a telephone. Somehow I doubted it had managed a real address for itself either. Bogus references indeed. Deirdre had apparently pulled the wool over McCafferty and McGlynn's eyes completely, a fact that should have caused them considerable embarrassment, but didn't. She was able to do it, I was sure, because they were miffed at having to do such a menial task for the family, but too afraid to say no to their new, rich, and powerful client. They needed the money to restore that lovely Georgian town house of theirs.

So where did this leave me? Nowhere, I thought sadly. Absolutely nowhere. I went out for a walk to think about it some more. Large buses of the touring variety were parked on the edge of town. The music festival was about to begin. Already the streets seemed more crowded as tourists clogged the area. All the shops, thrilled no doubt by the business, had posters in their windows advertising the special events, and canned music blasted from many a store. Despite all the noise and excitement, I continued to noodle the problem around for some time.

Deirdre would have been a good bet for the murders except for two things. The Byrne family, with the exception of Eamon himself, who'd apparently died quite naturally as a result of his illness, were all still alive. As Rob had pointed out, if she was bent on revenge, why kill the staff? Unless, of course, Herlihy and Michael had figured her out. That could be the explanation. Herlihy as the butler couldn't help but notice Deirdre didn't have a clue what she was doing when she arrived. But she'd lasted almost five years there. If he was going to rat on her, it should have been right away. And Michael? Probably much too nice to reveal her as a fraud. Somehow this didn't work.

All that aside, the most compelling reason for eliminating her as a suspect was that she was very dead, and a murder victim at that, a fact that almost automatically disqualified her as a candidate for perpetrator of the other deaths.

I decided to go back to the Inn to see if I could find Jennifer and have a bite to eat with her. Aidan, the proprietor greeted me as I came in. "Miss Jennifer says you're to read this before you go upstairs," he said smiling and handing me an envelope.

I tore it open. Inside was a hastily scribbled note. *Aunt Lara—Dad's here. I'm going upstairs to tell him about Paddy. Stand clear! Love, Jen.*

Chapter Seventeen

WHO CALLS THE STARS?

"Y OU, young lady, will go to your room," Rob shouted. "And stay there until I say you can come out. And you will never, ever, see that guy again!"

Do we suppose Jennifer has already told her father about the boyfriend, by any chance? I asked myself.

"But it's the music festival," Jennifer sulked.

"I don't care if it's the Second Coming," Rob said. "You are grounded, confined to barracks, under house arrest. Do you get my drift here?

"As for you," he said, his face flushed with anger, as Jennifer stomped across the hall to our room. "Have you aided and abetted in all of this? Have you set my daughter up with this Gilhooly fellow? I left her in your charge, you know."

"You did not leave her in my charge," I retorted. "And I did not aid and abet. I was as surprised as you are when I found out. Yes, I may have known about it a few days before you did, but that was because I was paying attention. You, on the other hand, have totally abrogated your responsibility as her parent. And furthermore, I do not think that yelling at her about it is going to change anything."

"Well, what is?" he yelled. He was totally out of control. It occurred to me that with this stress and the Irish cooked breakfasts he'd been eating, he might be on the verge of a stroke. However, I couldn't stop.

"She's an intelligent young woman. She'll figure it out for herself."

"What if it's too late?" he said.

Too late? Too late for what? "Oh for heaven's sake, Rob. Don't be such a drip."

I stomped out of the Inn. It was true, I was feeling guilty. But I still thought he was handling this situation all wrong. I wandered around the town for a while, holding imaginary conversations with him and her, and trying to calm down. From time to time, I'd see almost everyone in town I knew: Conail, out of jail and still drinking, Eithne and Fionuala—I took some pleasure in knowing Fionuala had persuaded her older sister to come into town—Paddy Gilhooly, who didn't seem to have allowed the disappearance of his young girlfriend to bother him too much. The only person I didn't see was Breeta. I carefully avoided the rest of them, not in the mood for conversation. I needed to think what to do.

Finally, in a fit of ill humor, I decided I was going to go to the music festival, whether I would enjoy it or not, just to spite Rob. I might even forget all about it, if I tried hard enough, I reasoned. I walked along the streets until I heard music I liked, the traditional Celtic jigs and reels, and went in.

The bar was packed, a haze of cigarette smoke, and very, very noisy. It was a friendly crowd, most of them, I could tell, out for a special Saturday night at their local pub. Young people crowded around the bar, and pints of beer, dark and creamy, were passed across to others in the room. Most were in couples, but there was a small group of women out for an evening together, and a crowd of young men on the other side of the room looking them over furtively. For a horrible moment, I thought I saw Rob and Maeve, which would entirely spoil the place for me, but when I looked in that direction again, I couldn't see them.

Over in one corner, two old women sat smiling, one toothlessly, at the crowd. They were of sturdy stock, both dressed in gray, one with her white hair held back from her face with a barrette, the other's hair covered by a small gray scarf. From time to time, the barman, a fellow with a hearty booming voice called across to them, "Ready for another round, dears?" and the two old woman would laugh and nod. The barman would then send a strapping youth to deliver the drinks to their table.

In another corner of the room, seated on a bench, behind a large low table on which were scattered dozens of drink glasses, some empty, some full, and several ashtrays heaped with butts, were four musicians: a raven-haired woman in a black sleeveless top and black pants playing a squeeze-box; a blonde woman, casually attired in sweatshirt and jeans, on the bodhran, the Celtic drum; another woman with short-cropped hair in jeans and sweater, the fiddler; and the leader of the group, a man in jeans and wool sweater, who played the flute. It was he who announced the tunes they were to play, or tried to at least, the din in the bar making it impossible for all except those closest to hear what he said, and marked out the beat with a thump of his heel on the wood floor.

Those patrons who wanted to hear the music crowded

in a large semicircle several rows deep around the table, those in front sitting on low stools. I stood near the back of that group, cheered by the music, as the musicians began to play. The first piece was a ballad, sung by the raven-haired woman, a song that all but me seemed to know. Her voice was clear and sweet, the refrain wafting over the crowd, some of whom sang softly along with her.

After a few minutes, the musicians broke into a jig, to a smattering of applause from the crowd, followed by a reel, then another jig. Faster and faster the music went, the fiddler leaning now into her instrument, her face a study in concentration, the bodhran thumping out the beat hypnotically, the squeeze-box wailing, the flute notes soaring, the crowd swaying, the man's knee moving up and down like a piston marking the time.

Then, I felt something hard pressed against my back, and a hoarse voice whispered, "Come along with me now, or I'll shoot." I felt myself being pulled away from the crowd, pushed down a hall, then out a door that led into an alley. Before I had any idea what was happening, or could even turn my head, I felt a cloth being placed over my mouth and the world went black.

I awoke, or perhaps I should say became conscious, to find myself in a place with no light and no sound. Perhaps this is what death is, I thought, no clouds or wings or pearly gates, nor on the other hand, the fires and sulphurous fumes of damnation. Just eternal nothingness. I thought with regret of all the things I'd left undone, and unsaid, and wondered if it might be possible to be given another chance, a reprieve. Dimly, I wondered if Eamon Byrne was somewhere nearby, wishing, in his case, that there were thoughts he'd left unspoken.

Gradually, however, nothingness became a cold, hard surface, the smell of dampness, waves of nausea, a glimmer of night sky way above me, and the roar of the wind outside my prison. And then, in the darkness nearby, I heard a groan.

"Rob?" I exclaimed. "Rob, is that you?" Another groan. I pulled myself up on my hands and knees, and felt about in the direction of the sound. A few feet away from my own resting place, I found him. He was still not entirely conscious, but he was coming around. I found his hand and held it.

"Who's there?" he said hoarsely, coming to with a start.

"It's me, Rob," I said. "You're with me."

He said nothing for a minute or two, and I thought he'd lost consciousness again.

"Any idea where we are?" he said finally.

"Nope," I replied.

He sat up slowly and groaned again. "It's coming back to me," he said. "The bar, the music, and you disappearing down the back hallway: I caught just a glimpse of you. It looked odd, somehow, so I decided I'd better take a look. I got as far as the back door. I wonder if there were two of them. Hate to think I'd be overpowered by just one. Must be seriously out of practice. It's all that desk work they're giving me back home. Has to be. You don't think it could be middle age, do you? Ether, probably, or something similar if I judged correctly in the split second between the time the cloth went over my mouth and I blacked out. And if this ghastly nausea I'm feeling is any indication. Primitive, but effective. I was out like a light. Whoever it was must have knocked you out first, and then got at me from behind the door, or something. Never even saw it coming. I'm definitely out of practice."

"It was nice of you to come after me," I said at the end of his soliloquy.

"That's what we policemen do. Stop crime, save the damsel in distress, that sort of thing. Not that I'm doing such a fine job of it on this particular occasion."

"Did you happen to see who was pushing me out the door?" I asked.

"Unfortunately not. I could just see the top of your head, and the back of someone else's, but it didn't look right."

"Man? Woman?"

"Couldn't say. How about you? Voice mean anything."

"No, it was deliberately disguised, though, which probably means I'd know this person."

"Mmmm," he said. I heard him moving in the darkness, and in a moment, the flick of his lighter and the small flame. "See!" he said. "There are some advantages to smoking. Don't think I didn't notice that you don't approve."

We stood up, and as Rob moved the tiny light about, surveyed our prison. We were standing in a circular structure of some kind, about ten feet in diameter. The walls, made of stone, curved inward and upward to a small hole about twelve feet off the ground. There was an opening, a small door with metal bars, and Rob leaned hard against it. It didn't budge. He turned off the lighter. "I want to save fuel," he said, "while I think.

"With these walls curving in like that, it would be virtually impossible to climb up there to see if we could make a bigger opening in the top," Rob said softly in the darkness. "You'd have to be a spider or a fly, or something. Maybe you could stand on my shoulders and see if you could push some of the top stones away to widen the hole. But," he sighed, "we still couldn't get up there. Maybe, if I stood near the wall and pushed you up? Probably not," he said, resignation in his voice. I was inclined to agree with him.

"I have a question for you," he said after a few minutes of contemplation, "this being the first opportunity I've had to be alone with you since we got on the plane."

And who's fault was that, I wondered, what with him spending so much time with his favorite garda? "Ask away," I said.

"Do you really think I'm a drip, and a—what was that other unpleasant term you used?—a poop?"

Really, the male ego. "No," I said. "Well, maybe sometimes. If you could just be a little more relaxed with Jennifer."

"How so?"

"Do you think this is a good time to discuss this?" I sighed.

"Why not?" he declared. "Not much else doing around here, is there?"

"All right. Then I would submit that she's going to grow up, she's going to have boyfriends. Brace yourself, she's going to have sex. Why, instead of putting your energy into scaring the boys off, which frankly probably has the opposite effect of what you intended, why wouldn't you talk to her about practical things like birth control and STDs and stuff?"

"That's a mother's job," he replied.

I was tempted to say that since she didn't have one, the role was his. But of course he knew that, and he had done the best he could with Jennifer, and not a bad job at all.

"Anyway, I'm not as much of a dinosaur as you

think. I know she probably won't marry her first high school sweetheart the way I did."

How could she when you won't let her have a high school sweetheart, I wanted to say, but kept my mouth shut.

"Don't say anything," he ordered. "Even in the dark, I know exactly what the expression on your face looks like right now. I just don't think Gilhooly is a good place to start," he continued. "She's a little immature compared to some of her girlfriends. I mean how old is he, anyway? Old enough to be her father? He can't be ten years younger than I am. Well maybe ten." He paused. "Okay more than ten, but you get the idea."

"You're saying he's too old for her, and you're right," I said. As tedious as a middle-aged man fussing about his age would normally be, this conversation about age struck me as rather interesting, suddenly. Could it be, I wondered, what with all this drama about Jennifer and her older man that I'd overlooked something rather important? How old would the lost child have been, I wondered. Because it would have had to be the child, wouldn't it? The mother, father, father's sister, and grandparents were already dead. Eithne said her parents had been married for thirty-four years. Byrne had been away a year before that. That meant his sister's child couldn't be any younger than about thirty-six, maybe more. Thirty-six to forty, say. Could Padraig be the lost child? It was possible, I supposed. You'd think that Eamon Byrne would have objected to his daughter taking up with his sister's son, assuming he wasn't in favor of a severely limited gene pool. But maybe he didn't know. He didn't seem to have known about Deirdre, perhaps because the family feud of his youth meant the families were not well acquainted. They'd inhabited quite different towns. Was it possible,

I wondered, that the child was alive and had tracked the family down?

"And anyway, I don't want her to get hurt," I heard Rob say. "It's just a vacation kind of relationship, admit it."

I turned my attention back to what he was saying. If he thought in my weakened condition I was going to agree with everything he said, he was sorely mistaken. "And you, I suppose, are setting a good example for her in that regard? Alex may be the soul of discretion where his roommate's comings and goings are concerned, but Jennifer knows perfectly well you've been creeping out very late and returning very early in the morning. And she doesn't believe the police business excuse, either!"

"I wish you hadn't said that," he sighed. "You didn't have to. I know. You're saying I'm a jerk and a poor excuse for a father." He sounded dreadful there in the dark.

"I'm sorry," I said. "I shouldn't have said that. And no, I don't think you're a poor excuse for a father, or a jerk. I mean, look at Jennifer. She's a lovely young woman, and very sensible. You should take credit for that. As for Maeve, she also seems very competent, and pleasant." Faint praise, I know, but it was the best I could do. "I gather the relationship is pretty serious," I added.

"Don't think so," he said quietly. I waited. "Two reasons: She's not really a widow. Her husband is still breathing. There's been no divorce in Ireland until very recently, so she bills herself as a widow for the sake of convention. He lives in Belfast."

"So maybe now she'll get a divorce."

"I think she's a little conflicted—is that the word?—on the subject, either because she doesn't entirely approve of divorce, or because she still has some feelings for him."

Oh dear, I thought. We both digested that for a moment.

"And the second reason?" I asked.

He sighed. "The second reason is that I'm not entirely sure that is where my heart lies. I'm not sure where it does lie, but I don't think it's there."

I wasn't sure I understood the details of that statement, but I did understand the sentiments expressed.

"And that fancy pants lawyer?" Rob said into the darkness.

"Don't think so, either," I replied.

"Reasons?" he said.

"One, I don't think I'm his type somehow, and two, I'm not sure that's where my heart lies."

"Mmm," he said. We sat in silence for a few moments.

"I've been meaning to ask you something for a while," he said, suddenly. "You can say no. But I was wondering if you would consider being Jennifer's legal guardian should anything happen to me. Her grandparents are getting a little frail for the job. You are the only person I know I would really entrust her to. She's eighteen, so she's almost beyond the need, but I think she could use some guidance for a while yet. You can think about it. I'm a policeman, remember, so the chances of being called upon to do this are higher than average."

"I don't have to think about it," I said. "If I had a daughter, and I confess lately I've wished more than once that I did, I'd be pleased if she turned out like Jennifer. So yes, I'll do it. You do realize, though, that if I'm your fallback, as it were, then you'll have to stop following me into these dicey situations."

"You're right, I will," he chuckled.

"What do you think will happen, here, I mean, and now? Be honest," I said.

"Are you sure you really want to know?"

"Yes."

"I expect whoever it is will either leave us here to rot, or come back to dispose of us."

"Wonderful," I said. "I'm sorry I asked." We both sat contemplating that lovely thought for a while.

"Where are we, do you think?" he asked. "Still in the Dingle?"

"Yes," I replied.

"North? West?"

"South-ish, I think."

"What makes you think so?"

"Because we're in a clochán," I replied. "And that's where most of them are."

"A what?"

"A clochán. A beehive hut. There are hundreds of them around here, on the slopes of Mount Eagle, most of them ruins, but some in good condition. I saw them when Malachy, Kevin, Jennifer, and I went looking for clues. Turn on the light, and look: Think of yourself on the inside of a beehive. See how the stones are placed to curve up to the top. It's called corbelling. A work of art, really. These beehive huts were little houses, dating back to the early days of Christianity and maybe even earlier. Monks lived alone in them, as hermits, to study and pray. Sometimes, they were built in clusters around a church. Or when they were used by ordinary folk rather than priests, around, or in, a fort for protection. This one is larger and higher than most. I think I've read that they were usually only about four feet high, but this one is much higher than that, so perhaps it was a house, rather than a monk's cell."

"Very interesting, I'm sure," Rob said. "Now can we think of any way of getting out of this clochán thing?"

"Not really," I replied. I thought for a moment. "Give me that lighter!" I said. I swept the tiny light over the surface of the walls, looking for what I desperately wanted to find. The walls were made of rows of stones placed on top of each other in rather tidy rows, tiny little stones filling in the spaces between them as necessary. For the first few feet, the walls angled in barely perceptibly, but as they got higher, you could see how each row of stones overhung the one below it just a bit, so that the wall curved up to the top, where an opening of about six inches had been left open.

"I'm thinking souterrain," I said at last.

"Sue who?" he said.

"It's not sue who, it's sou what," I replied. "Souterrain. Literally under the ground. If this was used as a house, there might be a souterrain."

"Dare I say, so what?" Rob said, just a touch irritably.

"So—sometimes the souterrain was just a place to store food where it would keep cool in the ground. But sometimes it was an escape route. These shores were often plagued by Viking raids, and people needed an alternate way out of their homes should the Vikings, or pirates, or whatever arrive suddenly. The Viking raiders were particularly interested in church treasures, if I remember correctly, the jewel-encrusted manuscripts and such. So people built low, narrow and curved underground tunnels, the easier to defend themselves from anyone following them, that led several feet or yards outside their houses. If some marauder came toward the front door, they'd go into the tunnel and out the back way.

"Look here," I said moving the light toward one side. "See where the stone pattern changes. Some of the stones are vertical rather than horizontal here, like a lintel over a doorway. And see, the stones are not as regularly placed. Perhaps this souterrain was filled in at a later date!"

Rob looked impressed. "Dry mortar," he said, "no cement or anything. Just the stones themselves. It should be easy to take apart, relatively speaking. Let's get to it! Here, you hold the light, and I'll start."

It was difficult at first, with the stones so closely packed, but in a matter of minutes, Rob had created a small hole in the wall. He reached back for the lighter, and carefully placed it into the hole, and peered in. I held my breath. It could easily just be a storage chamber, I thought, in fact it was more likely to be. I hardly dared to hope.

"I think it's a tunnel," he said at last. "Who'd have thought all that history of yours would be so useful." I almost sobbed with relief.

Within minutes, we'd pulled out enough stones so that we could slip into the tunnel.

"You go first," Rob said. "I'll protect the rear, in case someone comes in before we get away."

I pushed myself feet first into the tunnel. It was dank and cold, and I could see nothing in front of me. Rob passed me the lighter and I moved into the tunnel. After a few feet I was able to stand, although bent over at the waist. The tunnel jogged slightly, then narrowed, and after another few yards, I had to get down on my knees and crawl again. By the time I reached the end of it, I was lying on my stomach and pulling myself along with my elbows.

The end was blocked by a large stone. I pushed as

hard as I could. The stone trembled slightly, but didn't give way.

"Small problem," I called back to Rob who was now just a few feet behind me. I held the light up to the rock.

"Mmm," Rob agreed. "We'll both have to push." He pulled himself forward until we were lying side by side in the tunnel. "Turn on your side," he said. "I need some more room."

We were nose to nose and hip to hip by this time. I could feel his breath on my face. All I could think of was that if our captors came after us, we'd not be able to maneuver at all. Being a man, Rob saw it differently. "This is nice, isn't it?" he said. I just knew he was grinning there in the darkness. I glared back, even if he couldn't see.

"One, two, three, push!" he said. We both pushed as hard as we could on the stone. It rocked slightly.

"Again!" Rob ordered. We pushed again, then again. The stone started to rock, and finally, with a jerk, moved, then rolled away from the tunnel. Rob pushed me out in front of him, and we were free.

Chapter Eighteen

ON WHOM DO THE STARS SHINE?

So you want to hear the story of how the Celts came to Ireland, do you? The last great invasion of Ireland. That and the judgment of Amairgen.

Well, the story begins in Spain with a man by the name of Mil. He had a number of descendants as did his brothers. Now one of these boys was called Ith, and one fine day he climbed up on a high tower to see what he could see, contemplating the world about him. And on that clear day in winter, what do you think he saw?

Ireland did I hear you say? 'Twas. Ireland for sure. 'Twas just a shadow on the horizon, but he decided to go there. Now some of his relatives were sure he was daft. 'Twas clouds you saw, not land, they told him, and they tried to stop his going. But he went anyway, yes he did. He took some followers and his son Lugaid. And when he got there, he asked the inhabitants—and we know who they were now, Tuatha dé, Tuatha dé Danaan, Children of the goddess Danu—he asked them, "what do you call this place?" "Inis elga," the people replied. "And who's in charge?" Ith asked again. "Mac Cuill, Mac Cecht, and Mac Greine are the kings," they said.

So Ith and his son went to Ailech and met the three kings, and Ith said many good things about the land, so that he and the kings parted on good terms. But now the story takes a turn for the worse, for some of the Tuatha dé worried that Ith and his followers liked their country so much they would take it by force, so they hunted Ith down and killed him. His people took his body back to Spain where his brothers were sorrowful and angry, and vowed revenge.

So they collected their warriors, and all the sons of Mil and their relatives, the poet Amairgen among them, and in sixty-five ships sailed for Ireland. But when they got there, they couldn't see the island, for the Tuatha dé had placed a spell on it, and the Milesians circled the island three times, before finally coming to Slieve Mish. You know Slieve Mish. Then they went on to Eblinne.

Eventually, the Sons of Mil went to Uisnech of Mide. Uisnech you see was, and still is, if only we knew it, the sacred center of Ireland. It sits within the mystical fifth province—the Irish word for province is cóiced, don't you know, and that means a fifth. Now that causes problems for some amongst us. Because there are only four provinces, you see: Ulster, Connacht, Leinster, and Munster. Oh, they argue it away by saying that at one time or another Munster was actually two provinces, but those who hold the ancient stories in our hearts know there were five, and the fifth is called Mide—the place where the other four provinces come together.

And so Mide and Uisnech are a very special place. From there, on Uisnech Hill, you can see a ring of mountains all round. The whole of Ireland, if you had the vision, can be seen from there: the sacred sites and political centers of the other four provinces in olden times, Rathcroghan in Connacht; Emain Macha in Ulster; the Hill of Allen in Leinster; and Aine's Hill and Lough Gur in Munster, all lining up across the mountaintops. And just across another hill, Tara, Seat of the High Kings of Ireland.

And in the old days, the Beltaine fires lit at Uisnech could be repeated on the mountaintops all round, and seen from all of Ireland. Yes, Uisnech is the eye of the fire of the gods. And on its slopes sits Aill na Mireann, the Stone of Divisions, a huge stone cleft in four, yet still together. Just like Ireland. It was a magical place for a long, long time, until St. Patrick cursed its stones and the magic disappeared.

But that was much later. Who would Amairgen and the Sons of Mil meet at such a special place? The goddess Eriu, none other, the third goddess. Eriu, Fotla, Banba, three goddesses in one, like the shamrock or the holy Trinity. She welcomed them to the island, telling them it had been prophecised that they would come and hold the island, the best place in the world, forever. And she asked that her name remain on the island. Amairgen made a solemn promise that hers would be its chief name forever. 'Tis too, as Erin.

Next, they went to Tara, where the three Tuatha dé kings, Mac Cuill, Mac Cecht, and Mac Greine, husbands of the three goddesses reigned. The Sons of Mil gave the three kings three choices: Give us a battle, the kingship of Ireland, or a judgment of some kind, they said. The kings chose the judgment and they asked that Amairgen himself deliver it.

Amairgen, in making the very first judgment in Ireland, said the land would belong to the Tuatha dé Danaan until the Sons of Mil returned to take it by force, *and, so that the Tuatha dé would not be taken by surprise, that the Milesians would sail nine waves away from the shores before returning.*

The ships sailed away the nine waves, magic waves they were, and the Tuatha dé called upon their druids to cast a spell. A mighty storm overtook the invaders' vessels, and there were many losses, but Amairgen thought it was a druidic storm and not a real one. He sent a man up the mast to see if the storm was higher than the mast of their ships. It was not, but the man died in the telling of it. Then Amairgen made a spell of his own, for the poets in those times were druids, you see, and the sea became calm. At last Amairgen stepped again on Ireland's shores. "I am the sea-swell, I am a furious wave," he said, casting a spell on this isle. Then the Milesians, the Celts as we now know them, made their way to the Slieve Mish Mountains, right here in the Dingle, where a mighty battle was fought with the Tuatha dé Danaan; then another battle at Tailtiu, where the three kings of Ireland, and the three goddesses, Banba, Fotla, and Eriu died. And from that time till the Christian era, and some say long after, Ireland belonged to the Celts.

We picked our way carefully across the fields and stone walls heading down toward the sea and the road along the coast. It was very late, but at last we came upon a farmhouse. "I'll go to the door," Rob said. "You hide well back, just in case we've picked the wrong place."

But it was all right. The farmer and his wife, once roused, called the local gardai station, and within a few minutes we were on our way back to town. We made statements to the police, and then they dropped me at the Inn, while Rob said he was going to take the police back to try to find the clochán we'd been thrown in.

Wearily I climbed the stairs to my room. It was almost dawn now, and I was very tired. I carefully unlocked the door to the room I shared with Jennifer in order not to wake her. She was not in her bed. On the desk was an envelope with my name on it.

Paddy and I think we can find the treasure, the note read. *We're taking his bike. Don't worry, I'll call you tomorrow. I left Dad a note too. Hope he isn't too mad. Love, Jen.*

I went straight to the restaurant. It was closed, but I could see a light at the back in the kitchen. Breeta wasn't there. I begged to know where she lived. "I shouldn't tell you," the cook said. "But you seem to be very upset. She's two doors down, the blue door, second floor."

But Breeta, when she saw me, tried to slam the door in my face. I was ready for her, and I was desperate. I shoved the door open and pushed past her into the room. She was thinner now, and the bulge in her tummy more prominent. "Okay, Breeta," I said almost yelling. "Enough is enough. I know this has been a very bad time for you. I know that losing your father was bad enough, but then Michael, in such a violent way. Well, it has been terrible. But you have had long enough. From now on, you're just wallowing in it. Talk to me." She said absolutely nothing, and kept her eyes averted from my face.

"Here," I said pulling up the map in front of her. "I have narrowed down the location of your father's treasure to this area. The two nearest towns are Mullingar and Athlone. You need to understand that it is not the treasure I am after. Jennifer Luczka, whom you've met, a young woman who is very dear to me, has gone off to find it with Padraig Gilhooly. For all I know, he is the killer, and even if he isn't, then the killer will be after them. I must find her. Please help me, Breeta. I don't have anyone else to turn to. You'll be a mother soon. You must understand what responsibility for a young person like Jennifer means."

Still she said nothing. I felt tears of desperation forming in the corners of my eyes. "What would be here, Breeta, that your father would be interested in? Right here, Breeta," I said, pulling the map and pointing at the place where the lines Alex and I had drawn intersected. "I can't cover the whole area. There isn't time. This is life and death, Breeta."

Silence greeted my plea. I was too upset even to cry. I turned and walked to the door. As I put my hand out to pull it open, I heard her move behind me. I turned. Breeta was looking at me, really looking at me.

"Ooshna," she said. At least that is what it sounded like. "Ooshna Hill. Find the stone, Aill na Mireann."

"Thank you, Breeta," I gasped, and dashed from the room to my car.

I blasted up the Dingle peninsula to Tralee, then picked up the N21 toward Limerick, then the N6 through Ennis, Gort, and Loughrea, then on through Ballinsloe to Athlone. It was a frustrating drive, two-lane highways much of the way with few opportunities to pass, and it rained off and on, leaving the pavement slick. It took me almost four hours with one stop for a coffee and gas, and another to try to reach Rob at the Inn and the garda station. I was cursing the fact that I didn't have my cell phone. I'd left him a note, and I could only hope he too was on his way.

That was four hours to think, as well as drive, about treasures and broken geise, fathers and daughters, inappropriate love, ruined lives and revenge. I knew, just as I knew that it was Jennifer who mattered, not the treasure, that this was not about wealth, but about a stolen life. By the time I got to Athlone, I knew who would be there. It was all a process of elimination. There was really only one possibility left. Denny had told a true story. Oh, he'd changed the location just a little, had added a little fantasy, and a happy ending to bring a tear of joy to Eamon's eye. This ending couldn't be happy, that I knew. But I had to find Jennifer.

In Athlone, I pulled into a gas station for directions. The gas jockey was a young man. "I'm looking for a place called Uisnech Hill," I said, pronouncing it Ooshna as Breeta had.

"Never heard of it," he said. "Is it around here?"

"Yes," I said. "Somewhere between here and Mullingar."

He shrugged. "You could ask my Da," he said, tossing his head in the general direction of the office.

. "I'm looking for a place called Uisnech," I said to two men in the office, one I assumed to be the gas jockey's Da, the other, if I wasn't mistaken, his grandfather.

"Can't say I know it," the father said.

"What did you say?" the older man asked.

"Uisnech," I repeated.

"Sure," the older man said. "Uisnech Hill. Take the valley road," he said drawing me outside and pointing out the direction, "toward Mullingar. You'll come to a fork at the far end of town. I'm not sure if it's signed, and you'll probably get lost again. It's a ways yet, but once you're on the valley road, it'll be on yer left. You'll know you're just about there when you find the pub by that name. There'll be a small sign, not much else. People don't visit much these days."

"Thanks," I said. I sure hoped he knew what he was

talking about. But he did, because as I got into the car he called after me.

"If you go to the pub, raise a cup to the Stone for me, will you?"

As navels of the universe go, Uisnech, the sacred center of Ireland, is not much to look at these days, a rather unprepossessing hill gradually rising just a few meters from the floor of the valley between Mullingar and Athlone. There's a small sign, terribly worn, and a cleared area for a few cars. There was no sign of Padraig's motorcycle, nor the van he'd borrowed earlier, but there was another car, a rental like mine. I prayed I wasn't too late. The way up to the hill was gated and locked, with a sign on it that read DANGER, BEWARE OF BULLS AND SUCKLER COWS, DO NOT ENTER, LANDS PRESERVED & POISONED.

There was a old metal turnstile beside the locked gate and I went through, undeterred. Bulls and poisoned earth be damned, I thought. Theoretically, at least, you wouldn't have both poisoned earth and suckler cows in the same field, but I reminded myself to keep my eyes open for a bull.

The route up was relatively easy at first, an overgrown lane. Near the top of it, though, I had to climb up some old cement stairs and over a wire fence into an open field, which sloped gently upward to a small plateau. I felt terribly exposed there, feeling the killer's eyes on me at every step. The ground was wet and very, very muddy, and the climb was an effort, my feet making a sucking sound in the mud after every step. My pant legs were coated in mud.

A few hundred yards later on, I came upon a large cleared area. The rain stopped for a few moments, and the sky cleared, and I found myself on a small hill surrounded by a ring of mountains off in the distance.

With the exception of the view to the west, which was hidden by trees, I felt I could see forever. It was a very large space, and I had a feeling finding the treasure would be almost impossible, but then I remembered the Stone, Aill na Mireann, the Stone of Divisions, the large stone on the slopes of Uisnech that is supposed to represent Ireland. I wondered where that might be.

I went on a little farther to a standing stone surrounded by a ring of smaller stones. Seated off to one side of the ring sat Charles McCafferty. He was wearing rain gear, including rubber boots, and an umbrella. At his feet was a bundle, maybe a foot or two long, well wrapped in plastic and twine. And he was pointing a gun at me.

"I have been expecting you," he said.

"And I, you," I replied.

"Is it this you came for?" he said pointing at the bundle at his feet.

"No," I replied.

"No," he agreed. "You came looking for that young woman, what is her name?"

"Jennifer," I said. "Where is she?"

"Gone," he said. My heart leapt into my mouth. What did gone mean?

"Gone," he repeated, seeing my dismay. "She left with that man of hers. They had a bit of a disagreement. I believe he had a somewhat closer relationship in mind, a reward, perhaps for bringing her here. She didn't see it that way. She wasn't ready, apparently." He smiled. "Then he confessed he still loved someone else. All rather sweet, I thought. Quite right, too. He was entirely unsuitable for her. They didn't find this," he said, pointing once again to the bundle, "because I already had it. Nor did they see me, so I let them leave.

I am not entirely unprincipled. I see you are relieved. She's not your daughter, is she?"

"No," I said. "She's the daughter of a friend of mine. I care about her very much."

He nodded, and for a moment I thought he would cry. "That is as it should be. But it is not always so."

"The lost child," I said.

"Yes," he said. "The lost child. It sounds poetic, doesn't it? William Butler Yeats wrote a poem called 'The Stolen Child,' did you know that? It's a story about a child being enticed away from this vale of tears to a wonderful place by the fairies. Lovely."

I said nothing. He was going to say whatever he was going to say. I could only hope he would get distracted and I could get away, as difficult as that might be in the mud.

"But not so lovely when it's you who's lost, is it?" he went on. "Not nearly so lovely and poetic. Prosaic, perhaps, when compared to the gut-wrenching, heart-breaking stories of abuse so prevalent these days, some of them genuine, some of them not. Prosaic, yes, even perhaps, banal. But not when you're living it. Not when it's you. I was bundled off to an orphanage. Awful things, orphanages, but not nearly so bad as the home I was eventually sent to. I won't bore you with the details, just the highlights. Drunken, abusive father, feeble put-upon mother. Boy goes to bed hungry, gets up cold and even more hungry; beaten regularly; dirty, worn clothes, bad teeth, poor grades, scorn of class-mates. Father beats mother almost to death; lost child beats father, leaves home never to return. Boy hears his mother is dead, finally, by his father's hand. De-termined to be a success. Through hard work, desper-ately hard work, becomes a solicitor. Uses his new skills and knowledge to find his real family. That's it."

"And vows revenge," I said. "You forgot that part."

"Revenge," he agreed. "Beautiful, unadulterated revenge. I see it as a bright, white light of some kind, purifying, taking the blackened parts of my soul, and healing them."

Mad as a hatter, I thought.

"You think me mad," he said, as if reading my thoughts. "I prefer to think of it as focused, or even, perhaps obsessed. But you may be right. If I am, I was driven to it. These people, rich, so careless of others, they deserve everything that has happened, and will happen, to them.

"I found them, then I set out to destroy them. First, I had to get their legal work. I managed some introductions, all the right people, of course, and after giving Eamon some rather good bits of advice, if I do say so myself, took over his legal work. Then, it was just a matter of time. I looked after most of their banking and investments, and gradually I lost their money. Not in such large amounts, or so fast that they would notice it was done deliberately, but steadily. There was a period of time when it was actually difficult to lose money in the stock market, but I rather pride myself on having managed it. Not much, but a little. I'd waited a long time for this, and I wasn't for rushing it. It helped in a way that Eamon Byrne was ill. He wasn't there to see what was happening, figure it out, and he thought the reason his beloved empire was failing was on account of his inadequate sons-in-law.

"I did not benefit personally from this, you understand, not financially at least. To do so might have alerted various authorities who are charged with the responsibility to watch out for these things. But I derived enormous personal satisfaction, I'm sure you will appreciate, from the execution of my plan.

"It was something of a disappointment to me that Eamon Byrne managed to escape my clutches by dying. Very untimely of him. I had hopes that he would die in poverty, but unfortunately he did not. In that objective, I ran out of time. I was there when he died. You're the only one who knows that, although Deirdre may have guessed. And I told him just before he died. I came down to finalize his Will and to record the videotape. I had already hidden the clues to his specifications. When he was all alone, gasping for life, I told him what I was going to do to his family. He died minutes later. Shock, I like to think, in his weakened condition. Even so, I deprived him of only a few hours, or days, of life, hardly worth it. Possibly, he will try to haunt me from the grave. I think I might enjoy that. But I didn't want any of the family to die, not yet. I wanted them alive and suffering. Anyone else was, and is, expendable." His words were full of menace, but his tone matter of fact.

"I did consider wooing one of the daughters and marrying her. It was easy enough to split up Fionuala and Conail, and she would be an easy mark. There were two problems with that. One was that whether she knew it or not, she already had very little money worth marrying, my activities being so successful so quickly. The other is that I'm not really that way inclined: women, I mean. I see my adoptive mother's bleeding and bruised face in all of them. It would have been difficult, if not impossible, for me. Perhaps you sensed that. On balance, I decided to stay with the original plan.

"And it's working rather well. Second Chance, as you may have noticed, is on the market, at fire sale prices. Just a word or two on my part is all that is required to persuade potential buyers that the property would not be suitable for them. Byrne Enterprises is on a satisfying downward spiral. Sean and Conail, who might between them have managed to salvage something, I have set against each other. To each I blamed the other, when business affairs did not go well, and they were all too eager to believe the bad things I had to say about the other. It caused all kinds of strife in the family, all of which suited my purposes. I expect to be able to buy the company within a year. They'll be grateful, no doubt, for the pittance I pay them. It will not last them long.

"There was only one problem."

"The treasure," I said.

"The treasure. If they found that, then, if it was as fabulous as Eamon said it was, and I had no reason to believe it wasn't, it would solve their financial problems. I could ruin them again, of course, but time is important to me. I want to be able to enjoy their downfall for as long as possible, and we never know how much time there will be for us on this earth."

"Why didn't you just destroy the clues? You could have told Eamon you'd placed them. He wouldn't be able to check up on you."

"Because he insisted John Herlihy come with me while I placed the clues."

Poor John Herlihy; poor all of us, I thought.

"You did rather well finding this place," Charles said. "I had all the clues, both sets. I copied them of course, before Herlihy hid them, but still, it took me some time to figure it out. Not schooled in either ogham or the old stories. You did well. It's a big place, as you can see," he said, waving the gun around. "I had a lot of looking to do. It was near the stone, Aill na Mireann. I expect that was where you were heading just now."

I nodded.

"Every moment I could, I came up here, once I'd figured it out. It was simply a matter of getting here before anyone else."

"So who hid it, the treasure, I mean, if you didn't?"

"John Herlihy, of course. I thought you knew that. I believe that Byrne had instructed him to tell the family eventually if they didn't find it. Eamon was not as heartless as that video might indicate, and he was genuinely hopeful they would all work together. He even told me that Herlihy would get it to them when I told him what I had planned. I suppose he thought that would thwart me. He can't have been thinking clearly, in his weakened condition. John Herlihy merely presented a small, but easily dealt with, obstacle."

"By which I assume you mean you killed Herlihy." It was a statement, not a question.

"I did. Not difficult, even if it never occurred to Eamon that I was capable of it. If it had, I assume he wouldn't have told me. I asked Herlihy to tell me where the treasure was. He wouldn't. It was a simple matter to send him over the side. I lured him to the cliff and pushed him over. Next, no doubt you'll ask about the others. Michael, for example. Michael crept into the house the night he was killed. He was hunting about the place, going through wastepaper baskets and such—I have no idea why he came back nor why he was creeping around."

Would you believe it if I told you he was looking for a tortoise? I thought. And I suppose the destroyed clues.

"In any event, he overheard Deirdre and me—did you realize Deirdre was my aunt, Owen Mac Roth's sister? Yes? When I traced my roots to Connemara, I found her first, working, as you know, in a dry cleaners. It was she who told me the whole sordid story, about how my grandfather had died shortly after my father was incarcerated, having spent the family nest egg on his son's defense, I might add, and how she'd been left alone, without prospects to use that rather antique term, and had sunk to a pitiful state. In any event, Michael heard us talking about my plans, and he was heading off to tell the rest of the family. Unfortunate that. I had killed once, the geis was broken. I killed him too. I actually had the poison with me— I'd got it from one of my less salubrious clients—and had thought to use it on Eamon, although in the end I didn't need to. Called to Michael to stop, that I could explain everything. He did, too. Much too nice and polite a young lad. Death of him, really."

"And Deirdre?"

"She lost her nerve, that's all. She was going to tell you. Unfortunate that I involved her at all, but I had to, you see. I needed someone at Second Chance, so that I could manipulate the strings from far away in Dublin, unsuspected, but still have the information I needed about what was happening there. I sent her back, although she didn't want to go. I wanted her to wreak some more havoc—I thought her statement to police about Conail was inspired, don't you?—and also to keep her eye on you, after your rather insistent questioning of me when you came to Dublin. I made her call me from town every night to report, and so that I could bolster her resolve and keep her anger at the family stoked. But then one evening she didn't call, and I knew what that meant, although I didn't know why."

"Because Eithne Byrne told Deirdre how grateful they were she'd come back and promised to look after her."

"Interesting," he said. "After I got back to Dublin with Ryan, I turned around and drove much of the night to get there before she could do anything, then all the way back to Dublin to be at my office at the usual time. You know, I thought that because she had suffered too, like me, she must want, no need, revenge, that she was the perfect ally, but she hadn't the stomach for it."

I thought of how Deirdre had tried to warn me off, right at the start, out there on the road in the rain. She'd known what would happen to anyone who persisted in looking for the treasure. Charles was right: she hadn't the stomach for what he planned to do.

"Hated to do it, really, to kill her, I mean, but I'd come this far," he went on. "She'd had a hard life. Death might be a blessing for her." He paused for a moment or two, but his eyes never left my face.

"It's important to me that you understand that I do not kill casually or without reason," he said, suddenly. "In fact, I have gone to some lengths to avoid it. I am not a monster. I locked you and your friend up in the clochán to give me time to find the treasure, as you call it, before you did. But you moved too fast. If I had found it and left before you were able to get here, I would have made an anonymous call to the police and they would have sent someone to release you. There would be no need for this," he said, waving the gun in my direction. "The family could look for the treasure forever, as far as I was concerned, as long as there was absolutely no chance they would find it. And now, of course, they won't."

"So are you going to look at it?" I said.

He looked startled. "The treasure, you mean? I suppose so. It was never about the treasure, but now that I have it, why not? A bonus, perhaps. Here," he said pushing it toward me with one foot. "You open it. I need to keep my hands free," he said, tilting his head toward the gun.

My fingers were shaking so badly I had to struggle with the knots in the twine. It had started raining again, and the wet was soaking into my clothes and dripping off my hair into my eyes.

"Take your time," he said. I was, desperately hoping that help would come, and surreptitiously trying to look about me. The trouble with being at the sacred center of ancient Ireland, the Axis Mundi, a place from whence all of Ireland could theoretically be seen, and a fire burning here could be repeated from hilltop to hilltop until it could be seen across the island, is that there is nowhere to run. Or more accurately, I could run, but there was nowhere to hide from the maniac with whom I found myself inhabiting the place, except perhaps, a very small clump of trees on the downward slope to the west. To get to it, I would have to pass him.

"Your father did look for you," I said, desperately hoping to buy myself time, or distract him for a moment. "Owen Mac Roth, I mean. Your birth father. He looked everywhere for you."

"Did he now? How touching. I'm sure he was to be pitied. As I was."

"Eamon did too. They wouldn't tell him, the authorities, I mean."

"Need I say, too little and too late?"

"But the family, Margaret and the three daughters, are innocent. They know nothing of all of this. Surely you know this."

"I too was innocent," he replied. "But I suffered immeasurably because of Eamon Byrne. If I cannot have my revenge on Eamon Byrne, I will have it on his children. Besides, they have lived a life of luxury in their innocence. Whatever they wanted, I'm willing to wager, Eamon would have given them. And now I will bring them to ruin. Please continue with that package."

I did. I knew he was getting angry, and I didn't want to provoke him. But I wanted to tell him, although I didn't dare, that he was wrong. He wasn't going to destroy Eamon Byrne's children. Oh yes, he could ruin them financially. But I had seen the determination in Eithne Byrne's eyes, and I didn't think she could be defeated.

Thinking about that kept me going, looking for some way out of the horrible predicament in which I found myself. But I knew I was running out of time. At last, the knots loosened. Whoever had wrapped this package, had known what they were doing. Carefully I rolled open the plastic, to find another roll, this one of unbleached linen.

"Stop," he ordered. "Let's have a little fun. What do you think it is?"

"Nuada Silver Hand's sword," I said.

"Interesting. How did you arrive at that conclusion?" he said.

"The first letter of each of the clues, starting at the end, with the last one, like ogham, bottom to top, spelled out Nuada Argat-lam," I said. "Eamon Byrne was always looking for the treasures of the gods, so I figure this has to be the sword, one of the four gifts of the gods. It's long enough, isn't it?"

"Ah, interesting. Let's see if you're right," he said. "Proceed. You've come this far, you might as well finish it."

I thought that whatever it was, it would have to be pretty spectacular to distract him for a moment or two so I could try to get away. I wasn't sure a worn-out old iron sword would do it.

But it wasn't Nuada's sword. As the next layer of wrapping was pulled aside I saw a hand, a silver hand. Across the lower knuckles of the silver fingers were four large jewels, rubies, I'd say, and at the second joint were four little windows, in a clear stone, polished quartz, perhaps. It wasn't pagan, though, not something that would date to the time of Nuada, if ever he existed. It was Christian and very old, what is referred to as a reliquary, something to hold the bones of someone very special, a bishop perhaps, or even a saint. There was scrollwork etched into the silver in Celtic patterns, and it was one of the most beautiful works of art I had ever seen.

"Let's see!" Charles said, and I handed it to him. It was heavy and for a second he set down the gun. I lunged for it, but he saw me coming, also reached for it, and it spun to the ground a few yards away. As he scrambled to retrieve it, I made a dash for it, slipping and sliding down the side of the hill, trying to make for the shelter of some trees.

"Stop!" he yelled. But I didn't. I heard the report of the gun, felt a short burst of pain in my side. Nothing much, I thought. He can't really have hurt me. But then my legs wouldn't work and I found myself falling, then lying, facedown in the mud. I heard first some shouting, then a roaring in my ears, as the rain kept running in rivulets over my hands, and the world darkened around me.

Chapter Nineteen

WISE AM I

DYING, I can tell you, is not what it's cut out to be. I can personally attest that all that stuff about bright lights, long tunnels, and a transcendent feeling of peace is a crock, a figment of someone's imagination. I felt completely lucid but irritatingly cold, my fingers and toes blocks of ice.

I could hear everything, understood everything. I just couldn't move or speak, although I followed everything with a kind of detached interest as if it really had nothing to do with me. I had it in my mind, however, that I had something very important to say.

Gradually, I began to realize that some of the voices I could hear belonged to people I knew. I recognized Rob, Alex, and then Moira and Clive. Moira and Clive! Either I was having an otherworldly experience, or I'd been out for a bit, long enough for Moira and Clive to get themselves across the Atlantic to Ireland. And if the latter possibility was the correct one, then I must have been in pretty bad shape.

I heard a door swing open, and new footsteps in the room.

"Hello Breeta, dear," Alex said.

"How is she?" Breeta said. She sounded almost her old self. That was something, anyway. And I'd certainly be interested in the answer to her question.

"She's come through the operation all right," someone said, a doctor presumably.

How reassuring, I thought.

"But now it's a matter of seeing how she does over the next few hours."

What did that mean? I wondered.

"Can she hear us?" Breeta demanded.

"Possibly," the doctor said. "It's good to keep talking to her."

I heard footsteps come up right beside me and breath very near my ear. "I know you've had a very bad time, frightened for your life out there on the hill with that lunatic; shot and lying there in the mud and the rain," Breeta said. "And I'll grant you that Rob and the gardai cut it a little fine getting to you. And no doubt being operated on for hours and hours must have been very difficult whether you were conscious or not. But you've had long enough. From now on you're just wallowing. So pull yourself together, and wake up!"

People who hurl your own words back at you when you are in a weakened condition are a blight on the landscape, I decided. Not quite as bad as people who shoot you, perhaps, but a blight, nonetheless. I ignored her.

"This is all my fault," Jennifer sobbed. "She went after that awful man because she was worried about me."

"No, it's not," Rob said. "It's mine. I lied about

where I was going when I left the station. I didn't want anybody to know I'd gone to Maeve's place to discuss things. If I'd told someone, or gone back to my room sooner, we'd have figured it out and got there before she did."

Oh dear, I thought, I really will have to rouse myself and say something. I wouldn't want them to go through life thinking it was their fault. I was the one who'd persisted in this whole thing. Heaven knows, I should have known better. Deirdre had warned me after all. But I couldn't wake up, try as I might. Instead, I found myself drifting away. Soon, I was sitting in an empty theater, empty, that is, except for me. A single spotlight made a bright circle on the stage.

After a few minutes of silence, I heard loud echoing footsteps, and a man in bowler hat, black suit, and umbrella, his face painted completely white, stepped into the circle of light. I kept staring at him, thinking I should know who he was, but I couldn't figure it out, and in the end I gave up trying.

"And now, for your viewing enjoyment," the man said. "For one last time on the silver screen, sailor, world traveller, scholar, antiquarian, successful entrepreneur, and family man, from County Kerry, Ireland, please welcome, ladies and gentlemen, Missssster Eamonnnnnn Byrrrne!"

The screen behind the man lit up, as his footsteps died away, and there, larger, much larger, than life, was, as announced, Eamon Byrne. "I suppose you're wondering why I called you all together," the giant face said. "Particularly," and here he coughed, "particularly seeing as how I'm dead."

"I've seen this one," I said to the empty theater. "This must be summer reruns."

But it wasn't.

"I wish," Eamon Byrne said looking right at me. "I wish more than anything, that I'd told them, all of them, my sister Rose, my friends, my business partners, my staff, Kitty, John, Michael, even Deirdre, my wife Margaret, but most especially my darling daughters, my little Eriu, Fotla, and Banba—I wish that instead of saying those horrible things I did, that I'd told them that I love them."

And with that the screen went blank and I was back in my hospital room.

This, it seemed to me, called for decisive action. With all the strength I could muster, I opened my eyes. I must have been gone awhile, because Breeta was no longer there. All the rest of them were, though, and they were the ones I wanted to talk to.

"She's awake," Alex exclaimed.

"About time," Moira said, smiling at me.

I tried to move my lips. It was a slow and painstaking process. "I," I said, slowly and as distinctly as I could. They all leaned forward.

"Love," I said. Their eyes widened.

"Ou," I concluded, trying to take all of them in one glance. There was something about the Y sound I couldn't manage.

"Even ou, Clive," I said slowly. He hugged Moira and planted a sloppy kiss on my cheek.

"Brilliant!" Rob said, smiling down at me.

My next trip to Ireland was some months later, to testify at Charles McCafferty's trial. I was not there long, the trip cut short by an incident that still plays across the back of my eyelids from time to time, or drags me from my sleep, gasping and tearing at the bedclothes. On the first day of the trial Charles had looked relaxed and confident, as if certain his charm would carry the

day. And you know, it might have. On the second, as
he was being lead to the courtroom from the paddy
wagon, his arms shackled behind him, Conail
O'Connor stepped from behind a van, raised a rifle,
and shot him dead. The trial was a big one, covered
by media from all over the country, and the scene was
played over and over on television, Charles dying in
slow motion time and time again.

In my mind, he saw his killer, although I can't be
sure he did. I think he probably viewed his own death
with the same detached equanimity he had his life. On
the other hand, I'm not sure how I feel about all this.
While I consider him more sinning than sinned against,
particularly where Michael Davis is concerned, I feel
the occasional small tug of compassion when I think
of Charles. I can only hope the Byrne/Mac Roth blood
feud died with him.

On a happier note, Byrne Enterprises is making its
way back, led by a triumvirate: the three Byrne sisters.
The family is planning to donate the silver reliquary to
a museum, as soon as they have enough income to
qualify for the tax receipt, and will use the savings this
allows them over the next few years to expand the business. It's going to be a long road back, but somehow
I know they're going to do it. I like the idea of Byrne
Enterprises being run by the triple goddess of the Tuatha dé Danaan—Eriu, Fotla, and Banba. How can they
fail with all that magic on their side?

Sean McHugh is running one of the businesses
again, as vice president of something or other, report-
ing to his wife and sisters-in-law, but Fionuala and
Conail have permanently called it quits. Conail apparently thought that if he revenged the family on Charles,
his wife would stand by her man. He was wrong. Last
I heard, Fionuala, not one to be wasting time visiting

her ex-husband in prison, had set her sights on Ryan McGlynn. One can only hope, for her sake, that the resemblance between Tweedledum and Tweedledee goes only skin deep.

Second Chance has been sold. Margaret has made her way back to Connemara, and, much to my surprise, has actually written me to inquire about my health. The others have stayed in the Dingle: Eithne and Sean have a small house in town and Breeta is living quite happily in Rose Cottage with Paddy Gilhooly and their lovely baby girl. They've named her Rose. I found an absolutely wonderful antique bed for the little darling, and shipped it over. Alex has refused to charge them any rent, so Breeta and Paddy are gradually fixing the place up for him, including putting in electricity and a new lane from the main road. Alex says that someday, a long time from now, he plans to retire there. Vigs, I gather, stays with the cottage.

Jennifer Luczka is off to university. She's doing well at her classes. She also has a new boyfriend. She's bringing him home to meet us at Thanksgiving. Rob is steeling himself for the ordeal.

It is taking me considerably longer than I thought it should to get well again after the operation, the perils of being in your forties, I suppose. As Rob keeps telling me, middle age isn't for wimps. The doctors have told me to take it one day at a time, which I've tried to do, impatient though I usually am. I do feel reasonably well, at last, and am grateful to be alive.

Moira has decided that my life would be much better if there was a man in it, a view I'm not sure I share, and she has set her sights on Rob as my next partner. All I can say about this is that if Rob and I continue our current glacial progress toward a more intimate relationship, by the time we actually get there, we'll only

be capable of chaste kisses before we pass each other
the glue for our dentures. In the meantime, however,
I'm not much interested in anybody else.

Moira has also decided, in an indirect way, some
other things about my future. Greenhalgh & McClintoch is gone, but McClintoch & Swain is back in business. Sarah Greenhalgh, who didn't find retail nearly
as exciting as she thought it would be most of the time,
and way too exciting the rest of the time, asked me if
I'd care to buy her out. The decision for Clive and me
to reunite, in a business sense only, came at a three-
way conference at my kitchen counter.

"I have a proposal for you," Clive said carefully,
clearing his throat and glancing over at Moira as he
spoke. "With Sarah intent on leaving, and your having
been a little under the weather for so long, we've been
thinking you might like some help with the store. What
do you say to our getting together again? You have a
much better sense of the kinds of furniture and furnishings people like than I do, and you really do your
research on antiques. I like to think I'm good at the
design stuff, pulling it all together. What do you
think?"

I looked at the two of them, Clive his usual rakish
self, although somehow apprehensive, Moira looking
quite uncharacteristically diffident. I looked down at
my coffee cup, watching as a small pool of frothed
milk expanded across my saucer from the spoon, and
for a moment or two my life with Clive, the good times
and the bad, flashed before my eyes. For some reason,
I also thought of Charles, and a long, sad tale of inappropriate love, and I could feel myself getting angry
all over again, whether at them or myself I didn't
know.

Then I thought of all the laughs I'd shared with

Moira, the late night conversations, the support we'd given each other through the tough times in retail and in life. I remembered when we'd had our impacted wisdom teeth out at the same time, then taken a limo back to my place, where, curled up in blankets and flannel nightgowns purchased for the occasion, we sat up most of the night by a roaring fire, sharing a very fine bottle of scotch through clenched teeth, as our faces swelled. And I remembered being told that Moira, when she heard I'd been shot, had grabbed her handbag and passport, called Clive, then driven directly to the airport without so much as a toothbrush, calling her travel agent from the car and demanding to be put on the first flight headed in the general direction of Ireland. When I looked up, Moira had a expression on her face that was part hope, part pleading.

"You could think about it for a while," Clive said.

"No, I don't have to. It's a good idea," I said.

Clive was angling to call our new shop Swain & McClintoch rather than its original name, which predates our divorce. His second ex-wife Celeste was not too inclined to advance him any cash, however, and my dear friend Moira wisely stayed out of it. Under the circumstances, the bank was keener on my signature than his, so McClintoch & Swain it is. We opened with a very splashy party to which we invited everyone we could think of, and where champagne—real champagne—flowed copiously. I would not normally throw such an extravagant party: I mean, we're still paying for it months later. But who cares? Under the circumstances, I felt I was celebrating my new life, not just the new store. I've learned many things in the last few months, not the least of which is that life is a precious, and fragile, gift.

As unconventional as it may be to work in partnership with your ex-spouse, it's going okay. Irish Georgian is doing reasonably well for us. Just as I hoped he would, Clive mixes the paint and does a sketch of the room, complete with color swatches; I, with Eithne Byrne as our part-time agent and picker in Ireland, get the furniture. Whatever we need, Eithne finds. She's working out really well, and having a good time of it, I believe. I expect she'll open her own shop in Ireland soon enough, once Byrne Enterprises is on more solid footing, but I think, I hope, our relationship will continue.

And if Irish Georgian doesn't work for you, name your place. We'll see you get the complete look, furniture, furnishings, plants, lighting, window and wall treatments, whatever it takes. So far, we've done the Mediterranean, Tuscany, Mexico, Bali, and beyond. There's a whole world out there, and before I waft off again into that great silver screen in the sky, I plan to see it all.